How the hell did we miss this?...

Dean could clearly hear wood snapping. Given that the apartment was completely empty except for some shiny new hardwood on the floor, Dean figured it to be the flooring. *Wasn't one of Poe's stories about hiding a corpse in the floorboards?*

Mackey ran in, and promptly tripped and fell on his face.

Glancing down, Dean saw that someone had taken the precaution of laying a tripwire a few feet into the front room.

Sam jumped over the tripwire and into the next room, where the sound was coming from.

Or, rather, he tried to. Mackey chose the moment when Sam was jumping over him to try to get up, and his shoulder collided with Sam's long legs. The two of them went down in a tangle of denim and polyester.

Dean stepped over them both, pistol ready. "Hold it!" he yelled, but he only saw two legs going out the window onto the fire escape. The stench of decaying meat made Dean's nostril hairs stand at attention.

Dean went straight for the window, pausing to turn around for only a second. "Stay with that jackass!" he said to Sam, pointing at Mackey. Dean also caught sight of several pieces of ripped-up hardwood and bits of wormwood.

He turned and climbed

How the hell did we mi

SUPERNATURAL Books
From HarperEntertainment

NEVERMORE

Coming Soon

WITCH'S CANYON

SUPERNATURAL™
NEVERMORE

Keith R.A. DeCandido

Based on the hit CW series SUPERNATURAL
created by Eric Kripke

HarperEntertainment
An Imprint of HarperCollinsPublishers

HARPERENTERTAINMENT
An Imprint of HarperCollins*Publishers*
10 East 53rd Street
New York, New York 10022-5299

ISBN: 978-0-06-137090-8
ISBN-10: 0-06-137090-8

First HarperEntertainment paperback printing: August 2007

Printed in the United States of America

Visit HarperEntertainment on the World Wide Web at
www.harpercollins.com.

10 9 8 7 6 5 4 3 2 1

To the late great Scott Muni, for informing so much of the music of my childhood . . .

To John, Jack, Ray, Doug, Kathy, Janyce, Arleen, Kevin, and all the other nutjobs on *the paper*, Fordham University's alternative paper, who gave me my first great publishing experience . . .

To Edgar Allan Poe, who lived a hard life, but whose groundbreaking work will live on forever . . .

And in general to the Bronx, the place where I was born and live, the place where I grew up, the place where I was educated, and still New York's best kept secret. Boogie down!

Acknowledgments

There are a *lot* of people who have to be thanked for this, the first ever *Supernatural* novel. So get comfy . . .

To John Morgan, my wonderful editor, who came to me and said, "I'm going to be editing *Supernatural* novels, wanna write one?" So this book is entirely his fault. John and I have known each other going back to the earliest days of both our respective careers, but this is our first time working as editor and writer, and it's been an absolute joy to finally do so.

To Eric Kripke, who could've just done a show about two pretty guys who shoot monsters in the head, but has given us something far more than that in *Supernatural*. It's a show about two brothers, it's a show about family, it's a show about demons both physical and internal, it's a show about the importance of music, and it's a show about *people*. Thanks also to his crack team of writers, in particular Raelle Tucker and Sera Gamble, who've provided some of my favorite moments on the show, and Ben Edlund, who has rocked my world ever since the glory days of *The Tick*.

To my other editor, Emily Krump; my wonderful agent, Lucienne Diver, who both rocks and rolls; to the good folks at the café who plied me with hot chocolate during my marathon writing sessions; and to CGAG, the bestest writers group ever.

To Anthony C. Greene of the Bronx County Historical Society, who generously gave me an informative tour of the Poe Cottage, and filled me with all sorts of useful facts. Also to the BCHS in general for their books by Lloyd Ultan and Gary Hermalyn about the Bronx, in particular *The Birth of the Bronx, 1609-1900*, and also to Kenneth T. Jackson's superlative reference, *The Encyclopedia of New York*, and Susan Blackhall's *Ghosts of New York*.

To Jensen Ackles and Jared Padalecki, the voices and faces of Dean and Sam Winchester. Again, they could've just stood around and looked pretty, but they've infused their characters with, well, character, which made it much more fun to get inside their heads for this novel.

To Constance Cochran, GraceAnne Andreassi

DeCandido, Heidi Ellis, Marina Frants, and Lesley McBain, for invaluable feedback that made the book a lot better.

To the various online resources, from the "Superwiki" at supernatural.oscillating.net, to the official *Supernatural* site at supernatural.warnerbros.com, to the *Supernatural* entries on the main Wikipedia, to the various other folks on the Internet who support, discuss, overanalyze, and lust over the show.

To Dr. Judith Richardson, who really does offer a literature class at Stanford University called "American Hauntings," to the NYPD's website at www.nyc.gov/html/nypd for research assistance, to Susan McCrackin for financial aid neepery, and to Steven H. Silver and Rachel Ward for bringing the Latin.

To Gregory Mcdonald, from whose *Fletch* books I stole the "Park in Rear" joke.

Finally, it should be noted that, while most of the details about the life of Edgar Allan Poe and his home and family are as true as the author could determine, the historical figure of Percival Samuels is wholly fictional, as is his resurrection ritual.

Last, but not least, thanks to them that live with me, both human and feline, for constant companionship and encouragement.

I heard all things in the heaven and in the earth.
I heard many things in hell.

—EDGAR ALLAN POE, "The Tell-Tale Heart"

Historian's Note

This novel takes place between the second-season *Supernatural* episodes "Crossroad Blues" and "Croatoan."

ONE

Fordham University
The Bronx, New York
Sunday 12 November 2006

A chill November breeze blew John Soeder's hair into his face, Mother Nature's reminder to get a haircut in the absence of his actual mother being around to nag him about it. She was back in Ohio where it was safe, and also ten degrees colder than it was here in the Bronx. If Emily Soeder could see her son's shaggy mop of brown hair, she'd make that clicking noise she always made and offer to call to make the haircutting appointment herself.

John loved attending Fordham University for about a thousand reasons, but its considerable distance from his mother numbered high on that list.

He and his roommate, Kevin Bayer, were heading back to their off-campus apartment after a long day in the print shop in the basement of the McKinley Center. They were the coeditors of Fordham's alternative paper and had spent most of the day putting the latest biweekly issue to bed. The files had been e-mailed to the printer, and they would have the issues by Tuesday morning. That was critical, as they had to get it out before *The Ram,* Fordham's stodgy official student newspaper, especially because of the exclusive they got from the dean.

They were walking quickly through the campus, heading toward the exit at Belmont Avenue by Faculty Memorial Hall. From there it was only a few blocks to their battered, cluttered, tiny—but blissfully cheap—apartment on Cambreleng Avenue.

Once they hit the exit, John brushed his hair out of his face and said, "C'mon, let's motor. I wanna get home and change for the party."

"What party?"

"*Amy's* party, remember?"

Kevin winced. "I got an eight-thirty class tomorrow morning, dude, I can't."

Shrugging, John said, "Blow it off."

"No way. Dr. Mendez'll have my ass. Seriously, she takes *attendance.* I already missed three classes 'cause 'a production weekends, I *can't* miss another one."

They had come to the corner of Belmont Avenue and Fordham Road, and had to wait for the light—the traffic was sufficiently heavy, even this late on a Sunday, so they couldn't cross against the light. Prior to senior year, John had lived in the on-campus dorms, which were part of the lush greenery that characterized Fordham's campus, an oasis of academe in the midst of the largest city in the world. Well, not the *midst*—the Bronx was the northernmost part of New York City, just above Manhattan and Queens, and the only part of the city attached to the mainland. Before visiting Fordham during his senior year of high school, John had always assumed New York to be Manhattan. He had no idea of the outer boroughs, and was thrilled to find himself in a neighborhood that by itself was a more exciting city than Cleveland ever could be.

The transition still messed with his head a little, though. Fordham's campus was all trees and grass and a mix of old and new buildings—some dating back to the university's founding in the nineteenth century, others late twentieth-century additions—and wouldn't have been out of place in a sleepy town somewhere in New England.

But then you stepped through the wrought-iron gates and were hit with a cacophony of cars and buses zipping down Fordham Road—or crawling if it was rush hour—pedestrians, gas stations, fast-food

joints, car repair shops, and *people*. The neighborhood was a mix of Italians who had come in the
early twentieth century, Latinos who came in the
1960s, and Albanians who came in the 1980s. Just
down the street in one direction was Sears, Fordham Plaza, and the Metro North train; the other
way, the Department of Motor Vehicles, the Bronx
Zoo, and the Botanical Gardens. The "Little Italy"
neighborhood still thrived, filled with delis, wine
stores, restaurants, bakeries, pasta shops, and the
occasional street fair, and John had gained five
pounds that semester just by moving closer to a
source of canolis.

Of course, on a late Sunday night, there were
almost no people on the street, just the cars.

The light changed, and Kevin and John ran
across the street, since it was already blinking with
the red hand indicating DON'T WALK before they
made it halfway.

"Why'd you take a Monday morning class anyhow?" John asked. "You *knew* you'd be up late
most Sundays."

"It was the only medieval lit class I could take.
Only other one was opposite the Shakespeare sem-
inar, and that's a two-parter that I gotta take part
two of next semester."

They turned to walk up Fordham to Cambreleng. "And you're not taking a medieval lit class
next semester, why, exactly?"

"'Cause Dr. Mendez'll be on sabbatical, and that means Father O'Sullivan."

John, who was a history major and therefore had no clue about the English department, scratched his chin—he needed a shave, something *else* his mother'd be on his ass about were she here—said, "Yeah, and . . . ?"

Kevin's eyes got wide. "Father O'Sullivan's had tenure since, like, the *Dark* Ages."

"Middle Ages."

"What?"

"It wasn't the Dark Ages," John said defensively. "They don't call it that anymore, it's called—"

"Dude, the Roman Empire had indoor plumbing. The Holy Roman Empire peed out their windows. It was the Dark Ages."

John gritted his teeth and was about to respond, but Kevin got back to his original topic: "Father O'Sullivan got tenure in, I swear to *God*, 1946."

They turned onto Cambreleng. "Dude, my *father* was *born* in 1946."

"My *point*. The man's a freakin' *fossil*. No *way* am I taking a class with him."

"Whatever." John didn't really care all that much. "You should still come to the party."

"No way, I need my beauty rest."

John grinned. "Ain't enough sleep in the *world* to make *that* happen."

"Bite me entirely, dude."

Another breeze gusted, and John had to push the hair out of his face again. The farther they got from Fordham Road, the quieter it became, as Cambreleng was entirely residential. Most of the block was filled with red brick three-story town houses that were a few feet in from the street, a postage-stamp front area separated from the sidewalk by a waist-high wrought-iron fence. The rest of the block had five-story apartment buildings. Fewer buildings went higher than that, since once you went above five floors, city law required you put in an elevator. Many of the windows on the block were dark, and John and Kevin were the only people on the sidewalk.

"Well, *I'm* still going, since I had the brains to arrange a proper schedule, where my first Monday class is at twelve-thirty. Which means, par-*tay*."

Kevin chuckled. "Dude, Britt's not gonna dump Jack for you."

John tensed up. In fact, hitting on Britt was at the top of his list of things to do at Amy's party, but he saw no reason to share that with his roommate. "Britt's gonna be there?"

"Don't *even*. You lie like I snowboard."

"You don't snowboard."

"My *point*."

John started to say *Whatever*, but he'd already said that, and he hated repeating himself. Kevin may have been fond of that doofy catch phrase "my *point,*" which he used *all* the damn time, but John liked to be verbally diverse. That was the thing he always nailed in the articles he edited for the paper—repetition. You kept people interested by saying different things, not by using the same tired phrases. It was why he didn't like most stand-up comics and sketch comedians. They'd get some kind of catch phrase, and then it would become expected and desired, and the routine wouldn't be about being funny anymore, but about building to the catch phrase. That wasn't entertainment, that was conditioning.

"What the hell's that?"

Kevin was pointing at something, and John followed his finger to the plastic garbage cans in front of one of the town houses. It looked like someone was rummaging through the garbage.

Sadly, that wasn't so unusual a sight. There were plenty of homeless people around, and they'd often go through recycling bins to find cans and bottles they could redeem at the supermarket.

Then the figure raised its head, and John saw that it wasn't a homeless guy. They both stopped walking as they realized that it was some sort of simian.

"That's a baboon!" John said.

"Dude, that's an orangutan."

John frowned. "You sure?"

"Pretty sure."

The baboon or orangutan or whatever it was

looked over at them, opened its mouth, and *hissed*.

Both John and Kevin stepped back a pace or two. John whispered, "Dude, do orangutans hiss?"

"No, but I don't think baboons do, either. And why're we whispering?"

Before John could answer that, the—oh, hell, he'd just call it a monkey until he found out for sure—picked up the garbage can and threw it into the street. Unfortunately, the lid was off, so a torn garbage bag came rolling out, spilling rotten food, empty containers, and other stuff onto the pavement.

John said, "You got your cell?"

Kevin nodded.

"Good, 'cause my battery's dead."

"Who the hell'm I supposed to call, Lost and Found?"

Not taking his eye off the monkey, John said, "No, 911, you doof, now *call* 'em, before—"

Suddenly, the monkey ran toward them, screeching like it was on a meth bender or something.

John wanted to turn and run away, but found that he couldn't make his legs move.

And it didn't matter for very long, because this monkey could give Jesse Owens a run for his money. It was on them in a second.

As a general rule, John hated when he screamed. He always sounded like a girl. Proving that this was an unjust universe, his screams actually had gotten *higher* in pitch after his voice changed. It was embarrassing, really, so whenever he felt the urge to scream, he tried to keep his mouth shut, so it came out as more of a hum. To his mind, that sounded manlier.

But right now, with a crazed monkey screeching and howling and jumping on top of him and Kevin, and hitting them *really* hard with his big hands, he screamed like a girl.

He hadn't felt like this since he got into that stupid fight in high school with Harry Markum over who would be going to the prom with Jeannie Waite. The joke being, of course, that she went with that *loser* Morty Johannsen, so he got a black eye and a split lip for nothing. The monkey's fists pounded on him and Kevin both, and the pain was just *everywhere*.

Then one smack caught him in the side of the head, and he literally saw stars, something he used to think only happened in cartoons.

Only when he felt the cool pavement on his cheek did John realize that the monkey wasn't hitting him anymore. But he still heard screams.

Rolling over, which sent a shooting pain through his side, he saw the monkey picking Kevin up and throwing him into the fence in front of one of the town houses.

Then he heard a snap.

He didn't want to believe it. *Couldn't* believe it at first. It wasn't like a twig breaking, it wasn't like a piece of plastic snapping in two, it wasn't—

It wasn't like anything John Soeder had ever heard before. And because of that, he knew that Kevin was dead.

"No. Kevin!"

He barely noticed the orangutan or baboon or gorilla or *whatever* it was lumbering toward him. Instead, he just stared at Kevin, lying there on the Cambreleng Avenue sidewalk, his head at an impossible angle, and wondered how the *hell* this could possibly have happened. It couldn't have been real, monkeys didn't just show up on the street and beat people to death. It couldn't be!

The monkey leapt on top of him then and started whaling on him, and he didn't even raise an arm to defend himself, because he simply couldn't believe it.

The second boy took forever to die.

At least the first one was taken care of quickly. But the other one, the one who kept muttering to himself after the first one died, the orangutan had to keep punching and punching until he finally gave in.

Once the second one breathed his last, he spoke the incantation one final time, then stepped on the burning wormwood to put it out. A few charred bits of wormwood leaf were left on the pavement, but the wind would scatter that in due course. And even if they found it, no one was likely to connect it to an escaped orangutan beating two people to death.

It wasn't pleasant, but it was necessary—and it had to be done tonight, in the last quarter of the moon, just as the first one had to be done on the full moon on the fifth. True, they discovered the body two days later, which was sooner than he'd expected, but nobody from the constabulary had come to question him, so all his precautions had obviously been successful.

More to the point, it had to be done on this spot. The second spot of the sigil had been traced with the appropriate ritual.

Once he was sure the small flame was extinguished, he stepped out from the narrow passageway between one of the town houses and the apartment building—and wasn't it revolting, the way people just tossed their garbage into the dark places, hoping nobody would notice it?—and unholstered the tranquilizer gun. Taking careful aim, he shot the orangutan in the neck.

It fell face first into the pavement a second later.

Running onto the sidewalk, he quickly removed the dart with a gloved hand. There would be no trace of his presence here.

Turning, he ran toward his car while pulling out a disposable cell phone he'd bought earlier that afternoon at one of the delis on Arthur Avenue and dialed 911.

"There's some kinda wild animal! Beatin' two kids at Cambreleng an' a hun' eighty-eighth! Come quick!"

Then he tossed the cell phone into a metal mesh garbage can on the corner of East 188th Street and got into his parked vehicle.

Two down, two to go. Then, at last, the answer will be mine!

TWO

Bowles Motel and Lodge
South Bend, Indiana
Wednesday 15 November 2006

"That's the problem with the job, Sammy, sometimes you hit a dead end."

Sam Winchester silently agreed with his brother Dean as they did their final check of the motel room before hauling their stuff out to the car. Their father had drilled into them from a young age always to scour a room before checking out, as it wouldn't do to leave personal stuff lying around.

Especially when some of that stuff included exotic weaponry and ancient grimoires.

Generally, they were good about cleaning out the room. There was that one time in Key West when Dean had left the tin of salt next to the bed, and he'd insisted on turning the car around on Route 1 and heading back to retrieve it. Sam had asked why they couldn't just go to a supermarket and get another one—it was a pretty common household item, after all—but Dean had insisted that it was the principle of the thing.

Which had been fine right up until the clerk asked why the two brothers had a big tin of salt in their hotel room, and Dean had gotten that wide-eyed look he got when somebody went off the script. With Sam watching and not even bothering to hide his grin, Dean had stammered for about half an hour before coming up with something about lactose intolerance. ("Dude," Sam had said as they went back out to the car, retrieved tin in hand, "you *do* know that salt has, basically, *nothing* to do with lactose intolerance, right?" "Thank you, Mr. Wizard," Dean had replied through clenched teeth.)

Today, they were checking out and hitting the road, their latest job not having been a job at all.

Dean was still talking as they headed out to the car. "But at least we got to see beautiful downtown South Bend."

"Yeah, real hot spot," Sam muttered as Dean opened the trunk.

"Hey, we go where the jobs take us."

"Or don't. It really was a suicide, Dean. A normal, run-of-the-mill suicide."

Dean shrugged. "It happens." He tossed his

bag into the rear of the trunk, rolling it over the boxes of weapons and supplies. Sam did likewise, using only his left hand, as his right was still in a cast from when that zombie girl broke it back in Lawrence.

Sam didn't have the same attachment Dean did to the black 1967 Chevrolet Impala, the family car their father had passed on to Dean. (Then again, Sam sometimes thought he didn't have the same attachment to his late girlfriend Jessica that Dean had to the Impala.) When the car was wrecked a couple of months back, Dean had rebuilt it pretty much from scratch, a process that took weeks of backbreaking effort.

However, even Sam had to admit that the massive trunk was a great benefit, given that they lived their entire life out of this car. The rear of the voluminous trunk was taken up with three bags: Sam's bag, Dean's bag, and the laundry bag. That last one was starting to bulge.

"We're gonna need to do a laundry run soon, man," Sam said.

"Not here," Dean said quickly. "I don't think that cop was too thrilled with ace reporters Anderson and Barre. We'd better split before he decides to run my face through his computer."

Sam nodded in agreement. Dean was still wanted for a series of murders committed by a shapeshifter taking his form in St. Louis earlier that year, and there was just no way "a mutated freak who looked just like me did it" was going to fly with the U.S. Attorney's Office.

Dean closed the trunk and they headed to the main office. Like most of the places the Winchesters stayed, the Bowles Motel and Lodge was dirt-cheap with minimal amenities. All they needed was a roof, a bed, and a working shower—though the latter was hit and miss with some of the places they stayed— and they weren't exactly rolling in dough.

Fighting demons and monsters and things that went booga-booga in the night was important, but it didn't pay. They lived off credit card fraud, and Dean's pool and poker winnings. That meant the Hyatt was not an option.

They entered the shabby office, which had cracked wood paneling, a badly stained beige carpet, and a pockmarked front desk. An older woman sat behind that desk, puffing away on a cigarette while sitting under a red NO SMOKING sign and reading a Dan Brown book. Her face was caked with enough makeup to allow her to attend a Halloween party as the Joker, and her hair was sprayed within an inch of its life into something that probably wanted to be a beehive. Sam was fairly sure he could have hit that hairdo with any weapon in the Impala's trunk and not done a lick of damage to it. She wore a name badge that said MONICA.

"Hey," Dean said, "we're checking out."

Monica took a final puff on the cigarette, then stubbed it out in the ashtray. "You're Winwood, right?" she asked with a scratchy voice.

Sam managed not to roll his eyes. Just once, Sam wished Dean would pick an inconspicuous alias.

"That's right," Dean said with a smile. "We're ready to check out."

"Yeah, there's a problem. Your credit card was declined. I'm gonna need another one."

There was Dean's wide-eyed look again, but this time Sam didn't smile. "Declined. Really." Dean looked at Sam helplessly, then turned back to Monica. "Could you try it again, please?"

She gave Dean a withering look. "I tried it three times. That's all they'll allow."

"Did they say why?"

"No, no reason. You wanna call the credit card company? You can use this phone." She picked up the desk phone—which, Sam was appalled to see, was a rotary dial—and held it up for Dean to take.

"Uh, no, that, uh—that won't really help."

Sam realized why Dean was stalling. He had other credit cards, but none of them said Dean Winwood on them.

Quickly, Sam stepped forward, reaching into his back pocket, and said, "I'll get it." He removed one of his own fake credit cards from his wallet and handed it to Monica.

She took it and stared at it, which Sam had been

hoping she wouldn't do, since this one didn't say Winwood either. "Thought you two was brothers."

Without missing a beat, Sam said, "We are, but I was adopted. By the time I tracked down my birth parents, they had both died, so I changed my name to McGillicuddy in tribute to them."

Monica's face split into a rictus that Sam supposed could've been called a smile. "That's so sweet of you. What a nice boy you are." She ran the card through the machine, then entered the total for the three nights they stayed.

The wait for the machine to check was interminable. Dean, to his credit, had recovered, and he had his best poker face on.

Finally, after several eternities, the machine beeped and the word APPROVED appeared on the small screen.

"All right," Monica said, still smiling, as the whirr of a printer could be heard under the desk. "Here's your card back, Mr. McGillicuddy."

"Thank you," Sam said, retrieving it and putting it back in his wallet.

"Such good manners. Mr. and Mrs. Winwood obviously raised you both right."

Dean smiled. "Yes, ma'am, they did a bang-up job."

Monica then handed the printout, as well as the credit card machine's receipt, to Sam. "Just sign here, and you can be on your way."

Once that was all done, they went back outside. "Nice save there, Sammich," Dean said with a grin. "Y'know, I'm finally starting to get it."

Sam frowned. This sounded suspiciously like the beginning of a lengthy diatribe, the end of which would be a joke at Sam's expense. "Get what?"

"Well, Sammy, we grew up together, and that whole time, nothing about you ever screamed 'lawyer' at me. So when you told me that you were applying to law school, it kinda threw me. But I've been watching you the last year, and I think I figured it out."

Here it comes. Sam tried not to groan.

"You can shovel manure as good as anyone I've ever met. That line you pulled on Monica there with the adoption? Beautiful. And with a straight face."

In fact, Sam's skills at lying—both in terms of pretending to be someone else and also misleading people as to the true nature of his life and of the world itself—had been one of the things that attracted him to the law. His life as the child of a hunter of supernatural creatures, and of being trained to be a hunter himself, had given him these skills anyhow, and it only seemed natural to put them to good use.

That wasn't what he told his brother, though. "Yeah, I can pull the wool over people's eyes. And I do most of the research and know most of the lore. And I'm good with the weapons and the hand-to-hand." They arrived at the Impala, and

Sam gave his brother a grin as he stepped up to the passenger door. "So, uh, what do I need *you* for, exactly?"

Before Dean could construct a reply, his phone started playing Deep Purple's "Smoke on the Water."

"For that matter," Sam added, "I'm the one who showed you how to download ringtones."

Pulling the cell phone out of his pocket, Dean scowled. "I would've figured it out eventually." He flipped it open and glanced at the number, which caused his eyes to go even wider than they had in the office. Putting the phone to his ear, he said, "Ellen?"

That surprised Sam. Ellen Harvelle ran a road-house that catered to hunters. He and Dean had recently learned that Ellen's late husband died when he was on a hunt with their dad, and it put a bit of a strain on their relationship—especially since they only found out because Ellen's young daughter Jo snuck out and went on a hunt with him and Dean against Ellen's very strenuous objections.

Years of listening to loud music and using fire-arms had played merry hell with Dean's hearing, so he kept his cell's volume up way too loud. That meant Sam could hear Ellen's tinny voice over the phone's speaker.

"Listen," she said, "I may have a job for you boys."

"Really? 'Cause—"

"It's for Ash. He wouldn't ask himself, but I figure he did you two a favor, so you might be willing to do him one back." Ellen seemed to be barreling through the conversation, not letting Dean get a word in.

Or, at least trying not to. Keeping Dean quiet was usually a forlorn hope. "Sure, I guess." He smirked. "Always had a soft spot for that mullethead. What's he need?"

Ellen gave the particulars of the case to Dean, and did it in a lower voice, so Sam couldn't make it all out. Ash was a deadbeat drunk who nonetheless was a genius and able to track demons via computer, a trick Sam had never mastered despite many attempts. As Dean had once said, Ash's geek-fu was strong. Sam didn't entirely believe his claim to have gone to MIT—for starters, he said it was a college in Boston, and anyone who'd gone there would know it was in Cambridge—but he did believe that Ash had the know-how, based on the times he'd helped him and his brother out.

"Okay. We'll check it out." With that, Dean flipped the phone shut and looked out the driveway. "That road'll take us to 80, right?"

Sam tried to remember the map. "I think so, yeah. Why, where's the job?"

Dean grinned. "The town so nice, they named it twice: New York, New York."

"Really?" Sam turned and went back to the trunk. "Open it up, I wanna show you something."

"Something in New York?" Dean said, joining him at the back, since he had the keys.

After Dean opened the trunk, Sam took a folder out of his bag. "It may not be anything, but I noticed a couple of murders that took place there."

"Sam—it's *New York*. They get, like, fifty murders a day."

"Which is why these two probably flew under the radar." He took the clippings, photocopied off newspapers he'd looked at in several different public libraries they'd visited recently. "First, we got a guy bricked up in a building's basement." Sam handed Dean an 8½ by 11 sheet of paper with a filler news story in a section of the *New York Daily News* dedicated to community news about a man named Marc Reyes, who was found bricked up in the basement of a house in the Bronx.

As Dean glanced over the photocopy, Sam went on: "And this past Sunday, two college kids were beaten to death by an orangutan."

Dean looked up at that. "Seriously?"

Sam nodded. "That's two murders that are right out of Edgar Allan Poe short stories."

"That's kind of a stretch," Dean said as he handed back the story about the bricked-up man.

"Maybe—but they both took place in the Bronx, and Poe used to live in the Bronx. Plus, the first murder was on the fifth—they didn't find the body until two days later, but it happened on the fifth, which was—"

"The last full moon," Dean said with a nod. "Yeah, okay, maybe, but—"

Tossing the folder back into the trunk, Sam said, "And the orangutan was on the last quarter." He didn't need to add that lots of rituals were based on the phases of the moon. "It's not that big a deal, but since we're going to New York anyhow, I figured we could look into it while we—uh, do whatever it is we're doing."

Dean slammed the trunk shut. "Haunting. Some friend of Ash's is having ghost issues. So who's he gonna call?"

Sam chuckled. They both got into the car, Dean in the driver's seat. "That's really weird."

"What, that there'd be a haunting? We see them all the time."

"No," Sam said with a shake of his head, "that Ash would have a friend."

With a chuckle of his own, Dean slid the key into the ignition. A grin spread on his face as the Impala hummed to life. "Hear that engine purr."

Squirming in the passenger seat, Sam thought, *I swear to God, if he starts petting the dashboard again, I'm walking to New York.*

However, he was spared that. Dean shoved a Metallica tape into the player, twirled the volume up, and the car was filled with the guitar opening to "Enter Sandman."

Dean turned to him. "Atomic batteries to power."

Glowering at his older brother, Sam said, "I'm only gonna say, 'Turbines to speed' if you don't make a comment about me in short green pants."

Dean pulled the gearshift down to R and said, "Let's move out." He backed out of the parking spot, then brought it down to D and sent them out onto the open road.

THREE

On the road
Interstate 80, approaching the
George Washington Bridge
Thursday 16 November 2006

"How can there be so many people on one road?"

Sam tried not to laugh out loud at Dean's plaintive cry, the fifth time he'd asked the question in the last ten minutes—a time span during which the Impala had moved forward maybe fifty feet.

They'd been driving all night. Sam had suggested they stop at a motel overnight, but Dean wanted to get there quickly. They had stopped in a motel in Clarion, Pennsylvania, to shower and change clothes, paying for it with one of the fraudulent cards, but didn't stay the night. Instead, they worked their way across Pennsylvania and New Jersey, taking it in turns to sleep or drive.

Unfortunately, that meant they arrived at the approach to the George Washington Bridge smack dab in the middle of the morning rush hour, and traffic was bumper-to-bumper.

Dean was about ready to jump out of his skin.

"There's gotta be a faster way to get into the city."

Sam didn't bother looking at the map, since they'd had this conversation several times already. "The Lincoln Tunnel and the Holland Tunnel are farther away from the Bronx, and they're tunnels—they've probably got *more* traffic 'cause they have to squeeze more cars into fewer—"

"All *right*." Dean pounded the steering wheel. Ash's friend lived in a neighborhood called Riverdale, which was also in the Bronx, which meant it would be easier for Sam to investigate the Poe murders. "That other thing you were talkin' about," Dean said. "You said they were all from Eddie Albert Poe stories, right?"

"Edgar Allan Poe, yeah."

"Right, whatever. He's the guy that did 'The Raven,' right?"

Giving his brother a sidelong glance, Sam said, "You've read a poem?"

"They did it on *The Simpsons* once. Hey, c'mon,

move it, will you!" Dean suddenly screamed at the car in front of them. "Christ, you don't have to leave fifty car lengths between you and the guy in front of you!" Again he pounded the steering wheel. "I swear, these people got their drivers' licenses from freakin' Crackerjack boxes."

"Anyhow," Sam said, as much to take Dean's mind off his frustration as anything, "the guy bricked up in the basement is from 'The Cask of Amontillado.' The orangutan is from 'The Murders on the Rue Morgue'—which, by the way, was the first detective story."

"Really?"

"Yeah, that story was an influence on Sir Arthur Conan Doyle when he created Sherlock Holmes."

"Well, thank you, Marian the Librarian."

Sam was glad to hear Dean teasing him, as it meant he wasn't letting the driving get to him—

"Hey! Use the freakin' turn signal, will you?"

—much. "I took a lit class as an elective at Stanford—it was called 'American Hauntings,' all about the use of the supernatural in American fiction, including a lot about Poe." He shrugged. "I was curious, after all the weird stuff we've seen, what the pop culture interpretations of what we do were like."

"What, *X-Files* reruns didn't do the trick?"

"Honestly, Dean, you should read Poe's stories.

'The Fall of the House of Usher,' 'The Masque of the Red Death'—some of this stuff sounds like it could've been right out of one of our jobs. You gotta wonder what he saw to make him write that. I mean, he practically created the horror genre."

"So, Professor, whaddaya think the deal is with these murders? Phases of the moon, re-creating old short stories—sound like any ritual you know?"

"Not offhand, but there's something else. Before, when I had the maps out? I was checking something, and both these murders were exactly one mile from the Poe Cottage."

"First of all, what's the Poe Cottage?"

"Poe lived in the Bronx for a few years in a little cottage."

"Dude, I've seen *Fort Apache*—the Bronx doesn't *have* cottages. Hey, jackass, pick a freakin' lane!"

Sam suddenly felt the urge to get a firm grip on the dashboard with his good hand. "It did in the nineteenth century. The Bronx didn't even become part of New York City until the 1890s or so. Anyhow, because Poe lived there, they preserved the cottage—and his wife died there."

Dean nodded. "Okay, so the place has some emotional significance. Still not connecting the dots."

Shrugging, Sam said, "Me, either."

"Second of all, why didn't you tell me this when you were playing with the maps? I thought you were trying to find alternate routes."

Amazed Dean even had to ask, Sam said, "You had *Led Zeppelin II* in the tape deck. I know better than to try to hold an intelligent conversation with you when 'Whole Lotta Love' is playing."

Dean opened his mouth, closed it, then opened it again. "Yeah, okay, fair enough."

They crawled ever more slowly toward the bridge, and Sam realized that they were approaching a toll booth. Dean saw that some lanes were moving faster, and he inched into them.

"Uh, dude, those are the E-Z Pass lanes."

"Aw, crap." The bane of the Winchesters' existence had been the proliferation of things like E-Z Pass, Fast Lane, I-Pass, and assorted other services that involved sticking a piece of plastic on the wind shield that a scanner would read, deducting the toll from a credit card or from payments made with a check. The former required a consistency of use with a card that Dean and Sam couldn't afford, since their credit cards were all phony. Sam had considered setting something up with the checking account he'd had when he was at Stanford, and through which he maintained his cell phone and Internet, but now, with he and Dean wanted by the law, it wasn't prudent for them to attach something to the car that could be used to trace their movements.

However, the cash lanes were considerably slower, which, Sam knew, would only increase Dean's dark mood.

Sure enough, the realization that he'd be stuck in slow traffic while dozens of other cars zipped through the E-Z Pass lane undid all of Sam's distraction work, and Dean was now holding the steering wheel with an iron grip in his right hand while punching the inner driver's side door with his left and muttering curses to himself.

Recognizing a futile endeavor when he saw one, Sam pulled out his Treo and made use of its web browser. It was slow—basically as fast as dial-up—but he was eventually able to find and call up the website of Ash's friend's band, Scottso.

By the time he was done reading up on it, they were next in the toll line. "Dude," Dean asked suddenly, "you got any cash?"

Sam whirled around. "Excuse me? I thought you were the keeper of the lucre, Mr. Pool Hustlin' Poker Player Man."

"Remember that girl in South Bend, the Notre Dame student who—"

Under no circumstances did Sam ever want to hear the end of any sentence of Dean's that began with the words "Remember that girl." "Fine, whatever." Sam tried to straighten his lanky form as best he could in the front seat and dug his left hand into his pants pocket. He pulled out a ball of fluff, three quarters, several business cards that read SAM WINCHESTER, REPORTER that he'd made up in a print shop back in Indiana, and his monogrammed money clip, which had four bills in it, one of which stood out as being a ten dollar bill, since they were all a different color now. He gingerly yanked it out and handed it to Dean.

Dean paid the toll with the ten, waited for the change, responded to the toll taker's request to have a nice day with an incoherent grunt, and then stuffed the four singles into his own shirt pocket.

Sam considered objecting, then decided that life was just too damn short, instead saying, "We wanna take the Henry Hudson Parkway, so stay in the right lane."

Dean nodded as they started over the bridge.

For a moment Sam just took the time to admire the view. The George Washington Bridge was one of the most famous bridges in the country, and while it didn't look quite as distinctive as, say, the Golden Gate—which he'd visited on a trip he and Jess had taken to San Francisco—or the Brooklyn Bridge right here in New York, it still had a certain grandeur that he admired.

As the Impala rolled over the bridge—still moving at less than twenty miles an hour, but that was an improvement on their pre-toll-booth pace—Sam turned to his right. It was a clear day out, so he could see the most famous skyline in the world: skyscrapers in gray and red and silver and brown all reaching upward, all different sizes and shapes, with the pinnacle of the Empire State Building rising above all of it. It was a complex mélange of constructed life, a monument to human achievement over nature.

The scholar in him wanted desperately to explore the inner workings of that monument, whether to play tourist and see the sights, like he and Jess had done in San Francisco, or to check out the underside of the place, see if the thousands of legends that had grown up around the city were true: the alligators in the city sewer system, the phantom subway conductor, the missile silos in eastside apartment buildings.

He sat back in the passenger seat with a sense of melancholy. Their lives didn't allow for that sort of thing. They came in, they did the job, they left. Hell, now Dean was on the feds' radar, and, while Sam couldn't find any specific warrant out for his own arrest (and didn't Dean love giving him crap about *that?*), he was pretty sure he wouldn't be ignored if they got the attention of law enforcement, either. They had to keep their heads down—which meant no self-indulgence. Seeing the Statue of Liberty, going to the top of the Empire State Building, exploring Central Park, even going underground to check to see about the alligators and the ghosts and the missiles, none of that could afford to be on the agenda. Them doing the job saved lives, which meant time spent *not* doing the job meant people might die.

That's the job. And it needs doing. One of the items on his eight-mile-long list of regrets was that it took Dad dying for him to realize that.

The exit for the Henry Hudson was right after the bridge ended, and to Dean's loudly expressed relief, most of the traffic that took the exit was going southbound, which would take them into Manhattan. Almost nobody else was going north.

However, Dean's desire to speed was tempered by the parkway itself, which was hilly, twisty, and turny, and Sam found himself once again holding the dashboard in a death grip.

Feeling the need to distract himself from the fact that Dean was using the lane markers as a guideline more than a rule, Sam said, "So I checked out this guy's band on the web. I'm starting to see why Ellen thought of us—they're a cover band, and they do seventies rock."

For the first time since the cars started moving slowly on I-80, Dean's face brightened. *"Really?"*

"Yeah, they named themselves after a DJ who died a couple years ago named Scott Muni."

"Dude," Dean said in a familiar tone. It meant that Sam didn't know some arcane and pointless piece of musical lore that Dean thought was essential to being alive. Sam steeled himself for the tirade even as Dean said, "It's pronounced 'myoo-nee,' not 'money.' They called him 'the Professor,' he was one of the greatest rock DJs of the sixties and seventies. You know Van Morrison's 'Caravan'? The 'Scottso' he's talking about is Muni."

Sam just nodded, despite not knowing the song or DJ in question, and not caring all that much. He'd gotten enough of a tongue-lashing on the subject of Robert Johnson's music during that Hellhound job.

"Well, Ash's friend," Sam said once he was sure Dean was done chastising him, "Manfred Afiri, is the lead singer, and he plays guitar. There's four other guys, a keyboard player named Robbie Maldonado, another guitar player named Aldo Emmanuelli, a bass player named Eddie Grabowski, and a drummer named Tom Daley. They play weekends at a place in Larchmont called the Park in Rear."

Dean shot a sidelong glance at Sam. "Seriously?"

Sam shrugged. "That's what the website says."

The road finally straightened, just in time for a sign indicating another toll.

"Oh, you have got to be freakin' kiddin' me!

Bad enough we had to pay six bucks to get into this town, now we gotta pay more?"

Raising his eyebrow at the use of *we* in that sentence, Sam pointedly said, "You've got four bucks in your pocket."

"Yeah, yeah." Dean pulled in behind several other cars in the one and only lane labeled CASH ONLY, while other cars zipped through one of the six E-Z Pass lanes. Sam was starting to think it was a conspiracy.

Once they got through and went over another, smaller bridge that welcomed them to the Bronx, Sam said, "We wanna get off at 246th."

"Okay."

The road continued to curve menacingly past several exits, most for streets numbered in the 200s, before they reached the right exit.

Within seconds they were completely lost. They drove up and down several hills, and went on several roads that did not go straight, and were frustrated by jumps in the numerical sequence of streets. The area was also surprisingly suburban looking, with some really big houses that had yards—neither were images that Sam associated with being in New York City, especially after the view of crammed-together skyscrapers he got from the GWB.

"I thought this city was on a grid," Dean said through clenched teeth.

"That's Manhattan, Dean," Sam said patiently.
"Great."

The road angled down and to the right, nearing a
T intersection. Sam caught sight of a green street
sign that identified the upcoming street as East 248th
Street. "There!" he said pointing, "that's 248th.
Turn right."

"I swear to God, Sammy, if it's not on this block,
I'm turning around and going back to Indiana."

Sam refrained from pointing out that regardless
of whether they were going to Afiri's house or back
over the bridge, they were still lost. Besides, he got
a look at one of the house numbers they passed.
"We're on the right block. There, that's his place."

There weren't any parking spots on the street,
but there was a driveway next to Afiri's place, so
Dean parked the Impala there.

Once the car came to a stop, Sam hopped out,
grateful for the chance to stretch his long legs for the
first time since they'd gassed up in Scotrun, Pennsylvania. His knees popped as they straightened.

"Nice," Dean said, and Sam had to agree. The
house was a three-story Colonial, with a stone
chimney on the side, a wooden front porch, complete with porch swing, and a dark wood front
door with a small stained-glass window.

All Ellen had provided Dean was a name and
address, as well as the name of the band the guy

was in, so they had no way of knowing if he'd be home. A ring of the doorbell followed by a full minute of waiting indicated that he wasn't.

"Fine, let's break in," Dean said, reaching into his jacket pocket for his lock picks.

Sam put a hand on his arm before he could remove the paper clip in question. "Let's not. We're supposed to be helping this guy, remember?"

"We'll tell him Ash sent us."

"And if he doesn't believe us and calls the cops? Dean, we can't afford to commit felonies unless we absolutely have to, and we're not there yet. Hell, we just got here. Look, he probably has a day job. Let's check out the Poe thing and come back in the evening when he's more likely to be home."

Dean stared at Sam for a second. The way Dean's eyes were going back and forth, Sam could tell that his older brother was trying to figure out a way to be right and for Sam to be wrong and was failing miserably.

Finally, Dean turned around and went back to the car. "Fine, but we ain't goin' nowhere until you figure out how to get us out of this nuthouse." He opened the driver's side door. "Which crime scene you wanna hit first, the house with the bricked-up guy or the street where the monkey spanked back?"

Sam smiled. "Neither. The orangutan that killed those two kids was from the Bronx Zoo. We should start there. Say we're with, I dunno, *Wildlife Conservation* magazine or something."

"No, not that—*National Geographic.*"

"Uh, okay." Sam shrugged. "Not that it matters, but why not *Wildlife Conservation*?"

"'Cause that's run by the WCS, who're the people who run the Bronx Zoo. It'd be like investigating something on the Skywalker Ranch and saying we were with *Star Wars Insider*. They'd know we were bogus right off." With that, Dean got into the car.

Sam opened his door and folded himself into the front seat. "Since when do you know so much about animal magazines?"

"Cassie was a subscriber."

That got a grin out of Sam. Cassie was one of Dean's ex-girlfriends. Given Cassie's crusading character, based on the one and only time Sam met her in Missouri, he wasn't at all surprised that she supported the Wildlife Conservation Society.

Sam pulled out the maps to figure out the best route to the zoo. While he did so, Dean asked, "Hey, does the Bronx Zoo have penguins? Like in *Madagascar*?"

Without even looking up, Sam said, "That was the Central Park Zoo. I mean, the Bronx Zoo probably has 'em, too . . ."

"Yeah, but they're probably not as cool as the ones in *Madagascar*. I mean, I doubt they can take over a freighter or do hand-to-hand combat."

"Well, Dean, if they *can*, then we'll have three jobs . . ."

FOUR

The Bronx Zoo
The Bronx, New York
Thursday 16 November 2006

Clare Hemsworth brushed the bits of grass off the Wildlife Conservation Society logo on her blue shirt as she headed out into the pavilion in front of the Wild Asia ride. The crowds were a bit sparse in November, but visitors to the Bronx Zoo still wanted to go on Wild Asia.

Clare remembered her mother talking about how thrilling Wild Asia was back when it first opened in the late seventies. For her part, she couldn't imagine why anybody would make such a fuss. The monorail was *so* retro, and it wasn't as if it was *that* big a deal to see animals wandering around free. Of course, back in the stone age when Mom was a kid, she guessed it was a big deal not to see animals in cages, but there wasn't any novelty to it now. The monorail was a cheesy piece of plastic that Clare was convinced was gonna fall off the rail any day now.

Then again, she was in a bad mood generally. Ever since what happened with those two kids, she'd been talking to reporters, to police, and to lawyers representing Fordham University, and she was really, really sick of it. The lawyers were the worst—okay, cops and reporters were doing their jobs, but why should she have to listen to crap from Fordham's legal eagles just because the two kids who died happened to be their students? They weren't even killed on campus!

"Excuse me, Ms. Hemsworth?"

Clare closed her eyes and let out a breath. She'd had about fifty conversations that started with those four words this past week, and they were always like having root canal, only without the anesthetic. If it wasn't someone from law enforcement or from the WCS, she was going to tell them to screw off *so* fast . . .

She turned, and saw the hottest man she'd ever seen in her life.

There was another guy with him, but Clare didn't pay much attention to him, she was focused on this one guy. He had such amazing brown eyes, and, if he was the one who'd called her name, the sexiest voice she'd ever heard. Right there and then, she decided that she would do whatever this guy asked. He was tall, too, but not intimidating the way some tall guys were. His semishaggy dark hair was combed neatly, and he had an adorable small nose. "Uh, yeah, I'm—I'm Ms. Hemsworth. Uh, Clare."

The other, shorter one, said, "Nice to meet you, Clare. My name's John Mayall, and my friend here is Bernie Watson—we're with *National Geographic*."

Clare blinked, and tore her eyes away from Bernie Watson—what a wonderful name!—to look at the shorter one with the close-cropped hair, blue eyes, and mouth that looked like it was in a permanent smirk. *John, was it?* "Uh, okay." Then the text message she'd gotten from Frieda, her boss, came back to her. "Right! Frieda said you guys'd be talking to me. What do you need?"

"We're doing a story on the orangutan that killed those two students, and we were told you were the one who cared for them."

Bernie added, "If it's too much trouble—"

"Oh no!" she said quickly, not wanting Bernie to go away, but also still not entirely clear as to why *NG* would be doing this kind of story. Frieda's text had said that they were cleared by the press office, as long as they stuck with the questions in the memo that had gone around on Monday, but

Clare was confused as to why they'd bothered in the first place. "This isn't really, I dunno—typical of you guys, is it?"

John grinned. "Hey, we can't have all our stories be naked pictures of pygmies."

Rolling her eyes, Clare ignored John, and looked up at Bernie's tall form and soulful eyes. "So what is it you guys want to know? I mean, I've already told this story, like, a *thousand* times. You can probably get whatever you want from the news-papers."

"They're being very sensationalistic," Bernie said. "We're trying to print the truth, and make it clear that this wasn't the orangutan's fault."

"Oh, it wasn't Dean's fault at all!"

The short one suddenly developed a coughing fit, and then said, "Dean? That was the orang-utan's name?"

"Well, that's what I called him. We've got two on loan from Philadelphia for a while, and I named them Hank and Dean—y'know, after the Venture Brothers."

Looking at John, Bernie said, "Actually, I think Dean's a great name for a big ape, don't you?"

"Not really," John said in a low voice, and Clare started wondering what was going on. But then John looked back at her. "So, Clare, can you tell us in your own words what happened?"

"Yeah, okay." She was feeling a little exposed, so

she led the two reporters to one of the wooden tables near a food stand. Taking a deep breath, and trying not to get lost in Bernie's eyes, she went through the whole story: how Dean suddenly went crazy and started jumping up and down, before retreating under a rock. "Nobody saw him for a while after that—we don't really keep an eye on them 24/7, y'know?—and then when I went to feed him and Hank, I couldn't find him. Now you gotta understand, both these guys never miss a feeding— like, *ever*." She found her eyes misting up, and she wiped them with the cuff of the sleeve of her blue shirt.

John said, "You must care about Hank and Dean very much. That's really admirable—I've always been impressed with the work people like you do."

"Thanks," she said quickly, then looked at Bernie. "So I knew something was wrong, and we instituted a search. Animals wander off sometimes, and Dean had been acting a little weird, but we usually have *really* good security. But we didn't find anything." Good security was an understatement. Allan and Jimmy had lost their jobs thanks to Dean's escape.

Bernie leaned forward while John suddenly got up. "The paper said that NYPD Animal Control took Dean in."

Clare nodded. "They called us first, since we're

the only people in the city who *have* orangutans. Our animals have transponders so we can verify who they are, so they sent me to Animal Control." She shuddered at the memory. "*God*, what an awful place. All these animals stuck in tiny metal cages and treated like crap. I mean, I know, most of 'em are involved in crimes and stuff, but *God*."

A napkin appeared in front of her face. She looked up to see John, with a look of what she guessed was concern on his face. "Thanks," she said as she took the napkin and wiped the tears away. She even almost smiled; John was trying *way* too hard.

He sat back down next to Bernie, across from her. "So you checked the transponder."

"Well, yeah, but I didn't really need to, y'know? I know my Dean." She wiped new tears with the napkin. "The poor little guy was scared to *death*. They did blood tests on him, and he was hopped up on amphetamines of some kind, can you *believe* that?"

"Who would do that?" John asked.

"Well, *duh,* somebody who wanted to kill those two kids." God, what kind of idiot *was* this John guy?

"So it wasn't Dean's fault?" Bernie said, sounding relieved.

Clare shook her head. "And we were *so* afraid that we'd lose him. Sometimes the families of victims insist that the animals be euthanized, and judges usually come down on their side."

"Really?" Bernie said. "That's awful."

At this point, she couldn't work up much outrage. "It's typical. They're part of this world, too, but try to get most humans to acknowledge that. In fact, I'm going to law school part-time so I can make the laws about this kinda thing tougher."

"Good for you," Bernie said. "I actually almost went to law school."

"Really? Why'd you give it up?"

Bernie hesitated. "Weird family stuff," he said quietly. "Anyhow, I'm real happy with what I'm doing right now, believe me."

"Well, good for you. Still, you should think about it. So many lawyers these days are just in it to represent corporations and make big money— we need more people who care about the world, y'know? Where were you gonna go?"

"Stanford—that's where I did my undergrad work."

Clare whistled appreciatively. "I'm at NYU. I wish I had more time for class, but it's expensive, and I work a lot of hours here."

John then said, "I'm sure you'll get through it fine. You seem determined."

"I am, yeah," Clare said quickly to John, then looked back at Bernie. *All that, and brains, too, if he made it through Stanford.*

But then John said, "You said families of the victims usually ask for the animals to be—to be euthanized." John pronounced the word as if he'd never used it in conversation before, which struck Clare as odd. "But they didn't ask for that this time?"

She'd been hoping to quiz Bernie more on his law-school aspirations, but John seemed determined to actually do their job, which Clare supposed she could understand. "No, Dean lucked out." Was it her imagination or did John wince every time she referred to the orangutan by name? "Both the kids were members of WCS, and their families were sympathetic. Once the blood test proved that Dean was drugged, they didn't insist, and the cops were in a good mood that day, so they let us have him back." She shook her head. "I remember one time—in Minnesota, maybe?—a meerkat bit a kid who was too stupid to actually pay attention to the sign that said not to stick your hand over the fence. The family refused to give the kid a rabies test, so the zoo had to euthanize the entire family of meerkats."

"Sounds to me," John said, "like the wrong family got put down."

Clare nodded, conceding the point to John, then turning back to lose herself in Bernie's eyes. "So Dean's back with us, but we won't put him back out in the habitat yet."

"Why?"

"You kidding? He's, like, *totally* traumatized.

I just came back from feeding him, and he wouldn't eat until I left. He won't go near Hank, and he won't let me hold him."

John's mouth fell open. "You *hold* him?"

Clare couldn't believe he'd even ask that. "Of *course*. But now when I try, he—he *hisses*."

Bernie bit part of his lower lip for a second, which Clare thought was just *adorable*. "Clare, can I ask a favor?"

"Of course," she said without hesitation. Then added with what she hoped was a coquettish smile, "You can *ask*."

"Can we—can we *see* Dean?"

That wasn't what she'd been hoping for, especially since it meant she would have to disappoint him. "I'm sorry, but I so totally can't. Right now, they're just letting me in there."

John leaned forward. "Well, if *you* say it's okay—"

"It's not up to me. They only let me in because I'm their handler. We may wind up sending them both back to Philadelphia because of this. I'm sorry, but I'll get in a *huge* amount of trouble, and—and then they won't even let me see them anymore." Bernie was cute, but he wasn't *that* cute. Hank and Dean were her boys, and she wasn't letting anything jeopardize her relationship with them.

Not even Bernie.

They asked a few more random questions and then they got up, which surprised and disappointed her. "Well," Bernie said, "thanks for your help. If you think of anything else to share with us, give me a call, okay?" He reached into his pocket and pulled out a ratty piece of paper. "I'm sorry, we're outta business cards. We ordered them, like, three weeks ago, and still nothing."

All of a sudden alarm bells were going off in Clare's head. Why weren't they asking more questions? And they hadn't been taking notes or anything.

Still, she took his phone number. She wasn't a complete fool. Maybe she could talk to him without his partner and his drooling.

John shook her hand for a little *too* long and said, "It was a real pleasure meeting you, Clare. I hope Dean gets better."

"Thanks." She broke the handshake before John did, and then watched them both walk toward the staircase that would take them up to other parts of the zoo, or to one of two exits.

And that was it.

Frowning, Clare stared at the number, which had a 650 area code. She was pretty sure that *NG* was located in Washington, D.C., and their area code was 202. She was also pretty sure that 650 was in California somewhere. Of course, that could've been Stanford's area code, in which case Bernie would've had it from when he went there, but why wouldn't he have changed it to D.C. when he moved there after leaving Stanford?

And why didn't they ask more questions about Dean or the drugs that were used or any of the other questions on Frieda's list?

She shook her head, got up, and walked over to the small wooden ticket booth near the entrance to Wild Asia.

"Hey, Clare," the woman in the booth said, her voice echoing in the small booth and coming out through the glass partition. "What's up? Who were those guys you were talking to? The shorter one was *hot*."

"Gina, can you call Bill for me? I need to talk to him."

Bill was the head of security—and the one who fired Jimmy and Allan. Much as she hated to admit it, she was pretty sure he needed to know about John Mayall and Bernie Watson . . .

FIVE

"Nice work, givin' her your phone number."

Sitting in the passenger seat, Dean had been hoping to get more than a sigh from his brother. But then, Sam was driving, since Dean had decided that he didn't want to get behind the wheel again until they were somewhere sane.

Sam was rationalizing like crazy. "I just wanted her to be able to get in touch with us, in case—"

"In case she wanted to stare at you some more? C'mon, dude, she was totally into you. I mean, I even brought her a napkin when she got all misty-eyed, and she barely noticed." He leaned back, clasping his hands behind his head. "She was tuned in to Sam-TV."

"Well," Sam said, "maybe she appreciated somebody not trying so hard."

"That was *not* trying hard. That was trying normal."

"Maybe you woulda had better luck if you gave your real name." Sam grinned. "I mean, she obviously likes to hold guys named Dean. Or maybe you're not hirsute enough."

Dean had been hoping Sam wouldn't bring that up. Not that there was a chance in hell that Sam wouldn't, but he liked to dream, sometimes. "Look, it's just—" Then Dean cut himself off. An orangutan had the same name as him. There was just no comeback for that, and he was a good enough poker player to know when it was better to lay down than to keep playing. "So what's the next step?"

"You're just embarrassed 'cause you don't know what 'hirsute' means."

"I'm not an idiot, Sam. It means hairy. Now will you focus for a second? What's our next step?"

"You're the one carrying on about how she was 'into me,' and *I* need to focus?" Sam kept going before Dean could answer that. "It's almost six, I think we should head back to Afiri's, see if he's home."

"Fine by me." It had taken the better part of a day just to get someone at the zoo to talk straight to them. It had taken all of his considerable charm and

Sam's sincere facial expressions to convince the zoo brass that they just wanted to ask some questions for a magazine. "All we got for a day's work is that someone drugged the monkey, brought him out to do the two students, and then left it for Animal Control—which we pretty much already knew."

"You think it was someone from the zoo?" Sam asked.

Dean shrugged. "Maybe. That'd explain how they got past security, but—well, c'mon, you saw these people. Clare, that Frieda lady, they were nuts about the critters. They'd have to be to work there. I can't see one of them abusing an animal like that, just for some kind of literary re-creation."

"If that's what this is." Sam sighed as he got off the crowded highway and into a tangle of traffic at the end of the exit ramp, making Dean wonder if there was an open road to be found anywhere in this stupid city. "I wish I could figure out what they're trying to do here."

"No bells going off, huh?"

Sam shook his head. "Not so far. I'll dig into Dad's journal tonight, see what's up. It's still another four days until the twentieth—that's the new moon, so that's probably when the next one's gonna be. So we've got time to figure it out."

Eventually, they worked their way back to Afiri's place. Dean, who prided himself on an excellent sense of direction and on being able to find anything as long as it was on a road, had no idea how they got there. This whole area of the Bronx was hilly and twisty and turny and it gave him a headache. *Give me flat, straight roads any day. San Francisco wasn't as bad as this.*

This time when they pulled up to Afiri's Colonial, there was a dirt-spattered four-by-four in the driveway with a bumper sticker that said, DON'T LIKE MY DRIVING? CALL 1-800-U-BITE-ME. However, there was a spot on the street next to the driveway, so Sam pulled into it. The front of the Impala was blocking the driveway a little, but Dean figured they were going to be in the house of the guy they were blocking, so no big deal, and it beat trying to find somewhere to parallel park.

"Whoa! Ash wasn't kidding, that is one *fine* ride you got there!"

Dean looked up as he got out of the car to see a man standing on the porch. He had long scraggly hair that was mostly brown, a thick beard that was mostly gray, and a pair of thick plastic tinted glasses. He wore a Grateful Dead concert T-shirt and ratty jeans that were stained with brown and green and yellow. Dean decided he could live a happy life without knowing what caused those stains. He was also barefoot.

"You gotta be Manfred Afiri," Dean said. "I'm Dean Winchester, this is my brother Sam."

"Yeah, Ash said you'd be comin' by. How is that

old bastard anyhow? Please, God, tell me he finally got a better haircut."

Smirking, Dean said, "Nope, still all business on the top—"

"—and a party in the back." Manfred shook his head. "I mean, hell, I ain't one to talk about retro 'dos, but at least mine is a retro that's respected, know what I'm sayin', man?"

"Absolutely," Dean said. He and Sam walked toward the front porch.

Sam said, "We heard you have spirit problems."

"Yeah, it's kinda harshing my mellow, y'know? But we'll get to that in a minute. I was just puttin' on a cuppa joe. C'mon in, put your feet up, and we'll rap." He grinned. "Sorry, retro slang to go with the retro 'do. We'll hang. It's hang, right?"

"Close enough." Dean looked at Sam and grinned. *I think I like this guy.*

That feeling was cemented when they came into the house and Dean heard the strains of Jethro Tull's "For a Thousand Mothers." Dean found himself involuntarily air-drumming to Clive Bunker's riff. "Good music choice."

"Yeah, I been on a Tull kick lately. I wanna cover 'em, but nobody can play the flute, and it ain't Tull without the flute, y'know?"

"Got that right," Dean said as he looked around the house. The front door opened to a foyer that was covered with framed concert posters that dated back to long before he was born: the Beatles at Shea Stadium, the Rolling Stones at Fillmore East, the Isle of Wight Show in 1970.

Turning left, he saw the massive living room, which was covered in dusty old furniture—a couch, an easy chair, and a rocking chair, as well as a big china closet and a sideboard that was covered with bottles of alcohol—piles of newspapers, magazines that had musical instruments on the covers, three guitars on stands in one corner, several amplifiers, an entire wall filled with vinyl records, another wall filled with tapes and CDs, and an entertainment center that included a battered old television and a shiny metal stereo system that included turntable, tape deck, and six-CD changer. At first, he couldn't see the speakers, then realized there were four of them spread around the room for maximum killer sound value.

It took Dean a second to realize that Manfred and Sam weren't around. Turning, he saw they were heading toward the kitchen, which was through the hallway next to the staircase, straight back from the foyer.

"You'll have to excuse my brother," Sam said, "he's in the midst of having an orgasm."

A grin peeked out from Manfred's beard. "Sorry 'bout the mess, but the housekeeper ain't come 'round this year yet. C'mon."

They went back into the kitchen, which was also

a mess, with dirty pots and pans in the sink. Manfred shoved some of them aside so he could fill the coffeepot with water.

"That's a nice setta wheels you got there, fellas." Manfred grinned again. "Sorry, what is it, 'ride' now? Anyhow, it's a 'sixty-seven, right?"

"Yup," Dean said with pride. "Had to rebuild it from scratch a while back, too."

"Whoa." Manfred poured the water into the coffeemaker and then opened the freezer and took out a jar filled with coffee grounds. "Special blend," he said at Sam and Dean's quizzical looks. "Where'd you find a 427 engine?"

"Got a friend with contacts. Runs a junkyard. He tracked it down for me." Besides giving them a place to stay after Dad died, Bobby Singer also had been vital in providing Dean with the parts to rebuild the Impala after the truck totaled it.

"Groovy. Or, maybe, cool. Sweet?"

"Sweet works, yeah," Dean said with a grin.

"Used to have one'a them back when it was a new car. Wouldn't do me much good now—the trunk's big, but it don't fit the rig, y'know? S'why I got the Soccer Mom-mobile. Anyhow, that old contraption died on my way down to Florida back in 'seventy-eight." He chuckled. "Funny, I was drivin' down there with Becky t'get married, and the damn car died. Shoulda seen that for the omen that it was. We split back in 'eighty-six."

"So, Manfred," Sam said, "you have a ghost?"

"Yeah, it's pretty bad." After scooping the grounds into the receptacle, Manfred put the jar back in the freezer and retrieved a carton of milk from the refrigerator, placing it on the kitchen counter next to the coffeemaker and a chipped sugar bowl. "I dunno how much Ash toldja, but I'm with a band called Scottso. We play up in Larchmont every weekend—Friday, Saturday, Sunday night, we do three sets. It's our thing, y'know? And every time I get home from a gig, there's some crazy broad makin' awful noises and screeching and goin' crazy, and I just gotta get outta the house."

"It's only on those nights?" Sam asked.

"Yup." The coffeemaker started making gurgling noises as the now-boiling water mixed with the grounds and were poured into the waiting pot. "Oh, wait, not every time. There was this one Friday night when someone rented out the Park in Rear for a private party, so we didn't play that night."

"And no ghost?" Sam asked.

Manfred shook his head.

Dean had to ask: "Is it *really* called the Park in Rear?"

Another toothy grin—well, mostly toothy, as Manfred was missing a molar or two. "Yeah, but don't try that in the phone book. Nah, it's called 'Nat's Place,' but nobody calls it that. See, there's this gigunda sign that says 'Park in Rear' real big on top, 'cause it ain't legal to park on the street there, and the parking lot entrance ain't easy to see from the road. So we all call it that." He pulled three mugs down from one of the cabinets and poured the coffee. Sam got the one that had the dictionary definition of the word coffee written on it, while Dean's said THERE'S TOO MUCH BLOOD IN MY CAFFEINE SYSTEM. Manfred kept the one with the Metallica logo for himself, which disappointed Dean somewhat.

Dean left his coffee alone, having always preferred it to be as black as his car. Sam, of course, dumped half a ton of sugar and then filled it almost to the brim with milk. For his part, Manfred just poured a bit of milk into his.

Sam picked up his coffee but didn't drink it. Dean, being no kind of fool, waited until after his brother took a sip before trying it himself. "So," Sam said, "this spirit is tied to the band, you think?"

"Damfino, Sam, that's why I called Ash. I knew he was into that spooky jazz. Me, I'm just a carpenter for the city who plays rock and roll. I don't know nothin' 'bout crap that goes bump in the night." He gulped down about half his coffee, which made Dean think his throat was lined with ice or something, since it was still boiling, even with the milk cutting it a bit. "Gotta tell ya, it's seriously interferin' with my life. I mean, there are times when I wanna bring someone home after a gig, know what I mean? It messes with the mojo, havin' some broad screechin' in the house."

"Have you ever seen it?" Sam asked. Then he took a sip, and cut off Manfred before he could answer. "Wow. This is great coffee, Mr. Afiri."

"Please, it's Manfred. Mr. Afiri is what my kids' teachers used to call me those few times I went to parent-teacher conferences back in the day."

"You have kids?" Dean asked, immediately sorry that he asked.

"Not to hear them tell it. Far as they're concerned, the only father they care about ain't me, it's that jackass Becky married in 'ninety-two. Nicest thing they ever say to me is, 'Ain't you got a haircut yet, Dad?' "

"Sorry to hear that," Sam said in a quiet voice.

Manfred shrugged. "Nothin' I can do about it. I do what I can for 'em, but they don't need me much. And hey, I just screwed their mom—that don't make me a father, since we split when they was just babies."

Dean might have said something in response to all that, but he was too busy savoring the taste of the finest cup of coffee he'd ever had in his life. Admittedly, his standards weren't all that high. Generally he and Sam made do with whatever they could get from cheap diners, motel lobbies, and gas stations, which usually amounted to caffeinated dishwater. Their father had taken to using the phrase "a cup of caffeine," since what they usually had was so bad, Dad didn't want to insult it by calling it "coffee."

Not this, though. Dean would drink this flavorful wonderfulness even if he didn't need a caffeine jolt after a day dealing with New York traffic, Bronx Zoo bureaucracy, and women hitting on Sam instead of him.

"So you've never *seen* the spirit?" Sam asked.

Shaking his head, Manfred said, "No, but I ain't looked, either, y'know? I mean, I hear that yellin', and I get outta Dodge. I don't even come home no more, just wait till sunup. That's a bitch on Mondays, though—I gotta get to work."

"You said you work as a carpenter for the city?" Sam asked.

Manfred nodded.

"If you don't mind my asking, then—how can you afford this place?"

Dean blinked at Sam's question, but now that he thought about it, it was a legit question. If Manfred was divorced, he probably had child support, and he couldn't believe that a city carpenter got paid enough to buy this place, especially given how much property cost in New York. True, he had the music, but if that was anything great, he wouldn't need the day job.

Another grin. "It's handy being the son of two

really rich lawyers. Well, Dad was rich—Mom was always doing pro bono work, but still. I was the shame of the family—doin' the whole Summer of Love–antiwar–goin' to Woodstock thing while Dad was representing oil companies—but I was also an only child, so I got the house when they croaked."

"I'm sorry," Sam said, again in a quiet voice.

"Nah, s'no biggie. Listen, I'm really grateful to you two for helpin' me out."

Dean sipped some more coffee. "We haven't done anything yet, Manfred. We'll check it out, though, see what turns up."

"Great. And hey, listen, you guys got a place to stay in town? 'Cause if you don't, I got a couple guest rooms upstairs."

That almost made Dean sputter his coffee. He managed to hold it in, which was good, as that would've been a waste of a fine beverage. "Seriously?"

"That's very kind of you, Manfred, but—"

"We'd be happy to," Dean said quickly, before Sam's politeness got them shoved into yet another motel room. He wasn't sure what excited him more, the prospect of sleeping in the same house as that record collection, being able to wake up to this coffee, or not having to share a room with Sam. He loved his brother more than anything in the world—except *maybe* the Impala—but they'd been sleeping in the same room (or, all too often, the same front seat of the car) with each other virtually every night for over a year now. If the opportunity to get separate rooms—for free, no less—presented itself, he was for damn sure taking it.

"Great! Listen, I got practice tonight—we usually rehearse in Tommy's garage. He's the drummer. We used to rehearse here—I got tons'a space in the attic—but the neighbors started bitching. Didn't want 'em callin' the cops on us, what with the weed and all, so we moved to Tommy's."

Sam shot Dean a nervous look at the mention of weed, and Dean just rolled his eyes. *Jesus, Sammy, didja think a musician's house was only gonna have coffee in it? Especially a guy who was at Woodstock?*

"And tomorrow night, you guys can come up to the Park in Rear and hear us. I'll get you two in as my guests, so you ain't gotta pay the cover. Still gotta buy the beer, though, but they got some good stuff on tap up there." Manfred gulped down the rest of his coffee in one shot, then put the mug in the sink. "You fellas make yourselves at home. Rooms're upstairs. The one all the way on the far end from the staircase, that's mine. The other three all got beds, so pick whatever you want."

"Thanks." Dean looked at Sam. "C'mon, let's unpack." He took a final sip of his coffee, then headed back through the hallway to the front door.

Sam followed him, waiting until they reached

the front porch to speak. "Dean, you sure this is a good idea?"

"What's the problem, Sammy?"

"This guy's got a spirit. Maybe this isn't the best place to stay the night."

Dean stuck the key in the Impala trunk. "Dude, we're the guys who kill the spirits. 'Sides, it's Thursday. Spirit won't show till tomorrow night, so that gives us time to give the place an EMF once-over and research the house. Maybe we'll even figure out the Poe thing."

"The thing is, Dean—" Sam hesitated.

After hoisting his backpack out of the back of the trunk, Dean said, "What is it?"

"I'm a little freaked out."

"C'mon, Manfred's an okay guy."

"It's not Manfred, Dean, it's *you*. It's like we're in Dean Disneyland in there with the Fillmore East posters and the amps and the record collection. I'm worried we're never gonna get you outta there."

Assuming Sam was just giving him crap, Dean grinned. "Dude, I can focus."

"Hope so. 'Cause we got a spirit we know's gonna show Friday night, and a murder that we know's gonna happen Monday night, and we're staying with a guy whose house is full of illegal narcotics when we're both wanted by the feds."

Dean slammed the trunk shut. "Anybody ever tell you you worry too much, Sam?"

Without missing a beat, Sam smirked and said, "You, about four times a day."

"Then consider this time number five. We'll be fine. C'mon, let's get settled."

SIX

. . . Mom pinned to the ceiling, bleeding from the belly, fire consuming her . . .

They're with Dad, following every one of his commands. "Boys, don't forget, you salt the entrance, they can't get in," he orders. "Sam, I want you to shoot each of those bottles off the wall," he yells. "Dean, stay with your brother," he barks.

. . . Jessica pinned to the ceiling, bleeding from the belly, fire consuming her . . .

Learning how to field-strip an M-16 before ever kissing a girl. Unable to get through Moby-Dick or The Scarlet Letter *for school, despite having already read the collected works of Aleister Crowley—not to mention Jan Howard Brundvand. Knowing the exorcism ritual in Latin, but unable to remember the words to the Pledge of Allegiance, which earns a detention sentence at one of the (many) grammar schools.*

. . . Cassie pinned to the ceiling, bleeding from the belly, fire consuming her . . .

"I gotta find Dad." "He wants us to pick up where he left off—saving people, hunting things." "Can we not fight?" "You're after it, aren't you? The thing that killed Mom." "I don't understand the blind faith you have in the man."

. . . Sarah pinned to the ceiling, bleeding from the belly, fire consuming her . . .

The fear never dies, never goes away, never leaves, no matter how many times you put on the brave face, no matter how many times you lie to people that everything will be okay, no matter how often you tell people that you'll fix it, no matter how close you come to dying or being caught or being put away forever, and then you won't be able to protect anyone ever again . . .

. . . Ellen pinned to the ceiling, bleeding from the belly, fire consuming her . . .

"All right, something like this happens to your brother, you pick up the phone and you call me." "Call you? You kiddin' me? Dad, I called you from Lawrence. All right? Sam called you when I

was dying. *But gettin' you on the phone, I got a better chance'a winnin' the lottery.*"

. . . Jo pinned to the ceiling, bleeding from the belly, fire consuming her . . .

"*He's given us an order.*" "*I don't care! We don't always have to do what he says.*"

. . . Sam pinned to the ceiling, bleeding from the belly—

—but the fire doesn't consume him. Instead, his eyes open, and they're yellow.

"*You have to kill me, Dean. Dad said so.*"

"No!"

Dean shot upright, drenched in sweat, pants damp, sheets twisted and soaked.

"Dammit," he muttered.

Untangling himself from the sheets of Manfred's guest bed, he walked over to the bureau, on which sat a giant circular mirror with a peace symbol etched into it in red. A haggard, sweaty face looked back at him. Hell, even his hair was mussed, and he barely had enough hair to do the job, but that nightmare—*latest in a freakin' series, collect 'em all*—had done the trick.

Since he was a little kid, Dean had seen every kind of horrible thing. Stuff that would make H.R. Giger throw up his hands and go into aluminum siding. Stuff that made Stephen King look like Jane Austen. Stuff that could—and had—driven other people to drink heavily, or blow their brains out, or both. And never once did he have nightmares. Sure, he had bad dreams, especially as a kid, but not the kind of bone-chilling, sweat-inducing, full-on nightmares he was getting now.

And it was all Dad's fault.

Years on the road. Years of training, of fighting, of hunting. Years of obeying Dad's orders to the letter, no matter how ridiculous.

Years of being the one stuck between Dad's immovable object and Sam's irresistible force, trying desperately to keep family harmony.

Years of living up to the first command Dad had given him after Mom died: "Take your brother outside as fast as you can—don't look back. Now, Dean, *go!*"

After all that, what were Dad's last words to him before he let himself be taken by the same demon who'd killed Mom and Sam's girl? "Good job, son"? "Keep up the fine work"? "I'm proud of you, Dean"?

No, it was an order for him to protect Sam—and if he couldn't, he'd have to kill Sam.

Christ almighty.

Dean stared at his reflection, partly colored red by the peace-symbol etchings, making it look like blood was streaking down the center of his face.

On the one hand, he had to tell Sam. Leaving aside the fact that it was only fair to Sam, he didn't want to keep carrying this by himself. But Dad had said one other thing: "Don't tell Sam."

Bastard.

Most of the time he was able to distract himself, lose himself in the job. They did important work, him and Sammy. All the lives they'd saved, all the souls they'd avenged—it was necessary. And dammit, they were good at it.

Most of the time. But then something like this . . .

Dean shook it off. He knew he couldn't let it get to him. They had a job. In fact, they had two.

He looked over at the clock radio next to the guest bed, which told him it was 6:30 in the morning. He heard the sound of a high-performance engine in need of a tuneup, and walked over to the window, pulling back the brightly colored curtains. He saw Manfred's four-by-four back out of the driveway. His heart sank when he realized it was heading straight for the front of the Impala, which was still partly in the driveway, but at the last second Manfred veered out to the right. The two right-side tires clunked down the sidewalk lip while the left tires remained in the driveway, easing out onto the dark pavement of the street.

Forcing himself to breathe regularly again, Dean turned away and looked at the rumpled bed. *No way in hell I'm going back to sleep*. Much as it pained him to be up at this hour, it seemed he was stuck. Besides, he had the world's best coffee waiting for him.

One piping hot shower in Manfred's incredibly cool claw-foot bathtub later, Dean changed into the last set of fresh clothes he had and, making a mental note to ask Manfred where the nearest Laundromat was, went downstairs in search of coffee, being sure to grab Dad's journal on the way.

Of course, once the coffee was made, he just *had* to explore Manfred's vinyl collection in more depth. He'd taken a glance last night—well, okay, *more* than a glance. Sam had yelled at him for only checking the EMF readings in the living room and neglecting the rest of the house, to the point where his younger brother almost took the EMF reader away from him.

They hadn't actually found any EMF, but that wasn't completely unexpected. The spirit hadn't shown since Sunday. Not all spirits left a ton of EMF around, and this one wasn't a constant presence, but a recurring one. Tonight, after Scottso's show, would be the acid test.

Until then he intended to hear music the way it was *meant* to be played.

The problem was picking just one. Every time he saw one LP, he was all set to put it on when another caught his eye. He'd made a pile that included *Dark Side of the Moon, The Most of the Animals, Houses of the Holy, Dressed to Kill,*

Metallica, The Who By Numbers, the Australian version of *Dirty Deeds Done Dirt Cheap, Thick as a Brick,* and *In-A-Gada-Da-Vida*—and he hadn't even gotten to the blues albums yet. He kept flipping through the records even after he settled on putting *In-A-Gada-Da-Vida* on, playing air guitar to the classic riff that opened the seventeen-minute title track.

Sam's voice came from upstairs, getting louder alongside the creak of the old wood of the stairs under his brother's weight. "Yeah, okay. Thanks so much, I really appreciate you letting me come on such short notice. Yeah. Great. Thanks! 'Bye."

Dean looked up to see Sam pocketing his Treo and walking into the living room while saying, "You're up early. Not used to you walking around before ten."

"Yeah, I been up for a little bit." Dean looked down at his watch and realized that it was almost nine-thirty. He'd completely lost track of time looking at the albums. While he intellectually understood the value of digital recording, the death of the vinyl record had seriously messed with the ability of artists to create cool album covers. No booklet in a dinky CD jewel case was ever going to match the artistry of the woodcut in *Stand Up* or the complexity of *Sgt. Pepper's Lonely Hearts Club Band.* Would anybody have remembered the prism on the cover of *Dark Side of the Moon* if it had only been a few inches big?

He didn't bother sharing these thoughts with Sam, though, as it would only serve to piss him off. The boy didn't appreciate real music. So he asked, "Who was that on the phone?"

"A guy named Anthony who works for the Bronx County Historical Society and gives tours of the Poe Cottage. I looked it up on the web—Manfred's got a wireless network, and he gave me the key—and they're only open by appointment. So I called, and they're free today. I'll be heading over around noon." He grinned. "I'd ask if you wanna come with, but seeing as how you've been reunited with your one true love and all . . ."

Dean pulled down *Zoso* and said, "Look, Sammy, you can have your CDs, your MP3s, your AVIs, but I'm telling you—"

"AVIs are movies, Dean," Sam said with a grin.

Ignoring him, Dean went on: "But I'm *telling* you, there is no substitute, none, for the beautiful sound of a needle on vinyl."

Just then the record started to skip, Doug Ingle singing "always be" over and over again.

Sam's grin practically split his face in half. Dean scowled at him, then walked over to the turntable and nudged the needle, and it skipped ahead to a guitar chord.

"Let me guess," Sam said, "next you're gonna

extol the virtues of leeches as a method of healing the sick? Or, I know! Why horse-drawn chariots are better than cars!"

"Bite me, Sammich." Dean went over to the easy chair. "I'm gonna go through Dad's journal, see if I can find anything that matches this ritual."

Sam nodded. "After I'm done at the cottage, I'll check the house where the guy was bricked up and the street where the kids were beaten to death."

"Yeah," Dean said, "maybe you'll find something the cops missed."

"I doubt it," Sam said sincerely. "Dude, we're talking about the NYPD here."

"So?" Dean had a lot more experience with cops than Sam, and his considered opinion was that they were fine as long as a case followed a pattern. The thing was, what he and Sam dealt with didn't follow any kind of pattern—or at least not a pattern any cop would ever look for—so police always looked in the wrong places, didn't see the right things, and jumped to the wrong conclusions. "Sam, cops go for the familiar. Don't believe the crap you see on TV—most of the time, the first suspect they have is the one they arrest. Something like this, they're not gonna see the forest *or* the trees. Trust me, I'm willing to bet you ten bucks you find something they didn't."

Sam just snorted, and then went into the kitchen,

Dean assumed in search of a cup of coffee that he would violate with too much milk and sugar.

Dean turned his attention back to the record collection. *Is that actually a copy of* Music from Big Pink? *Awesome!*

The hardest part was finding somewhere to park the Impala.

The Poe Cottage was located at the intersection of the largest thoroughfare in the Bronx, the aptly named Grand Concourse, and another major street, Kingsbridge Road. According to the Internet research Sam had done before leaving Manfred's place, Kingsbridge Road used to be a horse path that led to the King's Bridge, which went over the Harlem River to Manhattan. He had also found a Poe enthusiast's web site, which had actually mentioned both murders and their connection to the author. He left it up on the screen for Dean to look at—assuming his brother could tear himself from Manfred's record collection, which Sam fiercely doubted.

A park sat in the midst of the intersection, stretching across several blocks, and it included a bandstand and a playground, both looking rather new, and a small white cottage that looked incredibly out of place. He understood why Dean had been so reluctant to believe that there was such a place in the Bronx. The whole city—aside from Manfred's neighborhood in Riverdale—seemed geared toward cramming as many buildings as close together as possible. Even in neighborhoods with houses, they tended to be rammed up against each other.

And yet, there in the midst of a tangle of streets that were lined with apartment buildings at least five stories high, and often higher, was this park and this cottage.

Sam maneuvered around several side streets, most of them one-way, as well as the two big streets, and tried desperately to find a spot in which the Impala would fit. He drove around for ten minutes, getting particularly frustrated with the roller coaster of emotions as he'd see an empty space, only to discover that it was a fire hydrant, then find another, only to see another hydrant. *How many damn hydrants does this city* need, *anyhow?* On those rare occasions when the empty space wasn't a hydrant, it was way too small to fit the Impala.

While he was driving, Sam also noticed that the people were making the best of the crowded situation. While he and Dean moved around a lot with Dad, they tended toward smaller towns, in part because Dad felt that they had better public school systems than the ones in big cities—though Sam's later research revealed that not to be nearly the universal constant Dad had insisted. As a result, his experiences with big cities were few and far between.

The thing that struck him the most was the diversity and the harmony, which was on par with what he'd seen at Stanford—but you expected that at a college campus, especially somewhere like Stanford. Here, he saw people from about twelve different nationalities walking the streets, using the small storefronts on the ground floors of the apartment buildings, playing in the playground in the Poe Park, chatting with each other, saying hi on the street, and so on. His (admittedly minimal) experience with larger cities was that ethnic groups tended to congregate in particular neighborhoods, but he wasn't seeing as much of that here in the Bronx as he'd expected.

Like Dean, his primary reference point for the borough was the infamous 1981 movie *Fort Apache, the Bronx*, so he'd imagined a place filled with burned-out buildings, roving street gangs, and the like. What he'd seen so far, though, indicated a place that had the crowds of a big city, but within the neighborhoods were still communities.

Or maybe I'm just romanticizing the whole thing, he thought with a laugh as he passed yet another open spot in which maybe a Mini Cooper could fit, but not any car built in 1967.

Finally, he saw someone pulling out of a spot at the corner of East 192nd Street and Valentine

Avenue, right on the border of the park. It was a spot with a parking meter, which was annoying, but at least that meant the Impala would fit. The meters had been installed decades ago and were spaced according to typical car size at the time. The Impala was pretty close to normal size when it was first released, so he was easily able to slide into the spot.

Dipping into the laundry supply, he put in two quarters, which would keep the spot legal for an hour. Given the size of the place, he couldn't imagine his tour would last any longer than that.

Sam locked the Impala and then walked through the Poe Park, past the bandstand—empty on this chilly November afternoon—and the playground—where six kids were playing and screaming and giggling, while four women kept an eye on them. As he passed, he heard the women conversing with each other in what he was pretty sure was Spanish.

The Poe Cottage stood out even more close up than it did from the road. From what he'd seen on the Bronx County Historical Society's website, it had been built in 1812, and Poe lived in it with his wife and mother-in-law from 1846 to 1849.

As he approached the front door, he reached into his coat pocket and turned on the EMF meter. He wouldn't take it out in front of the tour guide, but hoped he might have a chance to glance at it when the man wasn't looking.

Standing in the doorway was the tour guide in question: a short African-American man wearing a beige trench coat. "You Anthony?" Sam asked as he approached.

"Yeah," the guide said. "Glad you could make it."

Grinning sheepishly, Sam said, "Yeah, sorry, couldn't find anywhere to park. And I drive a boat, so it's even harder."

Anthony's head tilted. "What do you drive?"

"A 'sixty-seven Impala."

Smiling, Anthony backed away from the wooden door and let Sam into the dark front room of the cottage. "I feel your pain. My Pop had a 'fifty-seven Buick. Spent half his life tryin' to find somewhere to park the stupid thing. Anyhow, welcome to the Poe Cottage."

Sam looked around and saw various old kitchen utensils, a fireplace, and, right by the front door, a desk with postcards and other souvenirs. Behind the desk was a glass case filled with books that ranged from collections of Poe's writing to books about New York in general and the Bronx in particular.

"Before we start," Anthony said, "we usually ask for a ten dollar donation for individual tours."

Of course you do, Sam thought, trying not to sigh. Once again he dug into his pocket, hoping that the ten he gave Dean at the bridge wasn't his last big bill.

Luckily, it wasn't. He found a twenty in the

money clip and handed it over. Anthony reached under the desk with the postcards, pulled out a cash box, and retrieved a ten for him.

"What'd you do to your hand?" Anthony asked, indicating Sam's cast with his head.

Where Dean probably would've had some kind of smartass response, Sam found he couldn't think of anything funny enough for a total stranger. And the truth would hardly suffice. *Oh, well, I broke my hand when I was fighting a zombie in a grave-yard. See, I was trying to lure her back to her grave so my brother and I could impale her in it so she'd die again. No, I'm not crazy, and why are you backing slowly away from me like that?*

"It's a long story," he mumbled.

That seemed to satisfy Anthony. "Okay. Well, this is where Edgar Allan Poe lived for the final years of his life." He proceeded to tell Sam several things he already knew from reading the website. "Unfortunately," Anthony added, "you can't really appreciate the view now." He moved past Sam to reopen the door. "But if you look over there—" He pointed to the left. "—you can see that it goes downhill right at Valentine Avenue?"

Sam nodded. He'd actually gone down that hill briefly in his endless search for a parking spot.

"The cottage was right on the top of the hill, and you could see all the way to the Long Island Sound from here. This isn't where it was originally built." Now pointing across Kingsbridge Road, he said, "You see that apartment building with the yellow façade? It was about there. It was moved here when the park was built. This whole area used to be farmland owned by the Valentines, a Dutch family. They're the ones the avenue's named after. The Poe family rented the cottage, and they could barely afford it."

"I saw that on the website," Sam said, "and I thought it was kinda odd. I mean, Poe's one of the most popular American writers. And he was broke?"

"Oh, definitely. I mean, yeah, he was popular, and still is. Aren't too many writers that get football teams named after them, even if it's one step removed."

Sam frowned, then remembered that the Baltimore football franchise was named the Ravens. Poe died in Baltimore, and was buried there, and the team was named for Poe's most popular poem.

"And none of his stories have ever gone out of print. But most of the money he made from his writing got sunk into magazine endeavors that failed. Anyhow," Anthony led Sam into the next room, "we've re-created the atmosphere of the cottage as best we can. Obviously, most of the furniture isn't available, but we've done our best to put the types of furnishings that would've been present, given the time and the Poes' level of poverty."

Sam followed Anthony into what had to be the largest room in the cottage, which included a fireplace—now closed, according to Anthony—a chair, a writing desk, and some framed pictures. There was also a hanging bookcase on the wall, each shelf filled with old-fashioned leather-bound volumes in what Sam knew was a popular binding style in the mid-nineteenth century. "These hanging shelves were more common in those days, since the floors were almost never even—as you can see," Anthony added with a grin.

Grinning back, Sam shifted his weight back and forth on the creaky wooden floors.

Anthony continued: "The wood warped when it got damp, too. A bookcase on the floor just wasn't practical." He pointed to the wall. "That's an illustration of the cottage."

Walking over to peer at it, Sam saw the exact cottage he was standing in, at the top of a steep hill that matched the contours of Briggs Avenue and East 194th Street when he had driven down and up those respective streets. The surrounding ground, though, was all grass and trees. It seemed idyllic.

"Poe's wife Virginia was very sick—what they called consumption back then, which we now know as tuberculosis. He'd come to New York in 1844 to engage in those publishing endeavors that bankrupted him, and when Virginia got more sick in 1846, they moved up here, hoping the country air would do him some good." Anthony smiled. "Y'know, I still have trouble saying that with a straight face. Don't get me wrong, I love it here, but country air?"

Chuckling, Sam said, "Yeah, it is a little weird. But different times, I guess."

"*Oh* yeah. The Bronx was a bunch of farms in the eighteenth and nineteenth centuries, owned mostly by families like the Valentines, the Johnsons, and, of course, the first settler, Jonas Bronck—the peninsula used to be called 'Bronck's Land,' and that's where the name comes from. Anyhow, Poe set up a room just for Virginia when she got sicker."

Anthony led Sam into the next room, which was actually a hallway that included a door to a stairway up, the cottage's back door, and another, much smaller room, that included a bed, a nightstand, and little else. The bed wasn't particularly large, had a solid wooden headboard and an uneven mattress.

"We're pretty sure this is the actual bed that Virginia died in. We've modified it a bit—the original had hay in it, but that gets disgusting pretty quick, so we replaced it with those Styrofoam popcorn things they put in packages."

Sam couldn't help but bark a laugh at that. "Really?"

"It's not period, but it doesn't stink up the joint,

either." Growing serious again, Anthony talked a bit about how Poe's mother-in-law Maria Clemm did most of the work around the house and took care of Virginia while Poe worked and took long walks, and a little about the upstairs and downstairs areas, which were converted for use by the Historical Society and not open to the public. Sam tuned much of it out, thinking more about what it meant that Virginia Poe died in this bed, in virtually this very spot. *Okay, moved across the street, but could the spiritual energy from that night still be present, even though it was a hundred fifty years ago?*

When he was done talking about Virginia Poe, Anthony left the bedroom, pushed past Sam in the small confines of the back area, and pointed to a picture on the wall. Sam ignored him, instead taking advantage of Anthony having his back to him to pull out the EMF reader.

Unfortunately, it didn't read a damn thing. *Well, it was a long shot.*

Anthony talked a bit more about the house, about Poe's life, and about the plans to renovate the house and the surrounding area, including a visitor's center, which was being held up by city bureaucracy. Sam made some sympathetic noises, bought a couple of postcards—a picture of the house and a portrait of Poe himself—and then decided to go for broke. "Hey, have you heard about those murders?"

Up until now, Anthony had been pleasant and genial and friendly. As soon as Sam asked that question, though, it was like a cloud came over his dark features. "Okay, that's it. Get out."

Feigning innocence, Sam asked, "I'm sorry?"

Moving toward the door, as if to crowd Sam toward it—though not actually touching him—Anthony said, "Look, it's bad enough I have read this crap on the Internet, I ain't about to—"

"Whoa!" Sam held up his hands and refused to be moved. Anthony, to his credit, stopped moving forward. "I just read something in the newspaper and it threw me, that's all. It's no big deal."

"It's a coincidence," Anthony said firmly. Sam suspected he'd gotten this question quite a bit since the Reyes murder. "That's *all*."

Sam quickly took his leave and went back to the car. While there wasn't any EMF reading, the death of a loved one was probably still a good focal point for a ritual. *The question is, what ritual?* When he got into the car, he pulled out a Bronx street map he'd picked up the previous day on their way to the zoo, and figured out the best way to the corner of Webb Avenue and West 195th Street, where the body had been bricked up.

It actually looked to be a fairly easy drive, as that intersection was just two blocks north of Kingsbridge Road. Unfortunately, when he got there he realized that he couldn't make the right he wanted to onto Webb Avenue, as it was one-way the wrong way. So he made a right onto Sedgwick, figuring to make a right onto 195th—which was also one-way the wrong way. Finding himself coming around to Dean's animus toward driving in this city, Sam drove up another block to 197th—*and what the hell happened to 196th?*—made a right, drove a block to Webb, and made another right.

His concerns about finding the right house were unwarranted. For one thing, that corner only had two houses on it, the rest of the buildings being apartments. For another, the house he wanted stood out by virtue of being brown stucco as opposed to the red brick that every other surrounding building was made of. It was also the only one with crime-scene tape, not to mention a sign that read FOR SALE.

Deciding it would be better to come back at night, and with Dean for backup, he drove off. Besides, he couldn't find a single parking spot in the area—maybe that would be easier at night.

As he drove off, he saw a battered old Honda Civic double-parking in front of the house, and a short mousy-looking guy with a big nose get out. He normally wouldn't have given the guy a second thought, but he was parked right in front of the house where the murder took place—and he also looked irritatingly familiar, though Sam couldn't figure out why.

Shrugging, he drove down Webb back to Kingsbridge, intending to head over to Cambreleng Avenue where the two kids had died.

SEVEN

The Afiri house
The Bronx, New York
Friday 17 November 2006

Sam could hear Pink Floyd's "The Great Gig in the Sky" from Manfred's house before he even parked the Impala—this time finding a spot between two driveways across the street from the house—and he wondered if the same neighbors who objected to Scottso rehearsing in the house would object to Dean blaring the stereo.

Inside, Sam thought he'd be deafened by the music, and was grateful that he came home when Dean was playing the more low-key strains of Floyd rather than, say, Metallica or AC/DC or Deep Purple.

Turning left as he came in, he saw Dean in the easy chair—it was a recliner, which he knew because Dean had reclined it all the way back, his feet up—air-drumming with his right hand while flipping pages of Dad's journal with his left. Albums were strewn all over the floor. Sam's laptop was on the coffee table, precariously balanced on some old newspapers and magazines. Wincing, Sam walked in and moved it to the couch—an action that also yanked the power cord out, which went some way toward explaining why Dean had been so careless with the laptop.

Only now noticing Sam's arrival, Dean grabbed a remote off the floor next to him and turned the volume down. "Sorry about that, Sammy, but the battery was running low, and the only free plug was over there." He pointed at the now slack power cord, which snaked around to a plug by the living room doorway.

"Whatever. Find anything?"

"Actually, I did." Dean reached down and pushed the brown lever on the side of the easy chair, which brought it back upright and the footrest down with a solid thunk. "And it isn't exactly what you'd call great news."

Not liking the sound of that, Sam said, "Hold that thought. I need some more of that coffee."

Dean grinned and grabbed a mug that was on the coffee table. "Just made a fresh pot ten minutes ago. Help yourself."

"Thanks."

Sam went into the kitchen, fished out a mug that had a shamrock and the words KISS ME, I'M IRISH—which struck him as odd, since Manfred Afiri didn't seem to be a particularly Irish name—and poured himself some more coffee. He dumped sugar in, but decided not to bother with the milk, since what he'd had this morning tasted like it was on the brink of going bad. Besides, this stuff was actually drinkable. He had never liked the taste of coffee all that much, but life both as a hunter and as a college student had made him appreciate the virtues of caffeine regardless of its taste. He tended toward what Dean called "froofy" coffees mainly because the extra flavors and the whipped cream and whatnot hid the fact that the beverage itself tasted like drinking hot sulfur. And for Sam, that wasn't just a cute simile, as he'd drunk hot sulfur once, by accident during a job, and he wasn't eager to repeat the experience.

Returning to the living room, he saw Dean removing *Dark Side of the Moon* from the turntable and flipping it over. "So whadja find?"

Dean gently placed the needle on the edge of the record. A moment later "Money" started playing. Sam patiently waited for the look of rapture to pass from Dean's features and his head to stop bopping back and forth in time with the cash register noises.

Then his patience ran out. "If you're not too busy . . ."

Shaking his head, Dean said, "Uh, yeah, sorry.

Anyhow, I found the ritual in Dad's notebook, but it wasn't where I figured it would be."

Dean sat back down in the easy chair and hefted the cracked leather-bound notebook. Overstuffed with papers, clippings, and other paraphernalia, every inch of every page was covered in Dad's unique handwriting—military neatness swimming upstream against the speed with which Dad was taking many of these notes, resulting in letters that were carefully penned for clarity but words that swerved and curved and were compressed for space and twisted around other notes. Sam had always thought that a handwriting analyst could retire on Dad.

When the demon who'd killed Mom became active again, Dad went off the grid, leaving the notebook to Dean (and by extension to Sam) to keep and use while continuing Dad's work of hunting.

That notebook was all they had left of Dad.

Long-term, Sam wanted to convert the notebook into electronic form so they could index it and cross-reference things and generally find items in it in a manner more suited to the twenty-first century than flipping through ink-filled pages, yellowed newspaper clippings, and hastily drawn charts, none of which was sorted in any meaningful way beyond "when it occurred to Dad to write it down." Unfortunately, their life didn't lend itself to long-term thinking, and Sam had only barely begun the process of converting the notebook. Realistically, it would take months of uninterrupted effort, and one could argue that his life was pretty much one big interruption these days.

"Where'd you find it?" he asked Dean.

"In the back."

Sam winced. That was where Dad filed all the fakes and phonies, the rituals that didn't do anything, the creatures that didn't actually exist.

Dean flipped through the notebook. "You ever hear of a nut job named Percival Samuels?"

"Doesn't ring a bell," Sam said with a shake of his head.

"Back in the late nineteenth, early twentieth century—he was a spiritualist, and he was pretty high on the nut-bar scale even compared to all the other nut bars."

"How crazy?"

Grinning, Dean said, "Well, Aleister Crowley once said he was insane, so I'd say this guy strayed pretty far from the pack, y'know?"

"So what about him? God, Dean, there must've been, like, a billion spiritualists back then. Most of them were con artists."

"Yeah, a whole mess of John Edward clones running around, but without the TV show. They'd do séances, try to contact the 'great beyond' so little old ladies could talk to their husbands who died and kids could talk to their great-aunt Sally to see if they really hid a million bucks under the floorboards. It was bogus, but there was a lot of cash if you were any good at it."

"So where does Samuels fit in?"

"He *wasn't* any good at it, so he tried to come up with his own hook." Dean finally finished flipping pages, having come to the right spot toward the rear of the notebook, and handed it to Sam. "He started peddling a 'resurrection spell' that could actually bring relatives back."

Sam took the notebook and saw the description of Samuels's ritual, written in Dad's distinctive hand. Reading aloud from the notebook, he said, " 'The sigil must be drawn in precision. The Central Point is a locus of strong Anima for the Resurrected. The 4 Outside Points is a re-Creation of events of Great Importance and Power to the Resurrected at each of 4 distinct times: the Full Moon, the Last Quarter Moon, the New Moon, and First Quarter Moon. When the 4 Steps are compleat, the Resurrected will return to life.' " Sam looked up. "Sounds familiar."

"Yeah, but it's bogus. Samuels sold it to a bunch of people, but nothing happened, and he was arrested. He committed suicide in jail."

Frowning, Sam asked, "Do we know for sure it didn't work?"

Dean shrugged. "Pretty sure. Samuels claimed he obtained the ritual from 'the rituals of the Hindustani Peoples of the Far East.' "

"Hindustani's a language, not a people."

"Yeah, and even if he meant the Hindu religion, it doesn't even remotely track with any Hindu ritual. He was pullin' it out of his ass, and trying to make it sound exotic. Remember, this was when the Brits colonized India and right after Japan and China started having serious contact with the West for the first time."

Sam grinned. "And here I thought you slept during history class."

"Not in the eleventh grade, I didn't." Dean broke into that half smile he got whenever he talked about women. "I had Miss Modzelewski. She was *hot*."

"Of course." Sam bit his lip. "Hang on." He got up and ran across the street to the Impala to fetch his Bronx street map. Bringing it back into the house just as "Us and Them" was starting up, he looked at the coffee table, covered as it was with Manfred's crap, shook his head, and then just sat down on the red patterned rug that rested on the hardwood floor, pushing aside some of the LPs that were strewn about. Pulling a pencil out of his pocket, he marked the Poe Cottage. Then he erased it and instead marked the approximate spot where Anthony had said the Poe Cottage was.

"What's across the street?" Dean asked.

Sam quickly explained what he'd been told by Anthony. Then he marked the corner of Webb and West 195th, then Cambreleng Avenue between

East 188th and East 189th. "Bring the notebook over, will you?" he asked Dean.

Dean did so, kneeling next to Sam. Sure enough, he could re-create a portion of Samuels's sigil just by connecting the three dots he had.

"Yahtzee," Dean muttered. "The location of the cottage—the *original* location, based on what your guy said—is the 'locus of strong Anima,' and we've already had the 're-Creation of events of Great Importance and Power.'"

Sam kept drawing, finishing the sigil. "Right, and nothing's more powerful than a spell that takes a life." He finished it and sat upright. "Well, if we're right, then the next Poe-inspired murder will be on Monday at either Fordham Road and Martin Luther King Jr. Boulevard or at Webster Avenue just south of Bedford Park Boulevard." After letting out a long breath, he said, "Now if we just knew *who* was doing this."

"Actually," Dean said, standing upright and moving to the couch and Sam's laptop, "I think you may have found prime suspect number one." He tapped the space bar to get rid of the screen saver— it was the generic Windows one, since Sam knew that any attempt to personalize his screen saver would just open the door for Dean to tease him about it, and he saw no reason to make it that easy for his brother—and revealed the Poe enthusiast website he'd found that morning.

"You found something on the site?" Sam asked, getting up to join his brother on the couch.

"Kinda." Dean traced a finger on the track pad onto an "about this site" link, which called up a description of the site and a picture of the person who ran it, who was named Arthur Gordon Pym. The man had a huge nose, small beady eyes, thin lips, a cleft chin, and thin brown hair. "Guy's got a serious hard-on for Poe—even changed his name. Pym's a character in one of Poe's books. Seems to me this guy'd die happy if he got to meet his hero, and we've seen nuttier motives."

Sam's eyes went wide as two different pieces of information in his head clicked together. "Oh my God."

"What? You know this dweeb?"

"No, but—" He shook his head. "I saw him, earlier today." Quickly, Sam summed up the rest of his trip to the Poe Cottage, and then his abortive attempt to check the house on Webb and 195th. "Somebody pulled up to the house—it was this guy," he said, pointing at the screen.

"All the more reason."

"Honey, I'm home!"

Sam and Dean both looked toward the living room door to see Manfred walking in, wearing dust-covered denim overalls, work boots, and a long-sleeve shirt under a leather jacket. "Damn—ain't listened to Floyd in a pooch's age. Good choice, fellas."

"Thanks," Dean said. "Uh, sorry 'bout the mess."

"Don't worry 'bout it," Manfred said. "Nice to have a house guest who appreciates the finer things in life. Anyhow, you guys're comin' up to the gig tonight, right?"

"Wouldn't miss it," Dean said.

Sam turned to look at Dean but didn't say anything until after Manfred said, "Far out. Or awesome, I guess. Gonna go change," and went upstairs.

"What?" Dean asked at Sam's look.

"If the spirit is always here after their gigs, maybe we should stay behind and see if it manifests."

"And if it doesn't manifest until Manfred gets home, then we'll miss out on some fine live tunes, won't we?" Before Sam could object, Dean said, "Hey, you wanna be a homebody, knock yourself out. I'm goin' to the gig."

Sam thought about it and then said, "Nah, I'll come with. It's obviously tied to the gigs somehow, so we should check out the gigs themselves." Also, he wasn't thrilled with the idea of being by himself in this house for some reason. While Dean had made himself right at home, Sam felt like he was intruding. Certainly, he had no problem using the guest bed and avoiding another round of the credit-card-fraud shuffle—especially now with Dean's face in every law enforcement database in the country—but just sitting here by himself as if he owned the place the way Dean had all day wasn't something he felt right doing.

He wasn't sure why, but the feeling was there. Besides, if the band really did play seventies rock, there was no way Dean was going to be paying close enough attention to anything odd about the band that might explain the ghost. He needed to be there to back his brother up.

"Sweet," Dean said. "So we'll do the gig, check out the spirit, maybe even get rid of it, then find the Poe geek tomorrow."

"Sounds like a plan," Sam said.

EIGHT

The Park in Rear
Larchmont, New York
Friday 17 November 2006

Dean decided that the only way this night could possibly get worse was if he actually stuck red-hot pokers into his ears. And that was looking like a viable alternative to listening to one more note played by Scottso.

In his life, he had heard a lot of live music by a lot of mediocre bands. The low-spending necessities of the hunting life meant that three-figure arena tickets to see his favorite bands were simply out of the question. Instead, he took his live music where he could find it, in dives like the Park in Rear.

He'd seen bands in roadhouses, art houses, converted houses, and outhouses. He'd seen blues musicians in Chicago, jazz musicians in New Orleans, and cover bands in Key West. He'd seen college bands play in converted garages and garage bands play in college towns.

And in all that time, he'd never heard a band as wretchedly awful as Scottso.

That wasn't entirely fair—he'd seen bands whose pretentiousness was only matched by the strain their emotional baggage put on their voices. As a follower of classic rock, he'd seen what years of bleating till their veins popped had done to the likes of Robert Plant and Steve Perry, and Dean's sole consolation in watching these losers had been that they, like Plant and Perry, would spend their latter days with severe vocal damage. That would be a blessing to the music community, especially since the songs they wrote were so bad.

But those bands didn't bother Dean as much because the only music they were ruining was their own. Sure, they played for crap, but they were playing crap anyhow, so what the hell.

Scottso, on the other hand, were covering some of Dean's favorite songs: "Cocaine," "Ramblin' Man," "Rock On," even, God help him, "Freebird." And they were mangling the holy crap out of them.

It started with the drummer. The only short-haired man in the band, he changed the tempo about once every six measures, kept missing the cymbals, and had this annoying tendency between songs to do a rim shot, whether or not anybody said anything funny. As if that wasn't bad enough, he also wore purple shorts and a puke green T-shirt.

Like most bass players, this one had the stage presence of a really bored redwood. He stood straight, wearing a black T-shirt, black vest, black jeans, and black cowboy boots. His almost-black hair was slicked back, extending past his shoulders. An unlit cigarette dangled from his mouth. The only reason Dean knew for sure that he was alive was that his fingers did actually move across the strings, plus he occasionally bent over between songs to sip from his beer, somehow not dislodging the cigarette. A good band had a rhythm section that was locked into each other, bass and drums feeding off each other and providing the foundation for the other instruments. Scottso, however, was not a good band. Dean wasn't even sure that the bass player and the drummer were on the same planet, much less playing the same song.

The keyboard player was the only one besides Manfred with serious gray in his hair, and also the only one of the long-haired set that tied his back into a ponytail, which just accentuated how much he'd lost on top. The bar lights glowed blindingly off his pate. He did an amazing job of matching the notes of the songs they were covering without managing any of the feeling. It wasn't that he did anything wrong—in fact, he was better at keeping tempo than the rhythm section—but he was just soullessly playing the notes. The best cover bands did one of two things: Some made the old songs their own; others perfectly re-created the original experience. These guys were only halfway to the latter because they didn't so much re-create as imitate. And at that, the keyboardist was only marginally good at it.

Then there was Manfred Afiri, a man whom Dean had respected right up until he opened his mouth on the stage of the Park in Rear. It wasn't that he sang off-key. He hit the notes—although on some, all he could manage was to slap them around a little. But he had no power, no oomph, no soul, no heart. Hell, if it wasn't for the microphone, Dean doubted he'd even be able to hear Manfred singing—which, thinking about it, would've been a blessing.

Dean went to the bar for something like his sixth beer—he'd lost track, knowing only that he hadn't had nearly enough yet—and hoped this time he'd get the cute girl bartender instead of the grizzled guy one. Normally, he'd just wait for the cute girl to be available, but Scottso had put the acquisition of alcohol at the very top of his list of things to do.

Both bartenders were helping people, so he squeezed between a couple who were making out on the bar stools on one side and two frat-boy-looking types on the other. He stared at the dark wood of the bar, which looked like half the universe had scratched something into it over the years.

The girl got the two frat boys a couple of froofy drinks that made Dean instantly dismiss the two from his worldview. Then she came over to him. In fact, the "girl" looked to be in her late thirties, but she was quite hot. Her brown hair was tied back into a ponytail, letting her nicely round face show off on its own. She had very small eyes—Dean couldn't make out their color in the dim light of the bar—and very full lips that he gave an eight out of ten on his personal kissability scale—maybe 8.5. Like the other bartender—who was a tall, lanky guy in his fifties—she wore a black T-shirt with a drawing of the outside of the bar in red. Unlike the other bartender—who wore it as a muscle shirt and really, really, really shouldn't have—she wore hers nice and tight, and had the curves to make it work *real* well.

" 'Nother beer?" She spoke with a fairly thick accent, which he figured to be local. All he knew from New York accents was how they talked on *NYPD Blue,* and she sounded sort of like that.

"Yeah, another Brooklyn." One of the points in the Park in Rear's favor was that they had Brooklyn lager on tap. Dean had last had it during a job in Pittsburgh, and he found that he'd missed it—besides, it was fitting to finally drink it in its hometown.

But the urge to switch to tequila was strong.

She grabbed a fresh glass and started pouring the beer into it expertly—holding the glass at the right angle—without even looking. "I ain't seen y'round here before."

Never one to pass up an opening, he said, "My first time. The name's Dean."

"Jennifer." With her accent, the last syllable was more "fuh" than "fer." "And I'm impressed. We don't get too many newbies, y'know?"

"We're friends of Manfred's, actually—from out of town."

"Got it." She finished pouring the beer with one hand, grabbed a napkin with the other, placed it on the old wooden bar, and gently set the glass down on the napkin. "Like I said, not too many new guys."

"Mostly just regulars, huh?"

Jennifer nodded. "Nice t'see a new face."

Dean took a sip of his beer and said, "Well, it's even nicer to see yours."

"That's five bucks for the beer."

Nodding, Dean said, "Right," and handed her a ten. She went over to the cash register, giving him the opportunity to note that her jeans were even tighter than the shirt, and while she was perhaps wider in the hips than he generally preferred, on her it worked. She rang him up and gave him five ones.

He left four of them on the bar. "Thanks."

She tilted her head. "Thank *you*. 'Specially since you only tipped Harry a buck."

"You're more fun to look at than Harry."

Jennifer made a noise like a pipe bursting. "Damn well hope so."

Scottso finally finished "Freebird," and then Manfred said, "We're gonna take a short break."

"Thank God," Dean muttered as Van Morrison's "Brown-Eyed Girl" started playing on the bar's PA system.

One of Jennifer's eyebrows shot up. "You don't like the band?"

"Uhm—well, the guitarist is good."

"Yeah, Aldo knows his stuff."

He was actually telling the truth there—the guitarist was the one bright spot. Called upon to re-create riffs by the likes of Eric Clapton, Jimmy Paige, Gregg Allman, and Ritchie Blackmore, he managed it brilliantly. His solos had been the only enjoyable part of an otherwise dismal musical experience. *It's too bad he's stuck with these other losers.*

Frowning at him, Jennifer said, "Thought you said you were a frienda Manfred's."

Dammit. "Well, yeah, but—let's just say he used to sing better."

The bursting pipe again. "Manfred's been singin' at this bar for long as I been here, and he never could sing worth a damn. And that's ten years."

Dean laughed, relieved. "I guess. I was trying to be nice."

"'Sides, you couldn'ta heard him ten years ago, you were what, twelve?"

Defensively, Dean said, "Seventeen, actually." Putting on his most sincere tone, he added, "Which can't be older than you were at the time, so what the hell were you doin' hangin' out in bars?"

"Very cute, Dean, but I got food in my freezer older than you. Now I 'preciate the tips and the compliments, but you wanna hit on someone, there's about a dozen girls come in here that might actually getcha somewhere."

"Nah." Dean took another sip of his beer. "Anybody comin' in here's gonna probably like the music, and that's just something I can't deal with. You, at least, I know aren't here by choice."

This time she laughed.

"Well, it's about damn time. I was startin' to think your smile muscles didn't work."

"Show me a bartender that smiles, I'll show you a crappy bartender." And then she smirked. "Or a bartender who's being hit on by a cute kid."

Dean held up his glass as if to toast. "Thank you."

"And honestly, I don't even hear the music anymore. I been doin' this too long."

"In that case, Jennifer, I envy you." Again he held up the glass, this time actually sipping more of the beer.

She shook her head. "You ain't like mosta

Manfred's friends, I'll give you that. For one thing, you ain't got enough hair."

Thinking of Ash, Dean had to smile. "Yeah, I can see that."

"'Scuse me, I gotta help somebody. You need anythin', just ask, okay?"

Dean hadn't even noticed the person who'd walked up to the bar. Jennifer went to take his order, which was apparently for an entire table. "Yeah, no problem." He'd flirted with bartenders in the past, and he knew that you could only do it a little at a time or they couldn't do their jobs. Bartenders lived off their tips, so he knew better than to do the long-form version of his methodology. Instead, he'd go for the gradual effect. When he finished this beer, he'd go back, ask for another, and find out what music she *did* like.

True, she was older than his usual, but she was also pretty and smart, and didn't seem at all interested in anything beyond taking his compliments—and tip money. Dean decided to take that as a challenge. *Food in her freezer, my ass.*

Besides, he needed something to distract him from the music.

His plan in motion, Dean worked his way back to the table in the back where he and Sam had been sitting. The Park in Rear had a lot of nooks and crannies. When you walked in the front door, the bar was against the wall on your right. Right in front of you were a bunch of small bar tables and chairs, and then to the left was a raised section with tall tables and bar stools at them. All the way at the back was the stage, with a small dance floor in front of it.

There were support pillars all around, on which people had scratched even more than they had on the bar, and they made it easy to hide in corners. However, the bar's PA system was such that one could not escape from the music on the stage—even if you had done as he and Sam had, and chosen the table in the corner of the raised section, the farthest spot from the stage that was still in the bar proper.

Sam was nursing a light beer—*freakin' lightweight*—and studying the scratches in the table. "You know," he said as Dean approached, "somebody actually scratched the words 'Kilroy was here'? I didn't think anybody did that in real life."

"I think I'm startin' to figure out who the spirit is," Dean said as he sat in the stool opposite his brother.

"Really?" Sam sat up straight.

"It's the ghost of the DJ they named themselves after. He's haunting Manfred in a desperate attempt to get them to stop desecrating his good name."

Sam chuckled. "C'mon, Dean, they're not *that* bad. I mean, they're not that good, but they're a cover band in a dive in Westchester County. Whadja expect?"

"Dude, did you *hear* what they did to 'Cocaine'?"

Showing his total lack of appreciation of the finer things in life, Sam said, "Whatever. I assume you took so long 'cause you were hitting on the bartender." He grinned. "He didn't strike me as your type."

"Funny boy," Dean said tightly as he sipped his beer. "Nah, I got the girl this time. Her name's Jennifer, and she has good taste in music. Or at least doesn't like this music." He looked over at the stage, where several women were practically throwing themselves at all five band members for no good reason that Dean could see, and added, "Which is more than I can say for most of the female population of this bar."

Minutes later Manfred walked over, with a very short girl hanging all over him. She was wearing a sweatshirt that said IONA COLLEGE. "Hey there, fellas, you havin' a good time?"

"We're having a blast," Sam said quickly. "This is a great place."

"Yeah, I love this joint."

The girl nudged Manfred in the ribs. "Freddie, intro*duce* me."

"Oh, sorry, baby. Sam, Dean, this here's Gina."

"Ja*nine,*" she said with a roll of her eyes. "*God.* You *always* get that wrong."

Dean Winchester had spent most of his life pretending to be other people in order to hunt more effectively, and also had spent a lot of that time cultivating a pretty damn good poker face, and even with all that, it took all of his considerable willpower not to scream.

Sam, thank God, saved him by speaking before he said something that would force them to look for a hotel. "It's a pleasure to meet you."

"Thanks! Isn't the band just *awe*some?"

In a tight voice, Dean said, "That wasn't the first word that came to mind, but it'll do, yeah."

"Hey, listen, fellas," Manfred said, "we got one more set, then we head over to this place in Yonkers for a few drinks and a smoke or two—th'owner lets us light up, 'long as we stay in the back, and it just ain't right smokin' a cigarette standin' outside."

Dean was very grateful he was only talking about cigarettes. He didn't think he could take these guys high.

"Anyways, you're welcome t'join us."

"You should *come*," Janine said, "it'll be *fun*."

"You'll be there?" Dean asked.

Janine let out a long sigh and rolled her eyes again. "Probably *not*. My stupid *mother*."

"Don't make funna your mother, baby, she's the best cousin I got."

Dean's eyes went wide. "Cousin?" He let out a

relieved breath, since the idea that this young woman—who couldn't have been older than Sam—was hugging Manfred for sexual reasons filled him with a slightly queasy feeling. But he could live with simple familial affection.

"Yup. My uncle Freddie's the *best*." She extricated herself from Manfred and said, "I gotta go pee. It was *so* great meeting you guys." With that, she flounced off to the restrooms in the back.

Manfred smiled his almost-toothy grin. "She's a pistol, that kid. Hate when she calls me 'Uncle Freddie,' though—makes me feel old."

He patted Dean on the shoulder, forcing Dean to resist the urge to punch him. *Remember the record collection.*

"I'm glad you fellas are havin' fun." Then Manfred looked up and saw someone. "Hey, Aldo, come over here!"

Dean winced for a second, then realized that it was the guitarist Manfred had yelled for. Aldo—who had hair as long as Manfred's, but styled a little more carefully, and also still all dark brown—came over with a big smile under a rather large nose. "Hey, what's up?"

"Aldo, these are the friends'a Ash's I was tellin' y'about. Sam and Dean Winchester. These guys're a coupla pistols."

Grinning, Aldo said, "Thought Winchesters was rifles."

Dean gave that a sympathy chuckle. "Thanks. And congrats, you're the one thousandth person to make that joke."

"Haw haw haw!" Dean almost recoiled from the powerful sound of Aldo's guffaw. Next to him, Sam actually jumped in his chair. "That's a good one."

"Uh, thanks. Hey, listen," Dean said, grateful for the ability to say this to the one member of the band for whom it wouldn't be a lie, "you sounded fantastic tonight. You really nailed those licks."

"Well, thank you very kindly, Sam."

"Uh, I'm Dean, he's Sam."

"Right, s'what I said, Dean. So you guys know Ash, huh?"

"Yeah, he—"

"That is one crazy-ass sumbitch," Aldo said, shaking his head. "Wouldn't know to look at him he went to no MIT, now wouldja?"

Sam raised an eyebrow. "Yeah, we thought that was a little weird, too. Can't imagine he fit in all that well there."

"Hell, I can't see him fittin' in nowhere, Dean."

"I'm Sam."

"Right, s'what I said, Sam. Anyhow, look, I'd love to chat, but I got somethin' to take care of, know what I mean?" He actually waggled his eyebrows.

"Long as you stay away from Janine," Manfred said sternly.

"Yeah, yeah, yeah," Aldo said, putting his hand in front of Manfred's face and then walking to the bar, where he started talking with an older woman.

"Listen, I gotta go drain the lizard, m'self. You fellas need anythin' at all, lemme know." Before Dean could even consider a response, Manfred went off to the bathroom.

"So," Sam said after a second, "whatever's going on here, it's staying hidden real well. I'm not picking up any EMF in the bar, and I've checked the walls and pillars and stuff. Nothing's jumping out at me as being any kind of symbol or sigil."

Chuckling, Dean said, "You sure 'Kilroy was here' wasn't a summoning?"

Sam returned the chuckle. "Probably not. It was a long shot anyhow—I'm pretty sure that this thing is tied to Manfred directly, even if it does relate to the music."

"Well, we should cover all the bases," Dean said before taking a sip of beer. After he gulped it down, he added, "If nothing else, we check everything tonight, we don't have to come back tomorrow night." *Although,* he thought, *if Jennifer's working again . . .*

"By the way, Dean," Sam said after a second, "I was thinking that tonight, after we deal with Manfred's spirit, we go check the house on Webb."

"Why tonight?" Dean asked. "I mean, we're probably gonna have our hands full with Casper the Surly Ghost. Plus, who knows how long we'll be out drinking and lighting up?"

Sam gave him his earnest look and spoke in a whisper. "Dean, if we're gonna break into a house, I want it to be as late at night as possible."

Dean considered arguing, but his brother was right. "Yeah, okay, fine, but let's play it by ear with the spirit first."

"Sure. But I really hope we find something, 'cause there wasn't anything at Cambreleng. Oh, by the way, you owe me ten bucks."

"For what?"

"You said I'd find something the cops didn't. I checked, and the place was clean—too clean for a New York street. The NYPD got *everything*."

Dean picked up his beer. "Sam, I told you—"

"It's got nothin' to do with what they're looking for, man. Remember what Frieda said at the zoo? That they'd been talking to everyone from cops to reporters to *university lawyers*. Those were Fordham students who died, and that means the college is in full CYA mode. I guarantee they put pressure on the cops to vacuum that crime scene within an inch of its life. It doesn't matter if they think it's important or not. *Anything* at that scene is in an NYPD lab somewhere."

Gulping down the rest of his beer, Dean set it on the table with a thunk. "Fine, you know more about college administrations and their weird habits. But we still have to check the house." He thought for a second. "Thing is—we probably *won't* find anything."

"Good," Sam said with a smirk, "I could use the ten bucks."

"No, I'm serious, Sammy, let's think about this. I don't think this is for us. I mean, we know the ritual's fake."

"Do we?"

Dean looked over at his brother. Now he had on his insistent face. Dean hated the insistent face, because Sam only used it when he was arguing with him. *As opposed to when he argued with Dad. That was always the angry face.* "Of course we do."

"Because Dad said so, right? Except what if he was wrong? I mean, he was the one telling us that vampires weren't real, but then in Manning, bingo, vampires."

Shaking his head, Dean said, "Dad knew about vampires, he just thought they were extinct."

"The point is, Dean, that we don't know everything. And Dad knew more than us, but *he* didn't know everything, either. I mean, this Samuels guy only tried the ritual a couple of times before he was arrested. How do we know it didn't work? Or that it won't?"

"C'mon, Sammy, the ritual was only performed by Samuels, he lied about where it came from, and nobody's used it before or since."

"That we *know* of."

Dean glowered at Sam. "It's not even *based* on anything, it's just a big con."

Holding up his hands in surrender, Sam said, "Fine, let's say it really is fake. We can't just not do anything. We *know* when the next murder will be, and we at least have an idea where. And the reasons why they're happening then *are* supernatural, and that *is* what we do."

"No." Dean looked at his brother. "We hunt *real* monsters, not fakes."

Quietly, Sam said, "I'd say someone who's killed three people and intends to kill more is a monster."

Dean sighed, continuing the argument out of habit and an unwillingness to admit that his baby brother was right. "We could just tell the cops."

"You really think they'd believe us? The only way to convince them would be to explain the ritual, and if we explain the ritual, they'll think we're nuts. And then they'd run our descriptions through their computer, and then—"

"Yeah, yeah, yeah." He didn't need to be reminded of the fact that he was America's Most Wanted. At first he'd thought it was kind of fun, but the novelty had worn off once the real consequences kicked in. "I'm gonna get another beer. You want anything?"

Insistent face came back. "So we're doing this, right?"

"*Yes*, Mr. Worry Wart, we're doing it. We'll check the house tonight, and tomorrow we'll try to track Mr. Pym down."

"Good. And I'll have another gin and tonic."

Dean stopped, turned, and stared at his brother. "Dude, I'm *so* not ordering that. I'll get you a screwdriver, I'll get you a Scotch and soda, hell, I'll get you a glass of red wine, but a gin and freakin' *tonic*? What is this, *Masterpiece Theatre*?"

Sam stared at him with his mouth slightly open. "I *like* gin and tonic. What, that's a crime now?"

"Yes, actually." He put up his hands. "Forget it—get your own froofy drinks. I'm gettin' a beer."

With that, he grabbed his empty beer glass, stepped down from the raised area and squeezed his way between two people to get at Jennifer's side of the bar.

"You're back," she said with a raised eyebrow. Dean noticed that a sheen of perspiration beaded her forehead.

"Big as life and twice as cute," Dean said with a smile, wincing even as he said it.

"Well, you're one'a those, anyhow," Jennifer said with a cheeky smile, which Dean found himself liking. " 'Nother beer?"

He nodded. "So I gotta ask—what kind of music *do* you like?"

As she poured another Brooklyn lager, Jennifer shook her head. "Don't ask me that."

Frowning, Dean asked, "Why not?"

Jennifer shuddered, though her hand remained steady on the tap. "Because you're flirtin' with me, and that's really sweet, and I'm kinda likin' it, and the minute I answer that question, you're gonna run away."

"C'mon, it can't be that bad," he said with a grin. "I mean, it's not like you listen to boy bands or anything, right?"

After she finished pouring the beer, Jennifer just stared at him.

His face fell. "No!"

Setting the beer down on a napkin, Jennifer held up her other hand. "I can't explain it, all right? I'm, like, twenty years too old for this stuff, but I can't help it. I love it! The harmonies, the dancing—and dammit, they're *pretty*." She pointed an accusatory finger at Dean before he could speak. "Don't say a goddamn *word*, Dean, I get enough crap about this from my kids."

That caught Dean off guard. "Kids?"

"Yeah, a ten-year-old daughter with a smart mouth and an eight-year-old son with a bad attitude."

"I guess they're home with their father."

Jennifer laughed. "Dean, you're about as subtle as a nuclear explosion, y'know that? Nah, I'm what-cha call your single mom. I got a girlfriend who takes care of 'em at night when I work, and I take care'a her kids during the day when they come home from school until she gets back from work." She chuckled. "In fact, tomorrow I gotta take Billy to soccer practice."

Dean raised his glass. "A regular soccer mom."

"Damn right. Excuse me." She went off to help another customer. Dean watched her go, surprised at how much more attractive she seemed now than she did a few minutes ago. Which made no sense at all to him, since he hated soccer moms, generally preferred younger women, wasn't all that big a fan of kids, and despised boy bands with a fervor he usually reserved for creatures of evil.

Of course, none of that changes how hot she looks in that T-shirt.

After taking a long sip of his beer, he heard Manfred say, "Okay pals'n'gals, Scottso's back." Turning, Dean saw the band members gathering up their instruments and getting ready to play.

The band started to play the opening to David Essex's "Rock On."

As soon as he heard Manfred's dreadful crooning of "Hey kids, rock and roll" to start the song, Dean drained most of the rest of his beer.

"Hey, it's Dean, right?"

Whirling around, Dean saw Janine, still wearing her Iona sweatshirt. Only now did Dean notice how tight her hip-hugging jeans were, and how short the sweatshirt was. She had a blue belly-button piercing that actually sparkled in the dim light of the bar.

"Uh, yeah—Janine."

"You rem*em*bered!" She stared past Dean at the stage area and said, just as the drummer went completely off the rails, "God, they're *so* good."

Dean decided there just wasn't enough beer in the world.

NINE

Over the course of his life, Sam Winchester had had many occasions to ponder on the exact nature of hell.

Raised more or less Christian—Dad was surprisingly devout, all things considered—Sam believed in God and in most things that your average, white American Christian believed in. He didn't often make it to church on Sunday—the only times he entered a church these days was as part of an investigation for a hunt—but he prayed every day. And he'd read the Bible, both as a child and again when he was at Stanford, taking a comparative religion class as a theology elective.

But the Bible wasn't particularly helpful on the subject of what hell was like. In the New Testament there was plenty of stuff about the kingdom of heaven—though, again, specifics were avoided.

Was hell a place? The evidence he had seen indicated that it was, as the demons had to come from somewhere. And, while he'd seen his share of restless spirits who couldn't move on, they were a tiny fraction of the number of people who actually had died—which meant that most people *had* moved on, which implied that they went *somewhere*. Of course, it was possible they just faded into the ether, but he couldn't believe that. After all, he knew there were Reapers—they'd encountered one in Nebraska, and Dean had met another one when he was in the hospital after the car crash—and their existence led one to believe that they were preparing the dead for *something*. After all, if people were just going to fade away, why bother *having* Reapers?

And then there were the demons who'd taunted them. The one on the plane who told him how much Jess was suffering, and the crossroad demon who'd said something similar to Dean about Dad. Now, demons lied, but still and all, there might have been some truth to it. Sam hated the idea that Jess was suffering in some weird nether realm just because she was stupid enough to fall in love with him.

In fact, that was the focus of most of his daily prayers.

Even if he knew there was *some* place that resembled the hell that folks like Pastor Jim always talked about, he had less evidence of heaven. But Sam had gotten a lot out of that comparative religion class, which he took for the same reason that he took "American Hauntings"—he wanted to see how people in the normal world dealt with the abnormal that had been part and parcel of his life since he was six months old. What particularly intrigued him was the concept of yin and yang from Eastern belief systems. It was impossible to have black without an equal amount of white—and there was a little white in the black and a little black in the white.

He'd heard it best expressed by a folk singer named Arlo Guthrie on an old album belonging to his freshman year roommate: "You can't have a light without a dark to stick it in. You can't have one thing without the other thing." So if there was a hell, and Sam had compelling evidence to indicate that there was, then there just had to be a heaven.

But still, there was always the question of what hell was. Was it the way Milton described it in *Paradise Lost,* the home of the fallen angels who had warred with God and lost? Was it the fiery pit that so many Calvinists portrayed in their brimstone-laden sermons?

Or was it the old joke about how hell is other people? Jean-Paul Sartre had embodied that in his play *Huis Clos,* in which hell was three people stuck in a room together.

Right here and now in the Shamrock Bar & Grill in Yonkers late Friday night—or early Saturday morning, however you looked at it—Sam was coming around to Sartre's way of thinking, that hell was being stuck between Janine Molina and Dean. Janine had apparently called her mother, and after Manfred got on the cell phone and assured said mother that he'd get her home safe, she was given permission to join them for their after-gig drink and smoke. Dean was having trouble reconciling Janine's looks—which, Sam freely admitted, were incredible—with her love for Scottso's music, which meant that his usually frisky brother was trying to avoid being caught in her web. So when they came in, Dean had been careful to make sure Sam was between him and Janine.

To add insult to injury, Aldo had sat on the other side of Dean and immediately started in on the Impala: "Where the hell'd you get a 'sixty-eight Impala in such fine shape, Sam?"

"Well, it's Dean, and it's a 'sixty-seven."

"S'what I said. Anyhow, it looks fantastic."

Grinning, Dean had said, "Rebuilt it myself."

That started the ball rolling on an in-depth conversation on the subject of motors, transmissions, various and sundry fluids, and other minutiae about cars that Sam had right near the top of his list of Conversations that Bored the Holy Crap Out of Him, just before Dean's Favorite Music and just after Dean's Sex Life.

This wouldn't have been so bad, except that Janine, having been stymied in her attempts to sit next to Dean, instead decided to sit next to him. In the brighter light of the Shamrock, Sam could see that her large eyes were brown, and wouldn't have been out of place on Bambi. In fact, the name Bambi wouldn't have been out of place on her. She proceeded to talk to him—about Dean.

"So what's your brother do for fun?"

Several uncharitable answers flew through Sam's head.

He likes to flirt with women who look a lot like you and pretend to be something really impressive and sexy so he can get into bed with them.

He and I troll newspapers and the Internet looking for supernatural phenomena so we can hunt them down and destroy them before they hurt people.

He hustles pool and plays poker, which are the two legal ways we make enough money to actually survive, money that mostly goes into crappy hotels, crappy food, Laundromats, and gas for the Impala.

He could have said any of these things. While they probably would have dampened Janine's ardor, they also would have had the ring of truth by virtue of actually being true.

But Sam was torn. A part of him didn't *want* to dampen an ardor that was driving his brother crazy, and he was all about driving his brother crazy. But a part of him wanted her to shut up about Dean already.

Finally, he said lamely, "You know, you could just ask him."

"Oh, I don't want to interrupt! 'Sides, he's talkin' with Aldo about cars. *So* not my thing. All I know about cars is if you turn the key it starts and you hit the brake it stops."

"Yeah," Sam said with a tilt of his head, "that's pretty much where I am." He gulped down some more of his beer.

The Shamrock claimed to be an authentic Irish pub, but looking around at the dark furnishings, the scuffed walls, the wobbly chairs, the ragged tables, and the ethnic diversity of the clientele (to wit, not all Irish), it looked pretty much like every other bar he and Dean had been in all across the country. The only thing that made it seem in any way like an Irish pub was that it had Guinness and Killian's on tap.

He then heard musical words: "I gotta take a dump." It was Aldo, getting up from his chair after finishing his Coke. For whatever reason, Aldo didn't drink—and he was the only member of Scottso who wasn't smoking a cigarette, either. Thinking back, Sam remembered that all the band members had beers with them on stage except for Aldo, who just had ice water. Dean had singled Aldo out as the only competent person in the group, and Sam was wondering if there was a correlation there.

Janine was out of her own chair like a shot and was sitting next to Dean almost instantly. "Hey, Dean," she said in a dreamy voice.

"Uh, hey, Janine."

"So, you havin' fun?"

Dean actually squirmed in his seat. Sam covered his huge grin by sipping more beer. "Uh, yeah, actually, this is a lot—lot of fun. Hey, listen, I was wondering, you know that bartender, Jennifer?"

"Yeah. She's cool. She used to babysit me, and she still does for my brothers. Why?"

Blowing out a long breath, Dean said, "Uh, nothing, really, I just—"

"So what do you like to do for fun?"

"Fun?"

Sam couldn't help himself. "Yeah, Dean, 'fun.' Three-letter word meaning 'enjoyment.'"

"Thank you, Ask Jeeves," Dean muttered. "I, uh—I like listening to music."

Another eye roll. "Well, *duh*. I mean, I figured *that* from you bein' at the *Park* in Rear. You know, I got to see Tull at Carnegie Hall last year? They *rocked*."

Dean frowned. "They're still together?"

"*Duh*. Of *course*. They tour, like, *all* the time. And Ian Anderson's, like, a *thou*sand years old, but he still prances around like—"

Manfred appeared out of nowhere. "Hey, Dean, is my niece buggin' ya?"

Sam could just see the war on Dean's face—tell the truth or be polite to the man in whose house he was sleeping?

The latter won out, but Sam could tell it was close to a photo finish. "Nah, she's cool."

Janine's already large doe eyes went as big as saucers, and she clasped her hands between her knees. "*Real*ly?"

Okay, Sam thought, *this was worth sitting between her and Dean babbling about cars.*

He then heard a tinny version of "China Grove" by the Doobie Brothers playing next to him. Looking over, he realized it was coming from Janine's purse, which was still on the chair next to him. "Uh, Janine," he said, "I think that's your phone."

She rolled her eyes again. "Ignore it. It's probably Mattie."

"Who's Mattie?" Dean asked.

Manfred said, "Her ex."

Letting out a dramatic breath, Janine said, "Who won't *stay* ex. I *so* hate guys who won't take 'screw off and die' for an answer. Hey, you got a cell phone?"

Slowly, Dean said, "Uh, yeah."

"I'm thinkin' about gettin' a new one. Can I see what you got?"

Shrugging, Dean said, "Okay, I guess." He took it out. It was a pretty standard flip-top model, one that looked like about seventy-five percent of the phones out there. Where Sam had gotten a Treo, preferring to have the most cutting-edge and versatile phone he could, Dean pretty much stuck with the simplest, most common model that required the least thought on his part.

She flipped it open and started pushing buttons.

Dean leaned forward nervously. "Uh, listen—"

"Cool phone." She closed it and handed it back to him.

"Listen," Manfred said, "I was thinkin' we might wanna head back to the ol' homestead."

"*Good* idea." Dean almost shot to his feet as he pocketed the phone. "Janine, it was great meeting you, really."

Also getting to her feet, Janine's face fell into an adorable pout that Sam just knew Dean would have to struggle to resist. "Aw, you're leaving? C'mon, Freddie, you can stay a *lit*tle while longer, can'tcha?"

Manfred shook his head. " 'Fraid not, kiddo. Gotta hit the hay. Ain't as young as I used t'be."

Dean added, "And, uh, we actually have some

stuff we gotta do tonight before we hit the hay ourselves."

"Well, you'll be back tomorrow night, right?" Janine asked earnestly.

This oughta be good, Sam thought, draining his beer.

"Prob'ly not."

"I was just kinda hopin' we could get to know each other," she said, moving a bit closer to Dean. Then she brightened. "Listen, call me, okay? I put my number in your phone—call me *any*time, day *or* night."

"No problem," Dean said.

They all said their good-byes—Robbie, the keyboard player, promised to drop Janine off at home—and then the three of them went out to the municipal lot across the street from the bar. At this time of night the parking was free, but there were parking meters that needed to be filled during the day.

As soon as they got in the car, Dean said, "Just shut up, Sammy."

"I didn't say a word, Dean. Though if I *did* say a word, that word would be, 'Wow, I can't believe you fell for the can-I-see-your-cell-phone trick.' "

Dean angrily slammed the key into the ignition and turned it. "That was at least a dozen words."

"Well, I still can't believe you fell for it. And

what's the big deal, anyhow? She was into you, man." He leaned back, clasping his hands behind his head. "She was tuned in to Dean-TV."

Turning around to back out of the parking space, Dean said, "I will kill you with my hands."

Lowering his hands, Sam said, "Seriously, Dean, what was the big deal about her? I mean, I've seen you hit on girls a lot younger."

"Yeah, but they all had taste."

Sam muttered, "That's arguable."

Dean pulled out of the parking lot and onto the road right behind Manfred's four-by-four, and then they followed him onto various back streets that Sam had a hard time keeping track of in the dark until they wound up on 248th and in front of the house. There weren't any parking spaces to be found, and Manfred just pulled farther into the driveway so the Impala could fit behind it.

Once they were parked, they shrugged out of their coats—yes, it was chilly at two-thirty in the morning in November in the Bronx, but they needed the freedom of movement—and tossed them into the backseat. Dean opened the trunk and pulled out two shotguns, one each for Sam and him. Sam took his and immediately opened it up to make sure both barrels were filled.

Walking down the driveway, Manfred looked at the two weapons with more than a little apprehension. "Uh, fellas?"

"It's okay," Sam said quickly. "These have rock-salt rounds."

"Rock salt? What, you wanna make sure the ghost don't slip on the ice?"

Sam closed his shotgun with a snap. "Spirits are vulnerable to rock salt. It dissipates them."

Manfred frowned. "What's that mean, 'dissipates'?"

"Means they go away for a while."

"I don't want it goin' away for a while, I want it *gone*."

Dean closed the trunk. "Only way to do that is to find the body the spirit belonged to and salt it and burn it."

"Again with the salt." Manfred shook his head. "All right, whatever, man, just get that damn thing outta my house."

"That's what we do. We see the ghost tonight, we blast it with the rock salt, we figure out who it is, and we salt and burn the body it belonged to. Nothin' to it."

Manfred stared at them a second. "You fellas do this every day?"

"Not *every* day," Dean said.

Sam added, "Just most of them."

They started walking toward the front porch. Sam put a hand on Manfred's shoulder. "Maybe you better stay out here."

Manfred hesitated, then said, "Yeah, prob'ly."

He chuckled. "Hell, I ain't been stayin' in the house when I see this broad anyhow."

Leaving Manfred to lean against the Impala, Dean and Sam slowly worked their way toward the front door, shotguns in a low ready position. As soon as they moved, Sam's body went on autopilot, the drills Dad had worked with them so many times when they were kids coming as easily as breathing. Dean hung back while Sam moved to the porch, Dean keeping an eye on the door while he did so, then moving to the door.

Of course, the front door was locked. They'd been standing next to Manfred when he locked it.

Dean turned to Manfred and mouthed the word *Keys!*

Manfred frowned, and mouthed the word *What?*

Sam sighed.

"Keys," Dean said in an intense whisper.

The lightbulb went off over Manfred's head. "Oh, right!" He dug into his jeans pocket, pulled out a huge key chain, and tossed it toward the porch.

It landed about a foot in front of the porch, skidding on the concrete path.

Dean let out a breath through his teeth and jumped down off the porch to get the keys. Sam saw that the keys were all labeled: House, Car, Garage, Locker, and so on. Given the various substances

Manfred had drunk, ingested, and smoked in his time, labeling the keys made sense.

First, Dean tried one of the ones labeled House, which didn't fit, but the second one did. It unlocked the bottom lock. The first one he tried got the top lock that was right next to the small stained-glass window.

The door opened inward, and Dean just let it go. It creaked, sounding distressingly like the front door in every haunted-house movie ever made.

John Winchester had been a well-trained Marine, and he taught his sons well. They moved in proper formation, Dean going in low first with Sam covering him, then Sam going in ahead of him with Dean covering him, and so on through the front hall.

The house looked pretty much the same as when they had left.

Then the rattling started.

Looking around, Sam saw that the framed posters on the hallway walls were vibrating, the metal of the frames banging against the Sheetrock. Several of the items on the small table in the hall fell off.

Stealing a glance to his left, he saw that the record albums Dean had left lying on the floor were now dancing across the floor, and the stuff on the coffee table was also falling off. Some of the CDs fell out of their racks, the jewel cases splitting open.

Slowly, Sam moved forward toward the kitchen, shotgun still in the low ready position, Dean covering him with shotgun raised.

It occurred to Sam that they never found out from Manfred what room he had to enter before the spirit manifested itself. Now, however, wasn't the time to go out and ask.

As they moved into the kitchen, Dean cradled the shotgun with one arm and pulled out the EMF with the other. It was lit up like a Christmas tree.

Not that they needed the confirmation, since the house was behaving like it was on a fault line. That was pretty much impossible, though—the house was built on solid rock. There was no basement, even—the laundry room, which Manfred had given them free use of, was located in a nook off the kitchen.

They checked it after they were done with the kitchen, but still nothing. The washer and dryer were rattling as if they were on, but both machines' dials were in the off position.

They went back through the hallway into the living room, where more items had crashed to the floor. Dean winced as he stepped on the broken glass from the frame of the Isle of Wight poster.

Still no phyiscal manifestation of the spirit, just the house shaking and—

"*Ah*-ha-ha-ha-ha-ha-ha-ha-ha-ha-ha-ha-ha-ha-ha-ha-ha-ha-ha-ha-ha-ha-ha-ha-ha-ha-ha-ha-ha-ha-ha!"

No matter how many times Sam encountered sudden noises in his life—and he figured he encountered more in the average month than most people did in their entire lives—his heart still skipped a beat when it happened.

Only one beat, though. As soon as he heard the cackle, he got down on one knee, shotgun raised.

But there was *still* no physical manifestation.

The cackling faded and the same voice started chanting the words "Love me!" over and over again.

Sam looked at Dean. Without any sign or facial indication, Sam knew that his brother agreed they should check upstairs next.

Dean went up first, Sam standing at the base of the stairs, shotgun raised. Once he made it up, Sam followed. Taking advantage of his long legs, he took two steps at a time.

The house was still shaking, and the cackling was now intermixed with the exhortations to be loved. Manfred had hung pictures of people Sam assumed to be family on the walls, and some of them had fallen down to the floor. Others rattled on the nails that held them to the wallpaper-covered wall.

"Love me!"

Sam whirled around and saw the face of a woman with bottle blond hair that was flying out in all directions—and couldn't help but think it was a little ridiculous that the woman's *spirit* had a dye job—as well as a body, but no discernible arms and legs. Her shoulders and hips kind of just faded off. She floated down the hallway toward him and Dean, her mouth wide with her cackling, her eyes looking somewhat demented. Her entire form was also transparent—which wasn't true of all spirits, but this one barely had any substance. Plenty of spirits—especially angry ones—could manifest physically, but this woman seemed to focus most of her ectoplasmic energy on laughing and wanting to be loved.

Just before he fired his shotgun, Sam noticed that her T-shirt had some kind of funky design on it.

The rock-salt rounds did their job. As soon as the salt hit her form, it started to dissipate, features dispersing across the hallway until there was nothing left.

Though the echoes of her last cry of "Love me!" sounded throughout the old house, the interior had stopped shaking, and once the echoes faded, there was silence.

Dean looked at Sam. "What the hell's a spirit doing wearing a 'rÿche shirt?"

Sam frowned. "What's a rike shirt?"

He immediately regretted asking, as Dean gave him his most disgusted look, which meant that he had made the mistake of professing ignorance about music Dean worshipped.

"Dude! Queensrÿche. They did *Operation: Mindcrime,* which is only the best concept album ever created."

Unable to help himself, Sam said, "They're the ones with the umlaut on the *y*, right? How do you pronounce that, exactly?"

"Bite me, Sam."

"And I didn't realize that there were any *good* concept albums."

"Excuse me?" Dean cocked his head, his mouth hanging slightly open. "*Tommy, Thick as a Brick,* hell, *Dark Side of the Moon*, for Christ's sake, they're—"

Realizing he'd teased his brother enough, Sam said, "Shouldn't we tell Manfred it's safe to come into his own house?"

Dean blinked. "Right." Without another word, he moved back to the stairs.

Sam followed after pausing to chuckle at how easy taunting Dean could be sometimes, so Dean was already out the door by the time he got to the bottom.

Manfred and Dean came in together a few seconds later. "You *sure* it's safe?" Manfred asked, not sounding the least bit convinced.

Dean looked around the house. "You hear any cackling? Anybody asking you to love her?"

After looking all around, and actually putting a hand to his ear, Manfred finally said, "No."

"She'll probably be back tomorrow night, but for tonight, it's safe."

Manfred looked at Dean. "So you dislocated her?"

"Dissipated, yeah."

Shaking his head, Manfred said, "Man, I need a toke." He went into the living room, walking over to the sideboard. While dusty bottles of booze were piled haphazardly on top of it, the side had two doors with keyholes, a skeleton key sticking out of one of them. Manfred turned the key, opened the door, and reached into it, pulling out a Ziploc bag full of green leaves and a yellow box.

The brothers exchanged a glance, shrugged, and set their shotguns carefully against the hallway wall before joining Manfred in the living room.

Manfred was sitting on the easy chair, leaning forward while he put some of the stuff on the coffee table onto the floor, next to the stuff that the spirit had already knocked off, thus clearing space for him to construct his joint.

Sam and Dean both sat on the couch perpendicular to him. In a gentle voice, Sam said, "I'm sorry, Manfred, but we need to ask you a few questions."

"What, now?" Manfred didn't look up.

"We actually saw it," Sam said.

At that, Manfred looked up. "Really? Whoa."

"It was a girl," Dean said, "blond hair—"

"Dyed," Sam added.

"Right, dyed, kind of a hook nose, and wearing a Queensrÿche shirt. Ring any bells?"

Manfred shrugged. "You know how many women in 'rÿche shirts I see all'a time?" He gingerly finished rolling his joint.

Dean asked, "You ever take any of 'em home?"

"Maybe." Manfred shrugged again, then dug into the pocket of his leather jacket, which he had yet to take off after coming in from outside, and pulled out a lighter. "Honestly, I took lotsa women home, from the Park in Rear, from other places— Christ, I can't even remember last week, y'expect me t'remember that?" And then, to accentuate the point, he took a drag on his joint.

Dean looked at Sam.

Sam just shrugged back.

"You guys want a drag?" Manfred said in a much more mellow voice, smoke blowing out his mouth.

"No thanks." Sam got to his feet. "We actually have some stuff we gotta take care of tonight."

Manfred grinned. "Thought you was just sayin' that to blow off Janine."

Dean actually looked embarrassed. "Yeah, about that—"

Holding up a hand, Manfred said, "Don't sweat it, Dean. She flirts with anything that moves. You show up tomorrow night, she'll hit on y'all over again. You don't show up, she'll forget all 'bout you."

Sam looked down at Dean, who was still seated on the couch. "Gee, we don't know anybody like *that,* do we, Dean?"

Looking up, Dean glared, then also rose from the couch. "Yeah, we really do have something we gotta take care of."

"You takin' the car?" Manfred asked after taking another toke.

"Uh, yeah."

"Groovy, man. Jus' park it b'hinda truck when y'get back."

Dean smiled. "Thanks." He tapped Sam on the chest with the back of his hand. "Let's motor, Sammy."

They went out to the Impala and retrieved their coats from the backseat. Sam still had the keys, and Dean had shown no interest in doing any more driving in this city—nor did Sam have any interest in listening to Dean while he did—so Sam folded himself into the driver's side.

Driving to Webb and 195th took almost no time at all this late hour. There were other cars on the road, especially once they got out of Riverdale and drove on Broadway to West 225th Street, which turned into Kingsbridge Road once they went over I-87.

Unfortunately, Sam's belief that parking would be easier at night proved a foolish one. "I don't believe it," he muttered.

"Look around, Sammy," Dean said. "Most of these are apartment buildings, and I ain't seen too many parking lots. This time'a night, everyone's at home asleep, which means their cars are parked. Screw it, just double park."

Sam frowned. "Isn't that illegal?"

"So's breaking and entering, and that's kinda what we're here for."

"Yeah, but we're *good* at B and E, and we probably won't get caught. But the car's just *out* there being illegally parked. I mean, I saw tons of double-parked cars during the day, when I was driving around, but I haven't seen a single one since we left Manfred's. We'll stand out, is all I'm saying, and if some bored night-shift cop decides to—"

"You got a better idea, Sam?"

Sam steered the car down Webb back toward Kingsbridge. "Wasn't there a parking lot on Kingsbridge?"

"Is that the big street we came up?" Dean asked.

Nodding, Sam said, "We'll try there."

Making a right onto Kingsbridge, Sam saw the parking lot—then the rates they were charging, not to mention the sign that said, SORRY, FULL.

His head in his hands, fingers rubbing his forehead, Dean said, "Sam, just double-park."

Letting out a long breath, Sam said, "Yeah, okay." He drove down another block, turned right, made a broken U-turn using someone's driveway, turned left back onto Kingsbridge, then did the one-way-street shuffle once again to get to the house where the first of their Poe-inspired murders took place.

"I got an idea," Sam said. The house had a driveway next to it that was gated and locked. The driveway was *just* wide enough to accommodate the Impala. Sam pulled up as if to parallel park.

The first time, he aimed a bit off, and so had to start again. The second time, he came in at too wide an angle, so he had to start *again*. By the time he succeeded in parking the car more or less evenly, Dean looked like he was ready to chew off his own arm.

Glaring at Sam as he turned off the ignition, Dean reached over and yanked the keys out. "*I'm* driving back."

Sam shook his head and chuckled—it wasn't as if Dean was any *better* at parallel parking—and followed his brother to the wrought-iron gate that blocked the driveway they'd parked in front of.

Dean looked up at the house. "Nice place. Surprised they haven't sold it."

"Yeah, well, murder plays hell with real estate, y'know?"

Reaching into his coat pocket for his lock pick, Dean said, "Yeah." He knelt down and started working on the gate's padlock. After about thirty seconds' work—which seemed like an eternity to

Sam, feeling very exposed on the city street, even this late at night with no sign of anyone—it clicked open. Sam looked around nervously, unable to help noticing that several people in the surrounding apartment buildings had their lights on. *Hope none of them are looking down at the street outside their windows.*

Dean pushed the gate open quickly—something Dad had taught them, metal gates made *more* noise if you opened them slowly. Sam jumped forward and caught the gate before it collided against the house.

They both went into the driveway, Dean shutting the gate behind him so it would look normal. However, he didn't relock the padlock, as they might well need to make a hasty exit.

Dean knelt down next to the side door and started to work on picking that lock.

Several minutes passed, and Dean made no progress whatsoever.

Whispering urgently, Sam said, "Dude, will you hurry up?"

"It's a tough lock, Sammy," Dean whispered right back. "And it's dark. 'Sides, artistry takes time."

"So does incompetence. C'mon, Dean, I've seen you get through doors faster than this."

"Those doors had freakin' *porch* lights, okay? Just give me a sec, I think I—"

Suddenly, a light shone right in Sam's face. Looking down the driveway at the source, he saw a dark figure who appeared to be holding a gun in addition to a flashlight.

"Freeze, police!"

TEN

It had been several years since Detective Marina McBain had been up to the Five-oh in the Bronx.

Like most of the New York Police Department's precinct houses, the Fiftieth Precinct in the Bronx was a boxy white edifice with few windows and an American flag atop it flapping from a pole. McBain drove her Saturn—her own car rather than a departmental one, as technically she was off duty right now—up Broadway after getting off the Major Deegan at the West 230th Street exit. She turned left at West 236th, which had been renamed after Officer Vincent Guidice, a member who died in the line of duty a decade earlier. In fact, her last trip up here had been the renaming ceremony for the street back in 1999.

McBain searched desperately for a parking spot. Generally, the street outside a precinct house had angled parking, but cops *never* parked their cars neatly. Vehicles, both unmarked and blue-and-whites, were thrust up against the sidewalk at every conceivable angle, some of them on the sidewalk itself.

Eventually, though, McBain found a place to wedge in her Saturn. After locking it with the remote, she walked in the precinct's dirty glass front door, heading up the four metal-rimmed stairs and through the creaky wooden doors to the reception area. The public information desk was empty at this time of night, so McBain moved past it and to the left, walking by about half a dozen plaques for those officers who fell in the line of duty (Guidice most prominent among them). There, facing the large white wall with the Five-oh's insignia emblazoned on it, was the main desk, behind which sat a bored-looking night-shift sergeant. Hair in a crew cut, beady eyes barely visible under a ridged brow, a potbelly protruding over his gun belt, and with a name tag that said O'SHAUGHNESSY, the sergeant was perusing the sports pages of the *Daily News*. McBain could hear a voice, not really audible, on crummy speakers under the desk. She assumed it was the dispatcher, and as she got closer she heard familiar codes, confirming her presumption.

McBain also noticed the Derek Jeter bobblehead on top of the computer monitor. It was slightly askew, and obviously not attached to the monitor, so chances were good it belonged to this sergeant alone, who only kept it out during his own shift. In addition to his name tag, his badge, and the gold 50 pins attached to his collar, he was also wearing a decidedly nonregulation pin with the interlocking NY logo of the New York Yankees baseball team. If worse came to worse and she couldn't get O'Shaughnessy to help her out via friendly means, she could always threaten to report him for being out of uniform.

Without looking up from the paper, O'Shaughnessy said, "Can I help you?"

"So whaddaya think, the Yanks'll trade Johnson?"

That got the sergeant to look up. "Friggin' well hope so." He looked at McBain. She watched his face change as he regarded her. First he saw her dark-skinned face and short, nappy hair, and his disinterested expression said, *black female*. Then he moved down to her dark business suit, which altered his expression to vague interest, since it was now *black female who doesn't look like street slime*. Then he saw the gold shield on her belt. Only then did he set the paper down and change his expression to one of genuine interest, as now she wasn't a black female at all, but a member. "Never shoulda traded for the guy inna first place. He ain't no Yankee. Neither's A-Rod."

McBain smiled, dredging up the baseball knowledge she had absorbed from her fellow detectives in the Missing Persons Unit. She couldn't have cared less about that or any other sport, but you didn't survive in the testosterone-laden NYPD without being able to hold your own in any conversation about the Yankees, Mets, Knicks, Nets, Giants, or Jets. The Rangers, Devils, and Islanders were optional, which was good, as McBain drew the line at hockey. "Yeah, but A-Rod's still a good player. I don't think RJ has anything left in the tank."

"Got that right. 'Sides, after 2001, you don't let a guy like that onna team."

"I dunno, they let Johnny Damon on after 2004, and he's been pretty good."

O'Shaughnessy shook his head. "That's different— Yanks signin' Damon pissed off Red Sox fans. Pissin' off Red Sox fans, that's *always* good."

If you say so, McBain thought. She was already starting to use up all the knowledge she could bring to bear in a Yankees-related conversation. If she had to drag the endless Yankees–Red Sox rivalry into it, she'd flounder, and that was contrary to her purpose.

Luckily, O'Shaughnessy let her off the hook.

Now sitting up straighter in his chair, he asked, "What can I do ya for, Detective?"

"My name's McBain, I'm with MPU. You guys get any calls the last couple of days for a 10–31 at 2739 West 195th Street?" she asked, using the radio code for a burglary in progress.

O'Shaughnessy's pudgy face fell into a frown. "Don't think so. What's that gotta do with Missing Persons?"

Putting on an exasperated look, she said, "*Don't* ask. My sergeant's taken up lodging *right* in my ass until I get through this."

"Heard that." O'Shaughnessy sputtered a noise that McBain supposed could have been a laugh. He grabbed the keyboard with a meaty hand and dragged it toward him. "Lemme check."

Several keystrokes and a few mouse clicks later, O'Shaughnessy shook his head, causing his jowls to vibrate. "Nah, nothin' there since that homicide back on the seventh."

"Okay," McBain said. It had been a long shot, but she was just *sure* that—

The dispatcher's voice said, *"Nine-one-one call, 10–31 at—"* Here, the dispatcher enunciated each number. *"—two-seven-three-nine West one-nine-five."*

McBain had to fight to keep herself from grinning. *Knew I could count on the boys.*

O'Shaughnessy stared at McBain with an expression that she supposed was awe. "How the hell'd you know about that?"

"It was a guess," was all McBain would say. "Listen, let me take care of that."

"No biggie," O'Shaughnessy said, "I can get one of my guys down there and—"

Wincing, McBain said, "Sergeant, please—I really need to take care of this one myself. It's the only way I'll get outta the boss's doghouse, y'know?"

The sergeant stared at her for a second with his beady eyes. "This got somethin' to do with that homicide?"

"Sort of." That, at least, wasn't really a lie. "Like I said, it's a long story. If you want the whole thing, fine, but there *is* a 10–31, and—"

Waving her off with both hands, O'Shaughnessy said, "Fine, fine, what-the-hell-ever. Knock yourself out. Just leaves my guys free to bust more stupid college kids."

McBain chuckled. Both Manhattan College and Mount Saint Vincent were within the Five-oh's jurisdiction, and Friday nights usually meant lots of so-called SWIs—Stupid While Intoxicated.

Then O'Shaughnessy got a weird look on his face. "Hang on—you sure you don't need backup?"

Trying not to grit her teeth, McBain said, "If this is who I think it is, trust me, I can handle it."

"Yeah, but what if you can't? My lieutenant

finds out I let you out without backup, he'll have *my* ass."

"I can understand that," McBain said. She had been hoping O'Shaughnessy would be too bored to think through the implications.

O'Shaughnessy's eyes darted back and forth as he thought for a minute. Finally, he said, "Tell you what—I'll send one of my guys over in twenty minutes if I ain't heard from you."

That was a compromise McBain could live with. She was now grateful she'd had the foresight to program the Five-oh's number into her cell. "That's fair. Thanks a *lot*, Sergeant, I *really* appreciate it."

"No problemo, Detective," O'Shaughnessy said, picking up his paper. "An' hey, listen, I got me season tickets for the Stadium every year. I ever got a free seat, want me to let you know?"

"Sure," McBain said, confident that she would always be busy at those times, but preferring to keep the goodwill with the sergeant, just in case.

With that empty promise made, she turned and headed back to her Saturn.

It didn't take long to drive to the corner of Webb and 195th Street, and it took even less time to find an illegally parked 1967 Chevy Impala. *I swear, I'm gonna kill 'em.*

Double-parking her Saturn right next to the Impala, she checked to make sure her NYPD credentials were prominently displayed on the dashboard, in case one of O'Shaughnessy's "guys" decided to get overzealous with the parking citations.

The house in question was easy enough to pick out, as it was the only structure on the corner that wasn't red brick. Yellow crime scene tape was draped sloppily across the wire gate that led to the front door, probably a victim of eleven days of November wind. McBain was surprised the tape was still up, but then recalled that nobody actually lived in the house to take it down. Presumably, the real estate company representing the house—whose name, phone number, and website were listed on the For Sale sign—had declined to show the house for a while after it was a crime scene.

Walking back toward where her car and the Impala were parked, she saw a gated driveway. Normally padlocked, the lock was hanging open, though the gate was still shut. Peering past the gate down the driveway, she saw a side door, and two figures kneeling down in front of it. One was fairly tall and was staring intently down at the other one, who was crouched in front of the door. The tall one seemed to be speaking sharply at the short one, though not loud enough to be heard from the street.

McBain removed her nine-millimeter weapon from its holster and thumbed the safety. She also removed her flashlight, flicked it on and held both it and the nine-mil up as she kicked open the gate. "Freeze, police!"

Both of them looked up at her, like deer frozen in headlights as her flashlight shone on them.

Slowly, she walked into the driveway. The shorter one—that had to be Dean—started to rise up, and she said, "Which part of 'freeze' didn't you get?"

Dean stopped moving.

She finally came fairly close to the pair, though not near enough for them to be in arm's reach of her weapon.

Once she was sure she'd put on enough of a show for whoever it was who made the 911 call, she lowered her nine-mil. "You guys are complete idiots, you know that?"

Sam started to speak. "Officer, I can explain—"

"It's 'Detective,' and don't even *try* to explain it, Sam, 'cause I got *no* tolerance for Winchester-brand bull."

Both of them started opening and closing their mouths, as if unsure how to respond to her use of their name.

Deciding to put them out of their misery, she smiled and said, "Yeah, I know who you are. Sam and Dean Winchester, only sons of John Winchester, a man who, unlike his dumbass sons, knows to *call* me whenever *he's* in town."

"You knew our father?" Dean asked, sounding stunned.

"Yeah." She frowned, not liking Dean's use of the past tense. "The rumors I heard ain't true, though, are they? That he died?"

Both brothers looked at each other, and the expressions on their faces told McBain everything she needed to know. Far too many missing persons cases ended with a corpse, and she knew what grief-stricken people looked like.

"Damn. I'm sorry, guys, I didn't know. Look, my name's Marina McBain, and you are *damn* lucky I found you before the uniforms in the Five-oh did. You know there was a 911 call on your sorry-ass attempt at a B and E here?"

"How did you—" Sam started.

"Later. You wanna check out this place?"

They exchanged another glance, this time looking confused. "I, uh—yeah," Dean said slowly.

"Fine, get your ass back down on the ground and finish pickin' the lock. I gotta make a phone call. Here, this might help." She handed Sam the flashlight, which he held up so it shone on the lock.

"Thanks," Sam said.

"No problem."

"You *really* a cop?" Dean asked.

"Nah, I just like wearin' gold shields for kicks. *Yeah,* I'm a cop, now shut up and pick the damn lock." She started up the driveway toward the street.

"Or what," Dean said with a smirk, "you'll

show me that NYPD stands for 'knock your punk-ass down'?"

She turned back around. "Okay, first of all, white people should *not* quote Will Smith. Second of all, if you *want* me to put you on your ass, just say the word, brushy-top."

Leaving Dean to self-consciously touch the top of his head, McBain pulled her cell phone out from the inside pocket of her suit jacket, flipped it open, and continued up the driveway, calling up the number for the Fiftieth Precinct.

"Fiftieth Precinct, O'Shaughnessy."

"Sergeant, this is Detective McBain."

"You okay, Detective?"

He sounded genuinely concerned, which touched McBain. "It was the guys I thought it was. I took care of it, so you don't gotta send your guys over. Thanks, though."

"No problem, Detective. Hope this gets you back in good with your boss."

"Me, too," she said emphatically. Of course, she was actually off duty right now, and as far as her boss Sergeant Glover was concerned, she was a perfectly good missing persons detective who was currently at home asleep like any sensible day-shift detective would be at that hour. "Thanks again."

She turned and walked back down the driveway. "Okay, I got the Five-oh off the scent. If the 911 caller wants to know what happened, they'll say it was taken care of, but I doubt they will. Damn citizens don't follow up on anything."

Just as she got to the side door, Dean stood up and pulled it open. "Yahtzee."

Handing McBain the flashlight back handle first, Sam said, "Thanks."

"No problem. I'm gonna go out on a limb and assume you guys're checkin' out the basement?"

"Good guess." Dean then looked at her with an annoyed expression. "I suppose you wanna come in with us, huh?"

"You wanna try and stop me, knock yourself out."

"Lady, I don't even know who you *are*."

McBain smiled sweetly. "Lemme give you a clue, brushy-top. I'm the only person standin' between you and a couple uniforms from the Five-oh bustin' your asses, runnin' your face and prints through the system, turnin' up a federal warrant for your arrest, and lockin' you both up for the rest of your natural lives. You feel me, Dean, or you want me to call Sergeant O'Shaughnessy back and tell him I need backup?"

The two brothers looked at each other again, and seemed to come to a decision. McBain could swear they communicated telepathically.

Dean bowed slightly and indicated the door. "After you."

"Suddenly, you found chivalry?" McBain asked with a snort.

"Nah, it's just—you got the flashlight."

That elicited another snort. McBain went in the door.

The entrance led right into a staircase. To the left, it went up to an open doorway. McBain shone the light up to see an empty room—expected in an empty house for sale. There was also a whiff of spice in the air. The last owner had been a cook for a fancy restaurant in Midtown, and obviously her skills were plied at home as well.

To the right, the stairs went down into the basement, which was the actual scene of the crime.

She quickly got to the bottom of the stairs, which creaked with each step all three of them took, so much so that she was grateful that it was late and there was a driveway and a wall between this house and the place next door. The flashlight illuminated bits of the room: a washer and dryer, wooden support beams, a hardwood floor that had been put in within the last ten years or so, and incredibly hideous wallpaper on three of the walls.

McBain also found a light switch, and flicked it on. A forty-watt lightbulb dangling from a chain in the center of the ceiling lit up, making her think she was better off with just the flashlight.

The wall that wasn't covered with the wallpaper

was made of brick, and it was even newer than the hardwood—less than a month, in fact. Based on the reports she'd read, that had made it fairly easy to break the wall down after both the neighbors and the real estate agency complained about the smell in the basement. Sure enough, there was a large hole in the brick, more yellow crime-scene tape draped across the gap.

Sam stood behind her, peering over her head into the hole. "You can't even tell there was a body in there."

"Reyes, the vic, he died of suffocation. And one way you could've told there was a body in here was that the inside of some of the otherwise-brand-spanking new bricks had scratch marks on 'em. But they're all at the lab."

"Sammy, look at this."

McBain turned to see Dean kneeling down on the floor. Sam moved to kneel next to him. Deciding to respect the boys' need to do their own thing, McBain hung back.

Sam looked up at her. "Did the crime-scene report indicate any herbs found lying around?"

"Not that I can remember—but the woman who used to own this place was a gourmet cook."

Dean held up a small piece of greenery between thumb and forefinger. "I hope she didn't cook with this. This is wormwood."

McBain shrugged. "Well, you *can* cook with

wormwood—and make tea with it, for that matter—so I don't see—"

"It's also used in resurrection rituals," Sam said, "including the one this is part of."

"This is a resurrection ritual?" McBain shuddered. "Hell. I ain't exactly up on those."

Dean stood up. "What *are* you up on, Detective? Are you a hunter, a cop, a pain in the ass, what?"

Grinning, McBain said, "What, I can't be all three? I don't hunt that much, actually. Killed a vampire that was draining homeless folks for fun a few years back—and I gotta tell ya, takes *forever* to saw through a neck bone with a kitchen knife—but mostly I just keep an eye on things, help out hunters who come through town, and make sure the mundanes don't get word of it. I'm part of a network of cops, actually."

"Are you kidding me?" Dean didn't sound convinced. "A *network*?"

"Yeah, well, don't be *too* impressed, brushy-top. Right now, there's all of four of us—me, a woman in Chicago named Murphy, and a guy in Eugene, Oregon, named Lao."

"That's three," Sam said.

McBain smiled. "Well, you know the fourth. She's down in Baltimore. Kinda new, and she may not be a cop much longer."

Sam's eyes widened. "You mean Detective Ballard?"

Nodding, McBain said, "She's suspended right now, pending an IID investigation, and even if she comes out okay, she probably ain't gonna be able to stay in Homicide. Still, we reached out to her after she met up with you two, and she's joined up. We had another one, down in Mississippi, but she died in Katrina."

"You're right," Dean said, "I'm not too impressed."

"Well, just four of us was fine for a while," McBain said. "Up until about a year and a half ago, things were cool, but—" She shuddered. "The spooky stuff's quintupled lately. Gettin' harder to keep a lid on it."

Sam and Dean exchanged another one of their telepathic looks, then Sam said, "How come almost all of you are women?"

"Can we play twenty questions later?" Dean asked. He started checking out the rest of the basement.

Sam gave McBain an apologetic smile and started checking the hole in the wall.

For her part, McBain checked the ceiling. She didn't expect anything, but she also figured it couldn't hurt.

"To answer your question, Sam," she said as she got a good look at several cobwebs, "this ain't exactly normal police work. Your regular police, he ain't gonna buy this for a dollar. Only ones open to the spooky stuff are people already on the fringe. Usually, that's us womenfolk."

"And the one guy you mentioned was Asian," Sam said.

McBain nodded. "My training officer used to say that an Asian cop is like a Jewish Pope. And while they ain't *that* rare, they ain't common, neither." She let out a long breath. "So what resurrection ritual *is* this, anyhow? Like I said, that ain't exactly my area."

"It's not," Dean said. "It's a fake ritual some jackass in the nineteenth century made up to scam people out of their hard-earned moolah."

"Obviously," Sam added, "somebody believes it's real."

Not finding anything on the ceiling, McBain looked back at the brothers. "So this ain't just some fetish thing—someone's trying to, what? Resurrect Edgar Allan Poe?"

Dean said, "That's what it looks like." He turned to Sam. "You owe me ten bucks."

Sam looked outraged. "What?"

Holding up the wormwood, Dean smiled. "Cops missed the resurrection herb garden. You owe me ten bucks."

"Call my lawyer," Sam muttered, then turned to McBain and spoke quickly, probably to keep his brother from making a rejoinder. "Detective

McBain, if you don't mind my asking—how'd you know we'd be here?"

"Didn't know for sure till I checked out the Five-oh—that's the Fiftieth Precinct," she added when she belatedly realized that they might not have been versed in NYPD lingo. "This house is in their territory. Anyhow, the call came in on you guys right when I got there."

"Yeah, but how'd you know to check in the first place?"

Dean, who was looking at some kind of funky contraption that McBain realized was a goofy-looking homemade EMF meter, said, "I was wonderin' that myself."

"Well, I'd been keepin' an eye on the Poe thing from the git-go—I mean, this whole bricked-up thing screamed both 'The Cask of Amontillado' and ritual nonsense to *me,* so I figured a hunter or three might show up, and I thought it even more after the orangutan. Nobody here's put it together yet, but the two murders are different precincts, and not everybody's all *that* well read. I mean, 'Amontillado,' everyone knows that one, but 'Murders on the Rue Morgue' ain't taught in most English classes, and most cops don't even *remember* their English classes." She smiled. "And then the Five-two got a call from Bronx Zoo security about two guys, a tall one and a short one, claiming to be from *National Geographic* but not really being very convincing."

The boys exchanged another one of their glances, though this one, she noticed, was a bit more guilty.

"Ain't too many hunters that travel in a pair, and none'a the ones I know about match your descriptions, so I figured it was the pair'a you. Didn't know for sure till I got here, though."

"What would you have done if we were normal burglars?" Sam asked.

Shrugging, McBain said, "Busted you. And the Five-oh was gonna send backup if they didn't hear from me in twenty. Trust me, after ten years'a this, I've gotten real good at coverin' my ass. See, you guys can just leave town. Me, I gotta stay and clean up."

Dean put away his EMF meter. "Nothin'. All right, listen, we gotta motor. I don't think there's anything else to find here."

McBain said, "You think this is part of a ritual? I assume there's more to it, and the next piece is gonna be Monday."

Again the brothers exchanged glances. "Uh, yeah," Sam said.

"I follow phases of the moon—kind of an occupational hazard."

Sam quickly explained the ritual from some freak named Percival Samuels. "The next murder's either gonna be on Webster Avenue near Beford Park Boulevard or at Fordham Road and Martin Luther King Jr. Boulevard."

Scratching her nose, McBain said, "Yeah, okay. Tell you what, I'll help out—take whichever location you two don't." Dean got a sour expression at that. "You got a problem, brushy-top?"

"A couple, actually. First of all, *please* stop calling me 'brushy-top.'"

Sam broke into a wide grin at that.

"Secondly, I'm not sure I buy this whole 'crusading cop who fights demons on the side' crap—or that you knew Dad."

In truth, McBain had expected this—both that Dean would dislike the nickname and that the brothers would be hinky about the fact that she knew their father. Having met John Winchester more than once, it didn't surprise her in the least that he neglected to tell his sons about her. John wasn't exactly big on sharing. Besides, she'd gotten word of some of Sam and Dean's hunts, and while they hadn't made a lot of mistakes, the few they did make were ones she wouldn't have expected of John's sons—unless he held things back from them.

"John Winchester," she said, "white male, approximately fifty-three years old, six-foot-one, a hundred ninety pounds, dark hair, brown eyes, occasional beard depending on his mood, former U.S.

Marine, wife Mary, deceased, two sons, Sam and Dean. Came to New York City on three separate occasions, once to hunt a golem in Brighton Beach, once to deal with a haunting on the subway—"

Sam's mouth fell open. "The phantom subway conductor?"

McBain smirked. "Sorta. This spirit prob'ly was the basis for that crazy legend."

"What was the third one?" Dean asked.

"I swear to God, he slew a dragon. It was down in Chinatown—that was one crazy-ass case, lemme tell ya."

Sam's mouth fell even farther open. "Dad killed a *dragon*?"

Shrugging, McBain said, "Well, it was a small one."

Attitude still firmly in place, Dean said, "And you helped him?"

"Tried to. Mostly he snarled and spit at me— kinda like what you're doin' now, brushy-top—and told me to stay outta his way."

"Did you?" Dean asked.

"Not the first time. After we almost shot each other, we came to an understandin'. He kept me posted on his movements when he came to town, I told him what I knew, and I kept an eye on him from a distance."

Finally, Dean relented. "Yeah, that sounds like Dad."

"Listen, Detective, we'd better get going," Sam said gently.

McBain reached into her jacket pocket and removed her cardholder, picking out two business cards. "Here," she said, handing one to each of the brothers. "My cell's on there. You need me, use that one. If either one'a you calls to MPU, there's a record of it. The cell's my personal phone, so it's safer."

"Thanks," Sam said, pocketing the card.

The three of them went back upstairs, McBain switching the light off behind them, Dean closing and relocking the door once they were back out in the driveway.

After Dean clicked the padlock on the driveway gate shut and they were both standing at their respective cars, McBain said, "Listen, you two, be careful. I covered you this time, but it ain't gonna be easy, especially if you're gonna go pulling felonies on me."

"We can handle the cops," Dean said defensively.

"This ain't no red-state sheriff's office, brushy-top, we're talkin' the NYPD, and we're talkin' a federal warrant for multiple homicides. I know you hunter types like livin' on the edge, but right now that edge is pointed right at your balls, you feel me? You don't know me, you don't trust me, you don't like me, but right now, you need me. So don't do nothin' stupid, and we'll all get outta this alive."

Without waiting for either brother to reply, McBain got into her Saturn, turned it on, and drove off, heading toward Kingsbridge Road, which would take her back to the Major Deegan. That'd get her to the Triboro and back to her Queens apartment, where she'd get all of two hours' sleep before having to head into One Police Plaza to report for her shift tomorrow. Right now she was on a Wednesday to Sunday rotation, but at least that meant she'd be free to help the Winchesters out on Monday. *If we're lucky, we'll stop another poor bastard from getting killed.*

ELEVEN

Dean wasn't used to being the first one up—he was even less used to it when he got up at noon. But Manfred's door was shut, his snoring clearly audible even through the closed door, and a peek into the other guest room showed that Sam was not only out like a light, but drooling on the pillow. Pausing to get a picture of that with his cell phone, he then took a shower, went downstairs, and—after throwing a load of their dirty clothes into the washer—plunked himself down on the couch, opened up Sam's laptop, and found that crazy guy's Poe website.

Among other things, "Arthur Gordon Pym" had

archived a whole bunch of Poe's stories on his site, so Dean started reading them while drinking some of Manfred's killer coffee out of a mug that said, IBM: ITALIAN BY MARRIAGE, with the three letters in the red, white, and green of the Italian flag. That coffee also went a very long way toward reminding Dean as to what he liked about Manfred. So did the soundtrack for his reading, which was the dulcet tones of Rush's self-titled album. Both factors did a great deal to wash the taste of Scottso out of his brain.

By the time Sam stumbled downstairs wearing only a pair of pants, Dean put on his best mad-scientist voice. "It's *alive,* I tell you, alive!"

"Yeah, yeah," Sam muttered, heading straight into the kitchen.

Grinning, Dean looked back at the laptop, taking his third shot at reading this particular paragraph, and finally giving up.

When Sam came into the living room, clutching a mug that had a *Dilbert* cartoon on it, Dean said, "Dude, you told me that this Rue Morgue thing was the first detective story, right?"

"Yeah, why?" Sam said as he sat on the easy chair.

" 'Cause I gotta tell ya, this is the worst piece of crap I ever read in my life. I mean, the other stories weren't bad. Soon's I started reading 'The Tell-Tale Heart,' I remembered it from that stupid class I took back at that crappy Catholic school in Illinois. But this Rue Morgue story . . ." He trailed off.

Sam shrugged as he sipped his coffee. "What can I tell you, Dean, it was revolutionary at the time. And hey, if it wasn't for that story, we probably wouldn't have *CSI* today."

"No loss," Dean said. "There's better things on Thursday nights anyhow."

"It gets better once you get past the opening," Sam said.

Dean agreed with his brother only insofar as the story couldn't possibly have gotten any worse. The opening was just *stultifying,* going on for pages and pages about nothing. Where were the murders? The detecting? The *orangutan,* for crying out loud?

Just as "Working Man" came to an end, Sam gulped down some more coffee and then asked, "So whadja think of Detective McBain?"

Setting the laptop aside, Dean blew out a breath. "I can't believe Dad didn't tell us about her."

"Really? 'Cause I have no trouble believing that Dad didn't tell us about her. He didn't tell us about the roadhouse, he didn't tell us about Ellen or Jo or Ellen's husband, he didn't tell us about Elkins, he didn't—"

Throwing up his hands in surrender, Dean said, "All right, all right." He shook his head and gulped down the remainder of his own coffee, which had gone fairly cold. "I been thinkin' a lot about her, actually," he said, "and I think we can trust her."

Sam's eyelids had been half closed since he came down the stairs, but they opened all the way now. "Really? Not that I don't agree, but I'm surprised to hear you say it."

Dean shrugged. "Toldja before, I know cops. Dude, you and me—but especially me—we're the collar of the century. Any cop would give his left nut to bust either one of us right now. Last night, she had us *cold*. She coulda taken us in, gotten her face on the news, got promoted—hell, she'd have her choice of assignments, she brought us in. And she didn't. No way a cop does that."

"Unless there are extenuating circumstances."

"Exactly." Dean got up and said, "I'm gonna refill the java cup."

Sam unfolded himself from the easy chair and followed. "You know, I've been thinking about Dad—that's why I slept so late, to be honest, I was tossin' and turnin' with this half the night after we got back."

Crap crap crap, Dean thought as he entered the kitchen. The absolute last thing he wanted right now was to get into a talk with Sam about Dad. He wasn't ready to go there with Sammy, not yet.

Approaching the coffeemaker, Dean saw that Sam had only left the dregs in the bottom of the glass pot.

Grabbing it, holding it up, and sloshing the sludgy remains around the bottom, he said, "Dude! Coffeemaker etiquette. You finish, you make another pot."

Sam recoiled as if Dean had slapped him. "I didn't finish it—there's some left."

Dean glared at Sam. "You gotta be kiddin' me."

"Anyhow," Sam said as Dean dumped the remains into the sink. "I was thinkin' back to when we were at Bobby's and had Meg trapped in the circle."

Unsure where Sam was going with this, Dean just grunted noncommittally as he rinsed out the pot.

"Remember when Bobby told us that Meg was a possessed human?"

Dean nodded as he filled the pot with cold water. He had only thought of Meg as a demon, presuming that she had simply taken on the form of a cute blonde.

Sam, still clutching his mug of coffee, said, "I'll never forget the look on Bobby's face when he told us that—and he said, 'Can't you *tell*?' He couldn't believe that we couldn't recognize the signs."

"What's that got to do with Dad, Sam?" Dean asked, pouring the water into the coffeemaker, though he had a guess.

"That was something Dad could've taught us, but he didn't. He didn't tell us about other hunters, he didn't tell us about the roadhouse, he didn't tell us about vampires until we actually met some, he didn't tell us about goofer dust. Sure, he taught us the basics, and he taught us how to fight and defend ourselves, but that was it. Hell, most of the lore I know, I learned on my own. And for all that we fought about it—I think Dad was glad I was at Stanford."

Dean had moved to the freezer, and those words stopped him dead in his tracks. "What?"

"You don't just *get* a free ride at Stanford, Dean— or anywhere else. You gotta fill out a ton of forms, and a parent or legal guardian has to sign most of 'em, especially the financial aid ones."

This shocked Dean. "You mean Dad actually signed all that stuff?"

"At first, yeah. He bitched and moaned about it, but he signed *everything*."

Dean shuddered as he dumped the coffee grounds into the filter, remembering the nasty arguments during that time. Dad accusing Sam of abandoning the family, Sam accusing Dad of either running his life or ruining his life, while he tried desperately (and failed miserably) to get them to calm down and talk *to* each other instead of *at* each other. To find out now that Dad had *facilitated* the process . . .

"Maybe," Dean said slowly, "Dad didn't think it was real. I mean, sure, fill out the forms, humor you, but then when you actually said you were leaving . . ."

Sam tilted his head. "I guess that's possible. But still, that's a lot of paperwork just to humor me. And honestly, he could've killed my whole college career at any point just by not filling the stuff out."

None of this rang right to Dean. "You mean to tell me that Dad filled out that crap *every* year?"

"Uh—" Sam hesitated.

Dean knew that look on his brother's face. He was hiding something. "What'd you do, Sammy?"

There was a long pause. The coffeemaker started gurgling as the boiling water poured through the filter and into the glass pot.

"I—" Sam gulped down some more coffee to stall, then said: "I got them to declare me independent."

"*Excuse* me?"

"Dad wouldn't speak to me after I left, so I couldn't very well get him to fill out the paperwork for sophomore year, and I'm not a good enough forger to fake his signature. But I would've lost the scholarship, so I provided documentation that my father was missing and couldn't be found—which, by the way, was a pretty easy sell, since Dad *was* missing from a legal perspective.

So they declared me independent. I could fill out all the forms myself."

"So you're saying you disowned Dad?"

Sam opened his mouth, closed it, then lamely said, "He disowned me first."

Anger flared within Dean, but it burned to ashes almost instantly. *After the crap Dad pulled on his freakin' deathbed, I'm not about to defend the sonofabitch.*

Besides, it was over and done with. Getting into an argument with Sam about Dad right now would just about kill him, Dean thought.

"Fine," he said tersely, "so what's all this got to do with him not telling us about McBain?"

"Remember that air-traffic guy, Jerry?"

Dean nodded. He and Dad had saved Jerry Panowski from a poltergeist, and Jerry later called in him and Sam when a spirit was crashing planes. He wasn't sure what Jerry had to do with anything, though. "What about him?"

"He said that Dad went on about how proud he was that I was at Stanford. I couldn't believe it, but now I'm starting to understand."

Having pretty much lost all track of Sam's point— if he even had one—Dean threw up his hands. "Understand *what*?"

"Even while he was training us, he was protecting us. He yelled at me for going to Stanford, but he was proud of me—and *helped* me go in the first place. For everything he taught us, there's about fifty things we've had to figure out on our own or got caught off-guard by. Hell, Dean, the whole reason he up and disappeared a year ago was because he was trying to protect us from the demon, and he only let us come with him after we dropped a brick wall on his head."

Dean found himself staring intently at Manfred's sink, listening to the gurgling of the coffeemaker.

After several quiet seconds, Sam tentatively said, "Dean?"

Finally, Dean turned around and stared up at his brother, the man he'd come to find when Dad had disappeared, the man he'd been told to protect at all costs, and kill if he couldn't protect him.

In a very soft voice, Dean said, "You know what I think? I think Dad's need to fight evil was *constantly* fighting with his need to keep you and me safe. And I think he couldn't win that fight, and I think that fight killed him."

Sam and Dean just stared at each other for a few seconds.

Manfred's voice sounded from the staircase. "You fellas awake?"

Both brothers said "In here" simultaneously. Unable to help himself, Dean broke into what turned out to be a cathartic grin. Sam returned it.

Manfred, wearing a pair of hole-filled sweatpants

and a faded tie-dyed T-shirt, shuffled into the kitchen on bare feet. "You fellas all right?"

"Yeah," Dean said, "just had our daily allotment of emo-angst. We're over it. Oh, and I put in a load of wash. That okay?"

"No problemo, fellas. My *casa* is your *casa*."

"Thanks."

"Now, normally I wouldn't be up this early on a Saturday, but I jus' 'membered somethin' you fellas might wanna know about." He walked over to the cabinet, pulled out a pottery mug that had an ugly scrunched-up face carved into the side of it and the word GRUMBLE etched over it, and poured himself some coffee. "A while back Aldo had himself a girlfriend who was a real 'rÿcher."

Sam squinted. Dean rolled his eyes. "He means a Queensrÿche fan, not the first officer of the *Enterprise*."

Before Sam could say anything, Manfred went on: "Her name was Roxy—er, somethin'. I think."

"Was she a blonde?" Dean asked.

Manfred gulped down some coffee and then gave a gap-toothed grin. "Aldo only dates blondes. Anyhow, I'm gonna head upstairs and find me some porn on the Internet. Talk atcha later, fellas."

Wincing, Dean said, "Oh, no" after Manfred left.

"What is it?" Sam asked.

"We gotta talk to Aldo about Roxy. Which means we gotta go back to the Park in Rear."

Sam grinned. "It's hell bein' a hero, ain't it, Dean?"

"Screw you."

TWELVE

Dean's second trip to the Park in Rear was a marked improvement on his first for two reasons: no sign of Janine, and Jennifer was working the bar again. Better yet, Jennifer was wearing leather pants instead of tight jeans.

"Well well well," Jennifer said when he approached the bar with Sam, "look who's back."

They had just come over after helping Manfred lug in his stuff from the four-by-four.

"Why don'tcha grab us a table, Sam?" Dean asked without looking at his brother.

Sam smiled. "Plenty of tables, Dean, I wouldn't

worry. Besides, I figured I'd help you carry the drinks."

Now Dean did look at Sam. "I think I can handle carrying two beers—not to mention dumping one of them on your head if you don't get us a table."

Without another word—but with a particularly annoying smile—Sam went off to find a table in the raised section on the side.

Jennifer raised an eyebrow. "What, Dean, you don't like hittin' on older women in fronta witnesses?"

"First of all, I don't buy that you're an older woman. Sure, you pulled that 'food in the freezer' remark last night, but I think that's a load of crap, and you're really twenty-four. I'm thinkin' you get hit on by so many losers in here that you pretend to be a single mom to drive them off and that you're really a hot babe in her twenties who's just fussy."

By this time Jennifer had started pouring his Brooklyn lager without him even specifying what he wanted. "Y'know, Dean, you gave this a *lotta* thought."

"Yeah, I did." In fact, he had only just thought of it, as he'd been too busy breaking into houses, meeting cops, sleeping, psychoanalyzing Dad, and trying to find information on Arthur Gordon Pym. Unfortunately, they couldn't find anybody by that name in any city records. His website admitted to his name change, but it looked like he hadn't done it legally, and there was no indication of what name he was born with.

Placing Dean's drink on a napkin on the bar, Jennifer said, "Sorry to disappoint you, but it's all true. Took Billy to soccer practice this afternoon and everything. They're makin' him a forward."

"Good for him." Dean had no idea what that meant, really, but he assumed it not to be a bad thing.

"So what's Sam getting?"

"Uh, Bud Light for Mr. Wuss."

"Hey," Jennifer said, "whatcha got against Bud Light?"

"Nothing," Dean said, "I just prefer *beer*."

That finally got a smile out of her. She poured another pint full of Bud Light from the tap. "So I'm surprised to see you back. I figured you'd run screaming from another night of Scottso."

"What would you say if I said I came back to see you?"

"I'd say you're lyin' through your teeth."

Dean grinned. "And you'd be right. I need to talk to Aldo about somethin'. Getting to see you again was just a nice side benefit."

"What do you need to talk to Aldo about?"

"An old girlfriend of his."

Jennifer snorted. "Which one?"

"Blond girl named Roxy."

Another snort. "Roxy Carmichael? She ain't no girl. Hell, she was older than me."

That got Dean's attention. "Was?"

"Well, I guess she still is. She broke up with Aldo a couple years back, and I ain't seen her since. Too bad, they were a good couple—neither of 'em drank or smoked or nothin'. No, wait, I remember she and I used to go outside to smoke right after they made it illegal to smoke in bars."

Knowing that those laws varied from state to state, Dean asked, "When was this?"

Jennifer shrugged. "Couple years ago. Right before they broke up. Anyhow, she always drank ginger ale."

Before Dean could say anything else, the other bartender—not Harry, but another guy half his age and twice his height—said, "Hey, Jenny, move your ass, willya, I'm dyin' over here."

"Sorry," Dean said. "How much?"

"Catch me later." Again Jennifer smiled, but it wasn't the snarky one she usually used. This one was nicer.

A warm, pleasant feeling in his chest, Dean walked over to the table with the two beers.

That feeling got cold and clammy by the time Scottso reached the second verse of their opener, "Smoke on the Water." Dean swore right then and there he was changing his ringtone as soon as he figured out a way to ask Sam how to do it so Sam wouldn't tease him about it.

That may take a while, he thought forlornly.

By the time the set was over, he had gone back to the bar three times, the third time again talking with Jennifer until the other bartender screamed for help. He definitely had a good feeling about this.

Now, however, there was business to take care of. He made a beeline for Aldo, who was making a beeline of his own for the restroom. This worked out nicely, as Dean's own bladder was pretty loaded with Brooklyn lager at that point.

The men's room only had two urinals, and with the set just ended, there was actually a line. He got in behind Aldo and said, "Damn, I thought it was only women's rooms had lines."

"Haw haw haw!" Aldo said. "That's a good one there, Sam."

"I'm Dean."

"S'what I said, Dean. Good t'see you guys back."

"Thanks. You really kicked some ass tonight. Loved the way you nailed 'Sunshine of Your Love.'"

"They didn't call Eric Clapton God for nothin', my friend," Aldo said.

"Hey, listen, Aldo, Manfred was telling me you used to date someone named Roxy."

Aldo frowned. "Uh, yeah."

"Said she was a major 'rÿcher. I used to know a blond chick named Roxy who was a major 'rÿcher, and I was wonderin' if she was the same one."

"Coulda been, I guess," Aldo said with a shrug. "Name was Roxanne Carmichael." The two people at the urinals both flushed and left, and Dean and Aldo took their places.

Dean unzippered his jeans, and moments later it was as if a great weight had been lifted off his—well, not shoulders, exactly, but damn if he didn't feel ten pounds lighter after just peeing for two seconds.

"You know what they say about beer—the better it is, the sooner you have to give it back."

"I guess," Aldo said. "I just got my three-year cake from AA. Fact, that's where Roxy 'n' I met."

"Hey, I'm sorry," Dean said quickly.

"Nah, s'no biggie, Sam."

"I'm Dean."

"Right, s'what I said, Dean. Wouldn't last two seconds playin' tunes if I had a problem with booze and dope, y'know what I'm sayin'? Anyhow, 'bout Roxy—she was just some chick I dated. She up and disappeared one day, no forwardin' address, an' it was right after we had this big-ass fight, so I didn't really give a damn, y'know what I'm sayin'?"

Dean managed not to smile. "This fight wasn't at Manfred's house, was it?"

"No." Aldo zipped up. "Look, why you askin'?"

Realizing he had pushed it too far, Dean backed off. "No biggie, I just thought it mighta been the same girl." He finished off and zipped up himself, elbowing the handle to flush it. "In fact, she was big-time into the whole temperance thing, y'know?"

Aldo smiled, as if remembering something. "Yeah . . ." He shook it off. "Anyhow, I ain't seen her in, like, two years."

"Yeah, okay."

With that, Aldo walked over to the sink to wash his hands. Dean made for the exit, thinking, *Yahtzee.*

Someone else—the bass player, Dean realized, whose name he suddenly couldn't remember—said, "What, you don't wash your hands?"

"My dad was a Marine," Dean said. The bass player's blank expression indicated that he didn't get the connection—though with this guy, it was hard to tell, as that seemed to be his default look. So Dean explained: "Dad had this story. A Marine and a Navy guy walk into a bathroom together. They both take a piss, and then the sailor goes to the sink. The Marine heads for the door, and the sailor says, 'Hey—in the Navy they teach us to wash up after we take a leak.' And the Marine turns around and says, 'Yeah? Well, in the Marines they teach us not to piss on our hands.'"

The bass player actually cracked a half smile at

that. "That's funny." And then he walked toward the stage.

Dean headed back to the table, where Sam was chatting with Manfred and the drummer, whose name Dean also couldn't remember. Sam still had the remains of a light beer—he hadn't even tried ordering a gin and tonic again in his presence—while Manfred and the drummer had thick-bottomed glasses with clear liquids that Dean assumed to be ordinary vodka or good tequila.

The drummer was shaking his head and whistling. "Man, she was a bitch—but a *hot* bitch, I'm tellin' you *that* right now."

"What're we talkin' about?" Dean asked as he took a seat on the stool next to Sam, which was the only free one at the table.

Manfred said, "We was just wonderin' 'bout this old lady'a Aldo's, Roxy, the one I mentioned to you."

"Yeah," Sam said. "Tommy was just talking about her."

Tommy, the drummer, threw back some of his drink. "Wish I knew what happened to 'er, man. 'Cause if she wasn't Aldo's old lady, I woulda done 'er in a heartbeat, I'm tellin' you *that* right now."

Even more curious as to the answer to the question, Dean asked, "So what happened to her?"

"Nobody knows," Manfred said. "Aldo told us they broke up, and we never saw 'er again."

Tommy started pounding the table and laughing. "God, Manfred, 'member how she used t'get when we went t'your place?"

"How'd she get?" Sam asked.

Raising the pitch of his voice to sound girlish, Tommy said, "'Oh, wow, Manny, I wish I could marry somebody with a house like this.' Surprised you didn't propose, 'Manny.'"

Manfred shuddered. "I couldn't marry nobody that called me 'Manny.'"

They chatted awhile longer, and then Manfred and Tommy went back to the stage to set up for the second set.

Once they were gone, Dean filled Sam in on what he'd gotten from Aldo.

Sam had his fist on his chin. "So you're thinking maybe Aldo killed Roxy?"

"What, and you're not? C'mon, Sammy, it's the same old story. And things only become same old stories 'cause they happen all the time. They have a fight, he kills her, and he buries her somewhere."

Sam nodded. "And she comes back to haunt—Manfred? See, that's the part I don't get."

Dean shrugged. "Maybe Manfred's the one who killed her."

Shaking his head, Sam said, "Manfred didn't even remember her until this morning."

"He said it himself: He doesn't remember *last week*." He got up. "I'm gonna get another beer. Let's see if Roxy comes back tonight. Maybe if we call her by name, she might respond."

It was a long shot, but some spirits were communicative, at least to some extent. Unfortunately, her only words to date—"Love me!"—weren't very helpful, though they supported his working theory of death-by-spurned-lover, which kept Aldo as prime suspect number one.

He went over to the bar, muscling his way between two older guys who looked like they went to grammar school with Manfred, and signaled Jennifer.

She mouthed the words *one sec* at him as she prepared several drinks at once. Conveniently, Aldo had just started the solo to "Born to Be Wild," so Dean occupied himself by enjoying the music by the person he considered most likely to be a murderer.

My life is seriously screwed up, he thought with amusement.

Jennifer gave the drinks to the old guys, who cleared out for their own table, each holding two drinks.

"Another Brooklyn?" Jennifer asked.

"Uh, yeah." Something seemed off in Jennifer's tone.

She poured the drink in silence, then said as she put it on the napkin, "Dean, listen—I really appreciate what you been doin', but I gotta ask you somethin', okay?"

Shrugging, Dean said, "Shoot."

"Where you goin' with this?"

Dean frowned. "Whaddaya mean?"

"I mean, where you *goin'* with this? You said you're from outta town. I assume you're goin' *back* outta town soon, right?"

"Yeah, I guess, I just—"

"So, basically, the only place this can go is a one-nighter? Or maybe a two-nighter if you're in town long enough."

Dean found he had nothing to say to such brazen honesty. For starters, honesty wasn't usually a big component of his flirtation methods (or a lot of the rest of his life), so its use was unfamiliar to him.

"Look, Dean, you're sweet, you're bright, you're *incredibly* good-looking—"

At that, Dean couldn't help but beam.

"—and you're totally aware of it, but not in a vain way."

"Uh, thanks—I think."

"Oh, it's a compliment, believe me. But—" Jennifer let out a long breath. "Ten years ago I'da been right there with you, but now? I'm too old for one-nighters, Dean. I've been there and I've done that, and if I'm gonna be with a man, I wanna *be* with a man, y'know what I'm sayin'?" Then she broke into a huge smile. "Dean, you look like I ran over your cat."

Blinking furiously, Dean tried to wipe that look off his face, though he had no idea how it had gotten there. "Look, Jennifer, I'm—I'm sorry, I didn't—"

"Christ, Dean, do *not* apologize! Hell, you've made my *week*. Trust me, I'm gonna dine out on this with my girlfriends for a *year*. You know how long it's been since someone even *half* as hot as you hit on my fat ass?"

"Jennifer," Dean said, "of all the words I would use to describe your ass, 'fat' is the absolute *last* one."

"Thank you."

Then, deciding he had nothing to lose, he added, "And one other thing—you're right, with me it'd only be one night, maybe two." He grinned. "But it'd be a helluva night."

He ran back to the table before she could reply.

Of course, she was right—there was no chance of anything beyond a good romp in the hay or two. He had learned the hard way with Cassie that his life wasn't built for a relationship. And that was why he'd mostly focused his sexual energy on young women who were only interested in hooking up for one night. He was sure that half of them didn't believe the crap he spun to start talking to them, but just liked playing the game.

As soon as he sat down, Sam got all worried looking at him. "Dude, what happened? You look like someone ran over your cat."

Dean just drank his beer.

THIRTEEN

The Afiri house
The Bronx, New York
Sunday 19 November 2006

It needs to stop. Why won't he love me?

It had all started with the strange-looking man who looked a lot like Uncle Cal. Said he was a Reaper and his job was to prepare her for the after-life.

But that was wrong. If she was going to the *after*-life, it meant she was done with her *before*-life, and that meant she was dead, and that was something she just couldn't just *accept,* that was crazy, after everything she went through, she just couldn't just be *dead*!

She refused. No way, no how, she was *not* going with him, even if he *did* look like Uncle Cal, who was always so sweet to her, and the only one who'd still talk to her when she went into rehab, everyone else just *abandoned* her, the bastards, but Cal was always there for her and she trusted him completely.

She wouldn't go with him. That was where she drew the line. After *that* happened, she couldn't let go. She wouldn't let go. Couldn't couldn't wouldn't wouldn't.

The Reaper who looked like Uncle Cal tried to convince her that she was being foolish, that there was nothing left for her, that she couldn't do anything to change what happened, but she refused to believe that, refused to accept it, refused to even listen to it. She wasn't dead, she wasn't dead, she wasn't dead, she wasn't dead.

It needs to stop. Why won't he love me?

Throughout life, she hadn't asked for much. When things had gone wrong, she had owned up to them and fixed them. She was cured, as much as anybody could really be *cured*. She hadn't drunk anything since she got out of rehab, so that should've been that and that was all there was to it, period, full stop, end of sentence.

So there was just no way, no way, no *way*, *no* way, *no way*, she should die like *that*.

Something had to be done.

At first she just waited, figuring that everything would play out.

But no.

Manfred went out every morning to work. He went to the Park in Rear every Friday, Saturday, and Sunday to play with the damn band, and then he just came home.

Every time he came home, she hoped.

Every time he came home, those hopes were dashed.

After a while she couldn't take it anymore. How could she? How could she expect to just sit there and *take* it, just sitting there, just being there, just *existing,* not alive, not really dead, either, just floating around while *life went on without her and nobody cared!*

Eventually, she snapped.

Now, when the Scottso gigs were done, she was there. Over and over, every time he came back from the goddamn Park in Rear, she hoped, she prayed, she begged, she pleaded, but nothing, nothing, *nothing!*

It was terrible. It was awful. It was the worst thing in the world, worse even than dying, and she didn't think *anything* could possibly be worse than dying, but somehow this was.

She wondered if maybe she should have listened to the Reaper the way she'd always listened to Uncle Cal, who looked just like the Reaper—or was it the other way around? She didn't know anymore, didn't care anymore, she just wanted it to stop stop stop stop stop stop!

And then it got worse.

Yesterday, someone else came in who wasn't anyone from Scottso. It was two new people, and they *shot* her!

It was the worst feeling ever in the whole world, worse than dying, worse than rehab, worse than knowing nothing changed, worse than when she discovered her shellfish allergy, worse than *anything ever*.

And she would make them pay. Oh yes, she was *not* going to take this any longer, nosireebob, she would have what she wanted and that'd show *all* of them the truth!

As soon as she pulled herself together.

It had been *really* weird, actually. She saw the two guys, and they shot her, and then—

Nothing.

Emptiness. No longer tethered to Manfred's house, no longer tethered to anything, no longer able to see or hear or touch or—

Well, actually, she couldn't do most of that stuff anyhow, but she had *something*. She had consciousness. Didn't she? How else did the Reaper that looked like Uncle Cal *talk* to her if she wasn't able to be talked *to*?

But after those two guys shot her, pfft. Gone.

She had to get herself back together. They were coming. She could *feel* it. She couldn't feel much of anything, but she could feel that. They were coming. They were coming. She had to show them what was happening before they shot her again.

So she tried to focus.

That was a challenge—focusing was hard, even back when she was alive, and the more time passed after she died, the harder that got. She had no idea what it was that those two guys shot her with, but whatever it was was deadly stuff. Probably some kind of poison or something.

No, that didn't make sense. Poison? She was already dead. But it wasn't regular bullets. Or buckshot, or whatever it was that shotguns shot. What the hell did she know about that, she was a girl from Morris Park, all she knew about shotguns was that guys in cowboy hats carried them in old movies.

Uncle Cal always showed her those movies when he babysat her when she was a kid. Mom and Dad were off getting stoned somewhere every Saturday night, so Uncle Cal would take care of her, showing her his favorite old movies. *My Darling Clementine. Calamity Jane. Rio Bravo. The Good, the Bad, and the Ugly. The Magnificent Seven. A Fistful of Dollars. Unforgiven. Tombstone.* All the men wore funny hats and all the women wore poofy dresses and they were just so cool, she loved it so very very much.

They were coming.

It needs to stop. Why won't he love me?

She gathered up everything she had, however

she could, forcing herself to come together again as the two strangers who shot her walked through the door.

There they were—she saw them. She couldn't talk to them, though. Whatever they shot her with when they shot her last night was keeping her from talking, but she could *see,* dammit, and she saw that they were coming in, the tall one with the shaggy hair and the short one with the short hair. They both wore little black bracelets and dressed the same sloppy way kids in their twenties dressed these days. Dammit, when she was in her twenties, she knew how to dress *cool,* not like these post-Grunge losers.

She'd show them. She'd show them real good.

Concentrating harder than she'd ever concentrated in her life or in her death, she focused on that stupid picture of Manfred and his kids upstairs where Manfred had that stupid smile on his face and the kids were all squirmy like they wanted to be anywhere but with Manfred. Why did Manfred even *have* that picture anyhow? It was so pathetic. He didn't raise them and they didn't even care about him, so why have the stupid picture?

The picture flew off the wall and headed straight for the tall one. Unfortunately, he heard it coming—and he had, like, *killer* reflexes—so he batted it out of the way with his forearm, which took *all* the fun out of it.

"I think she's pissed at you, dude," the shorter one said.

The tall one she almost hit said, "Pissed, period, I think."

She tried again. She had to *hurt* these guys after what they did to her.

"Roxy, you there?" the tall one said suddenly. "Look, we don't wanna hurt you."

How'd they know my name?

And yeah, *right,* they didn't want to hurt her. How could anybody say that with a straight face twenty-four hours after they *shot you?*

Then the short one said, "But we will if you throw more picture frames at our heads. Look, this house belongs to a friend of ours, and—"

She hadn't been paying any attention to him, busy as she was trying to focus on the Fillmore East poster in its metal frame. Eventually she got it to fly free of the wall and hit the short one in the back of the head.

The tall one helped him stand back up, and the short one put his hand to the back of his head and winced. "Okay—*ow.*"

"You all right, man?"

"No, I'm not freakin' all right, some spirit bitch just hit me in the back of the head with a priceless concert poster!"

She couldn't help herself. She laughed at that. She laughed long, she laughed hard, and she laughed

loud. It was even funnier than that time when her
brother actually snorted glue, thinking that "sniff-
ing glue" meant you took actual glue up your nose
like you did cocaine.

The walls of Manfred's house shook, she laughed
so hard.

Both of the strangers lifted their shotguns, and
suddenly she stopped laughing. She couldn't face
that again, not yet.

Instead, she went away, like she always did once
Manfred left. She'd bide her time, be patient, like
they kept telling her to be in rehab, and then she'd
show them what she was made of the next time
they came back from that stupid bar. She had no
idea when that would be—days of the week no
longer meant anything to her, she just *knew* when
all of Scottso were together at the Park in Rear—
so she'd wait until it was time again.

It needs to stop. Why won't he love me?

Dean stared down at the EMF reader and shook
his head. "Nothing. There was that fit of the gig-
gles, and then nada."

Sam lowered his shotgun. "Weird."

"Yeah. And those two shots she took at us were
pretty weak."

Nodding, Sam said, "Yeah, I'm thinkin' she
hasn't come all the way back from the rock-salt
dispersal." He knew that it was different for every

spirit. Some only stayed dissolute for a few minutes. Others were permanently torn apart by the rock salt, though that was pretty rare.

"Well, it looks like she's gone," Dean said. "We can tell Manfred it's safe."

"Yeah." Sam sighed. "Tomorrow, I'm gonna do a little digging online, then Monday check the libraries, see if I can find out anything about this house. I mean, we're assuming it's Roxy because of that King's Reign T-shirt—"

Dean winced and snarled at the same time. "It's Queensrÿche."

"Whatever." Sam managed not to break into a grin, since he'd messed up the band's name completely on purpose just to annoy Dean. "But there may be another spirit here that we just don't know about."

Giving Sam a dubious look, Dean said, "That happens to look just like one of Scottso's ex-girlfriends, down to the same love for Queensrÿche?"

Sam had to concede that point. "Yeah, it's a stretch, but it's not like the band's been all that forthcoming. And I don't know about you, but *I* can't tell if she reacted to us calling her by name."

"Yeah, me either. Okay, we'll try that. What about the Poe thing?"

Sam shrugged. "Keep looking for Arthur Gordon Pym. I'll make some calls tomorrow—or Monday, I guess, since tomorrow's Sunday—and see if I can track down who owns the server space that website's on." Then something occurred to him. "Hey, didn't McBain say she was with missing persons?"

Dean tensed up. "Yeah, so?"

"Maybe we can run Roxy's name by her."

"We don't need to bring her into this, Sammy."

Sam sighed. "C'mon, Dean, I think we can trust her. Like you said, she didn't arrest us, and she knows Ballard."

"What the hell does *that* have to do with—"

"If it weren't for Ballard, we'd both be in jail right now, and you know it. She helped me dig up the body we needed to find, and she shot her partner and let us go. We trusted her, I think we can trust McBain. Besides, she *is* Missing Persons, and that means we can *check* for missing persons without having to make something up." Dean was still antsy, so Sam came up with a compromise. "Look, we're gonna need her help on Monday anyhow, so let's ask her then."

Frowning, Dean asked, "Why're we gonna need her help on Monday?"

"There's two more sites left to complete Samuels's sigil, but we don't know which one of the two it'll be. Dad's notes didn't specify what order the points had to be drawn in. So unless you want me on one and you on the other—"

Dean held up a hand. "Fine, whatever, we'll get

her to cover one, and then we can ask her about Roxy. Happy?"

Chuckling, Sam said, "Thrilled beyond all possible imagining."

"Hey, fellas, can I come in yet? Freezin' m'*ass* off out here!"

Sam turned toward the front door, through which Manfred had yelled. It was much colder tonight than it had been the previous night, and there was no reason to keep Manfred out of his own place. "It's clear!" Sam yelled.

FOURTEEN

Dean hated waiting.

There were a lot of reasons why he had gone to Stanford a little over a year ago to fetch Sam, but at times like this he liked to think the main reason was because Sammy was actually good at the piddly crap.

And the last two days had been chock full of piddly crap, ending now with the pair of them sitting in the Impala on Webster Avenue in the Bronx, waiting for something to happen.

Sunday had been pretty dull. Sam left messages on several people's voice mails, one of which was

finally returned this morning, saying that the Poe
website was paid for by a corporation called Pendulum Pit Incorporated ("Oooh, subtle," Dean had
muttered at the time). It took no time at all for
Sam to use his research-fu to find out that Pendulum Pit Inc. was a self-owned corporation owned
and operated by one Arthur Mackey.

Unfortunately, he didn't dig that up until after
sundown, and they needed to try to stop their Poe
nut—who Dean was still convinced *was* Pym or
Mackey or whoever he was—from killing someone
else.

Dean and Sam had volunteered to take Webster
Avenue and 199th, which was a major thoroughfare containing parking lots, auto parts stores, and
mechanics, with three or four floors' worth of
apartments over many of the stores.

McBain took Fordham Road and MLK
Boulevard—which was a huge intersection that had
the Church of St. Nicholas of Tolentine and Devoe
Park, as well as several more apartment buildings.
Webster was pretty quiet at night, whereas the other
location was fairly well traveled. They all agreed
that it was better for the two fugitives to take the
quieter spot.

The problem was, there were several spots where
the next killing could take place, most of which were
in apartments. Dean and Sam knew they couldn't

just wander around looking too much, as this was a predominantly Latin American neighborhood and they stood out.

At least the car wasn't as big a deal as it might have been. One of the mechanics had a couple of vintage vehicles, and a 'fifty-four Buick was in the parking lot down the street from where Dean had parked. Generally, the Impala was a bit conspicuous, and Sam once made the mistake of bringing up the possibility of abandoning the vehicle for something less distinct, since they were now on the run.

Dean made it clear that Sam was never to even consider the possibility of bringing *that* subject up again. He'd sooner cut off his left nut than give up the Impala.

Their third (and, God willing, final) excursion to the Park in Rear last night hadn't been much of an improvement. They had pretty much run out of excuses to bring up Roxy, and besides which, they seemed to have gotten as much intel as they were likely to get on that score. Roxy was just one of a long line of girlfriends these guys had bagged and tossed to the curb over the years, and Dean was convinced that half the stories they told about Roxy were actually about some other chick.

To make matters worse, Jennifer wasn't working Sunday night, and all the other women in the Park in Rear were part of a couple or simply not his type. He'd been hoping that Jennifer would at least call—he'd given her his cell number before they left Saturday night—but so far, zip.

Dean hadn't bothered with the "hot" handle on his shower that morning.

Roxy made the same cameo she'd made Saturday night—some cackling, some shaking, rattling, and rolling, and then disappearing. Both Sam and Dean agreed that she probably still hadn't gotten over the dispersal yet, but that come Friday, she'd probably be back to full-tilt-boogie haunting mode.

Sam had also found some lore about New York City ghosts, most of whom appeared to be famous people: Theodore Roosevelt, an NYPD commissioner before he was President, haunting the old police headquarters; Mark Twain haunting the place where he used to live at on West Tenth Street; Alexander Hamilton all up and down Jane Street, on the block where he died following his fatal duel with Vice President Aaron Burr; Burr's own ghost in the Barrow Street restaurant that now stood where a carriage house he'd lived in was; and, of course, John Lennon in the Dakota, the apartment building where he was assassinated. Sam assumed, and Dean agreed, that a lot of this was New York hype. There wasn't anything about Riverdale in general or this house in particular, or about women in band T-shirts screaming for people to love them.

For lack of anything better to do while Sammy was researching, Dean had read up a bit more on Percival Samuels. He had to admit, for a con artist, the sonofabitch was *good*. He put on a great show for his clients—which was good, 'cause they paid through the nose for it. That show didn't hold up if you paid attention, though. Even Dean knew that Hecate, Osiris, and Morrighan were gods from three different pantheons (Greek, Egyptian, and Celtic), and Loki was from a fourth (Norse) and *wasn't* the god of love and redemption. But it probably sounded cool to the rubes who didn't know any better, the same way that the psychics you saw on late night television sounded cool to the folks who missed all the reading tricks and leading questions.

For the nine hundredth time he cast a longing gaze at the radio—he'd found a local classic rock station, and it didn't even suck that badly—but he knew that blaring music would be a mistake. Headphones wouldn't improve things, as he needed to be able to hear if something bad happened—like, say, Sam screaming for help, or demon noises, or some other damn thing.

So he sat in silence, and waited.

Dean really hated waiting.

Finally, Sam came out of one of the apartment buildings, looked around to see if anybody was on the street, saw two people walking north on Webster, and then wandered slowly toward them, head down.

The two people were talking to each other, and each had one ear bud from the same iPod in their ears. They didn't even notice Sam, but he still waited until they turned up Bedford Park Boulevard before stopping, turning, and jogging across the street to the Impala.

"Nothin'," he said as he slumped into the passenger seat, slamming the large door shut. "I've checked both apartment buildings. There's that one other place over the auto parts store."

"What about the store?" Dean asked.

"Which one?"

Dean shrugged. "Any of 'em."

"I don't see it. Cars didn't exist in Poe's time. If it's gonna be something that has an emotional connection to Poe's life and work, it'd have to be in one of the apartments."

"A sidewalk near a college campus isn't in any of Poe's stories either, is it?"

Sam frowned.

Dean shifted in his seat so he was facing his brother. "The thing with the orangutan happened on a street—it was in an apartment in the book, though, right?"

"Yeah."

"So obviously our nut job is willing to fudge it to get the location right. Hell, for all we know, that garage over there has a big-ass pendulum in it."

Sam rubbed his chin the way he did sometimes when he wanted to make Dean believe that he was thinking. Dean never bought that, because he knew Sam was thinking all the time. No, this was Sam stalling.

"All right, then—why don't you check out the garages, and I'll take the last apartment building?"

Dean just blinked and stared for a second.

"What's wrong?"

"Nothing, I'm just shocked that you came up with a plan that doesn't suck."

"Hardy har har."

Grinning, Dean climbed out of the car, as did Sam.

After making sure all the doors were locked, Dean jogged over to the garage with the big yellow sign saying MANNY'S CAR REPAIR on the corner of 199th, even as Sam went around the corner—the entrance to the apartments over Manny's was on the numbered street, perpendicular to Webster. Dean assumed that Sam would wait for someone to walk out and make like he was a resident coming in at the same time—or just ring a doorbell and do the "I'm your neighbor, I forgot my keys" routine. The speakers on these buildings were so crappy that Sam could probably pull it off without too much trouble. Besides, he had that whole earnest thing going for him. People trusted Sam, which was another reason he liked having him along for hunts.

During the day, Manny's probably had the door wide open so cars could pull in. Now, though, the big metal garage door—which was about three car lengths wide—was shut, with a chain securing a thick metal bolt on either side of the door. Looking up, Dean saw that the door raised and fell automatically, which meant that he would need a remote to open it, even if he could pick the lock securing the chain to the dead bolts. Squinting in the dim light provided by the streetlight several feet away—there was a closer one, but it wasn't working—Dean saw that the chains were secured with one of the new special locks that were supposed to be harder to break. In the real world, that meant that with good light it would take him fifteen minutes to pick them instead of the usual two. He probably could pull it off, but he'd already had the cops called on him once, and this garage door was considerably more exposed than the side door to that house had been, and he'd have to pick *two* locks, which would take forever. Not worth the risk.

Then he noticed the small door inset into the garage door, which only had a regular key lock for a standard dead bolt. He knew he could open that in half a second.

As always, Dean marveled at how stupid people could be sometimes. They'd spend thousands of dollars on an alarm system, but then never change the code from the default provided by the company—or worse, would change the code to something obvious like their birthday or the house's address or something. Or they'd have four locks on the door, but leave the front window wide open because it was too hot. People were better at the illusion of security than they were at actually being secure.

And the owners of this garage were just as bad. Peering through the very small, very filthy windows of the garage door, Dean could just make out several cars, and the big locks that kept them safe from being stolen. But by leaving a door like this with just a crap lock on it, an enterprising thief could easily break in and make off with the smaller pieces of equipment or car parts that were there for the asking.

Reaching into his jeans pocket, he took out his lock pick and within seconds had the small door open.

At which point a loud beeping noise started, loud enough to make Dean's eardrums vibrate.

Looking around quickly, he located the alarm code pad, ran to it, saw which model it was and knew that it only required a three-digit code, and entered the garage's cross street: 199.

The beeping stopped as soon as he hit the ENTER button. *Let's hear it for stupid people!*

With the alarm silenced, he jogged back to the door and shut it. *No sense in advertising that there's a break-in.* The only cop he wanted to encounter this trip was McBain.

Dean considered leaving some kind of memento of his presence, just as an object lesson to Manny and his employees that their security sucked. Back when he was a kid, about eleven years old, he used to go looking for cars that had "No Radio in Car" signs on them. He'd take a removable radio, of a type that was very popular at the time, and throw it as hard as he could at the car window with a note wrapped around it that read, NOW YOU HAVE ONE. Really, did anyone think that sign would actually *stop* people from breaking into their cars?

"Ow, fiddlesticks!" someone screamed from the back room, just as something metal crashed to the floor.

Dean's eyes went wide. *Fiddlesticks?*

Slowly, removing the pistol tucked into the back of his jeans, he moved toward the back room, past two Geo Metros and a Prius. For a brief instant he gazed longingly at the Prius—not so much for its elegance, as it was a truly butt-ugly vehicle, but for the hybrid car's gas mileage. The Impala had many virtues, but it also guzzled gas like a sonofabitch, and at anywhere from two to three bucks a gallon, it was becoming increasingly difficult to keep her fed.

Once he got past the Prius, he saw that there was a flashlight waving around a back room. That room had an almost closed door with the word OFFICE stenciled in faded gold letters on a grease-streaked window.

Dean slowly walked up to the door, and saw a short guy with a patch of baldness on his crown surrounded by thin brown hair. The guy was kneeling down with his back to him, so that was all he could see of him, but he could also see that the guy was spreading some kind of dust on the office's red Oriental rug. He was wearing a brown polyester suit that wouldn't have been out of place on a used car salesman or a weekend golfer.

The man was chanting something under his breath. Dean didn't recall anything this guy was doing as part of Samuels's ritual, but that didn't mean it wasn't.

Kicking the door open, he thumbed off the pistol's safety and said, "Don't move."

To his credit, Ugly Suit Guy immediately stopped chanting and held up his hands, which were wearing grime-covered latex gloves. "Please, it's very important that you listen to me. I understand that I have broken into your place of business, but if you do not let me complete this ritual I have started, someone will die. There is a madman out there killing people in an attempt to resurrect the dead, and I *must* stop him before he kills again!"

Dean frowned. That wasn't the reaction he was expecting.

Then the guy turned around, and Dean recognized the big nose, small eyes, thin lips, and cleft chin from the Poe enthusiast's website.

"You're Arthur Gordon Pym."

The beady eyes went as wide as they could. "I'm afraid you have me at a disadvantage, sir—unless you are the Manny indicated on the sign for this—"

"Just shut up a sec, okay, Artie? And yeah, I do have you at a disadvantage, 'cause I got the gun. I also know that your real name is Arthur Mackey, that you live here in the Bronx, that you own Pendulum Pit Inc., and that you're the one trying to resurrect Poe, so cut the crap, okay?"

Very slowly getting to his feet, and, Dean noticed, being careful not to move suddenly, Mackey said, "I can assure you, sir, that I have no intention of resurrecting anyone. Edgar Allan Poe is quite dead, and I'm content to leave him that way. I've seen resurrected corpses before, and they're—" Mackey shuddered. "—rather disturbing."

Remembering the zombie chick who broke Sam's arm, Dean sympathized, but he wasn't ready to believe this goober just yet. "How do you know about the resurrection spell?"

"I learned of it at the Walsh Library at nearby Fordham University, actually. I am quite curious as to how *you* know of it—and who you are."

"Yeah, well, keep wonderin', 'cause I still got the gun and—"

The sounds of "Smoke on the Water" emitted from Dean's pocket. Then it stopped, then it started again.

Keeping the pistol cocked in one hand, he reached into his pocket with the other and flipped open the phone: two missed calls from Sam, which meant either he got crappy cell reception around here or Sam was signaling to him that he was in trouble and needed his help but couldn't actually talk on the phone.

After mulling for half a second, Dean waved his pistol. "Get up, Artie, you're comin' with me."

"Please, sir, I need to locate the killer before—"

"If these calls mean what I think they mean, my brother's already found the killer."

Mackey's thin lips pursed to the point where they pretty much disappeared. "Your brother?"

Grabbing the lapels of Mackey's ugly jacket, Dean yanked him out of the office. "Just move your ass, Artie."

Dragging Mackey across the garage, Dean went back to the front door.

"Sir, I must protest this treatment. If your brother—whoever he is, and whoever *you* are—

have found the killer, I'll be happy to come with you and assist in whatever meager way I can, but—"

Dean stopped, turned, and put the muzzle of the gun under Mackey's chin. "Do you *ever* shut up?"

Mackey swallowed, his Adam's apple sliding across the muzzle.

Letting out a snarl, Dean lowered the pistol, thumbed the safety back on, and stuck the gun back in his pants before going back onto the street. That was another reason to avoid getting the attention of any member of the NYPD not named McBain—the handgun laws in this state were among the nastier in the country. Of course, with the murder charge, it was the least of his worries, but it was also the kind of thing that drew attention.

They walked quickly down to the corner and then to the front door that Sam was supposed to have gone through.

Dean's concerns about how to get in that door were taken care of pretty quickly when he saw that Sam was standing in the doorway, propping the door open with his foot. He also wasn't moving, but Dean could hear someone talking.

Staring down at Mackey, he put his finger to his lips. Mackey nodded and stayed a step behind Dean as they both quietly moved up the small staircase to the front door. Dean took out his pistol. *Screw the handgun laws, if someone's messing with my brother.*

Sam was talking now, holding his hands up in a nonthreatening position. His Treo was palmed in his left hand, which was probably how he'd signaled Dean. "Look, I understand what you're going through, but—"

"And I'm tellin' you *right* now that it ain't *right* what the *right* is doin' to this country, it ain't *right,* and the *right's* gotta know what's *right,* 'cause it ain't *right,* you feel me? Do you? *Do* you?"

"Of course I do, now just please, sir, put the gun down."

Crap. From the sounds of it, some looney-tunes with a gun was off his meds and taking it out on Sam. They didn't have time for this crap.

Dean walked up behind his brother and next to him. He could see, now, that there was a bald African-American man wearing an undershirt and boxer shorts and waving a revolver around fast enough that Dean couldn't tell if it was cocked or not. He didn't particularly want to find out the hard way that it was. The man was pacing back and forth across the narrow hallway, right next to a metal door that was ajar.

"Sam?" Dean said, his own pistol pointed right at the guy's smooth head as he went back and forth.

"Who that? You 'nother one? 'Nother one from'a gummint? I ain't listenin' to no more from you white folks with your pills an' your gummint an' your doctors and *none*'a that! Flushed them pills down the *toilet*, let the alligators at 'em, that's what *I* did. Don't be tellin' *me* I need no pills for nothin'!"

"Sir," Sam said in his most reasonable voice, "I can assure you that we're not from the government. We're trying to stop a killer, and—"

"So, what, you cops? Don't like me no cops, cops be takin' me to the hospital, an' they be givin' me the pills! I don't *take* that, you feel me?"

"No, sir, we're private investigators. We've been hired to find a killer because the cops couldn't handle it."

"Damn right, the cops can't handle it. No cops in no town don't know nothin' 'bout nothin'."

"But, sir," Sam said, "we can't catch the killer unless you let me and my partner in."

Dean winced. Sam hadn't seen Mackey yet, and he hoped that this guy didn't bust a gasket when he found out Sam had *two* partners.

"Maybe you can help," Sam said. "If you help us, you'll be a hero."

That, finally, got the guy to stop pacing, which, if nothing else, gave Dean a clearer shot. "A hero? Like Superman?"

"Exactly, sir, like Superman. You'll stop a horrible killer and you'll be in the newspapers and on television."

"That'd be good. I like television. 'Cept the news, don't like that, but Oprah's cool. She knows what's *happenin'*, she knows what's *right*, not like the *right* don't know what's *right*."

"Sir, can you tell me if any of the apartments in this building are empty?"

Dean glanced at his brother, wondering if Sam was really expecting a straight answer from this garbanzo.

"They say they empty, but they lie, I know what goes on up there. Up in 2B, they say they ain't nobody there, but I know they plannin', they plottin', they doin' all *sortsa* stuff up there, I'm tellin' you *right* now, it ain't *right* what the *right's* doin', and they be doin' it in 2B, that's for *damn* sure, I'm *right* about that *right* now!"

"Okay, thank you, sir." Sam lowered his arms. "If it's okay, we're gonna go check out Apartment 2B, okay?"

"It ain't *right* what the *right* be doin' *right* up there, you feel me?"

"I know, sir," Sam said, "I know, that's why we're gonna stop it."

"You be tellin' those news people, it was Omar that done help you. Ain't no last name, though, 'cause that be my slave name that the *right* gave me, and they got no *right* to be doin' that to my *rights*, you feel me?"

"Absolutely, Omar. We'll tell the news people

you helped us catch the killer that the cops couldn't."

Omar nodded so fast Dean thought his head would fall off. "Damn right. Damn cops. Damn straight, those damn cops couldn't find no damn nothin'."

"Thank you, Omar. We really appreciate it."

"No sweat, my brother. You get that killer and show the *right* that they don't got the *right* to be givin' nobody no pills that they don't be needin'."

Sam gave Omar a quick nod. "We will."

"Good."

With that, Omar went through the metal door and slammed it shut.

Dean let out a breath he hadn't even realized he was holding. "Well, *that* was fun."

"We must hurry," Mackey said.

Sam turned around and looked down the stoop at Mackey, who was putting on a fresh pair of latex gloves. "You're Arthur Gordon Pym."

"I seem to be quite the celebrity," he said dryly. "Yes, I'm Pym, and we can't dally when there's a killer to be caught."

Looking at Dean, Sam said, "He's not the killer?"

Dean shrugged. "I found him doing some kind of ritual in the mechanic's office."

"I was endeavoring to pinpoint the locus of the spell."

"It isn't a spell, Artie," Dean said.

Mackey recoiled as if Dean had slapped him. "I beg your pardon?"

Sam said, "We're pretty sure the spell's bogus, Mr. Pym. So if you were trying to do a locator spell, it wouldn't have worked. There's no real magic here, we don't think."

"Well, much as I'm often willing to take the words of two young thugs whom I've never met, I prefer to believe my own tried and true methods over the rantings and ravings of callow youth."

Holding up the pistol, Dean said, "Uh, Artie? Still have the gun."

"Let's get upstairs," Sam said, glancing around nervously, "before somebody else notices we're here."

The trio all came into the narrow hallway, which was covered in grime and dirt that looked to Dean as if it dated back to the Reagan administration.

"Where'd Omar come from, anyhow?" Dean asked.

Sam shrugged. "He just burst out into the hallway waving the gun around and babbling like an idiot. I wasn't sure I'd be able to talk him down, which is why I signaled you."

At the back of the hallway was a narrow staircase that twisted around 360 degrees by the time it reached the next floor. Dean wondered how the hell anybody got furniture up.

There was also a faint smell of urine in the hallway. As soon as they got to the top of the stairs, Dean took the lead, heading straight to the door with the shiny new 2B in gold on it. He assumed that since it was empty and being shown off to people, the landlord was trying to make it look good. It was the only one of the four apartments on the floor that even had a label on it, though he could see worn holes where the number 2 and accompanying letters used to be.

Then he heard the sound of wood being snapped in half.

Turning to signal Sam, Dean was knocked aside by Mackey, who cried, "We've got to get in there, *now*!"

Next time yell a little louder, jackass, there are people in New Jersey who may not have heard you, Dean thought angrily as Mackey grabbed the doorknob with his gloved hand and pushed it open.

Now Dean could clearly hear wood snapping. Given that the apartment Mackey revealed was completely empty except for some shiny new hardwood on the floor, Dean figured it was the flooring. *Wasn't one of Poe's stories about hiding a corpse in the floorboards?*

Mackey ran in and promptly tripped and fell on his face.

Glancing down, Dean saw that someone had

taken the precaution of laying down a trip wire a few feet into the front room.

Dean and Sam both ran in, jumping over the trip wire, and went into the next room, where the sound was coming from.

Or, rather, they tried to. Mackey chose the moment when Sam was stepping over him to try to get up, and his shoulder collided with Sam's long legs. The two of them went down in a tangle of denim and polyester.

Dean stepped over both of them, even as Sam practically kicked Mackey off him.

"Hold it!" Dean yelled as he ran in, pistol ready. But he only saw two legs going out the window onto the fire escape. The stench of decaying meat made Dean's nostril hairs stand at attention.

Dean went straight for the window, pausing to turn around for only a second. "Stay with that jackass!" he said to Sam, pointing at Mackey, who was stumbling into the room, brushing dust off his polyester suit. Dean also caught sight of several pieces of ripped-up hardwood and bits of wormwood.

He turned and climbed through the window.

How the hell did we miss this? If he was remembering the Poe story right, the victim was killed and cut into pieces and buried under the floorboards. It was "The Tell-Tale Heart," one of the good ones—if nothing else, it was *short*. Did their bad guy commit murder quietly?

That was a question for later. Right now he had a scumbag to catch. The dark figure was already on the 199th Street sidewalk. Dean squeezed himself into the tiny opening that took him to the metal ladder that went down to the street.

His feet hit the pavement and Dean bent his knees with the impact. Turning, he saw that his prey had run up to the next street—Decatur Avenue—and turned left. Dean gave chase, thrilled to have some action after sitting on his ass for so long. As he ran up the hill to the next street, he started going over the different ways he was going to kick this guy's ass, especially since he'd managed to commit *another* murder right under their noses.

As soon as he got to the corner of 199th and Decatur, however, headlights shone right in his face. Holding up one arm to protect his eyes, Dean raised his pistol with the other, but the car attached to the headlights was moving toward him down Decatur.

Dean couldn't see anybody on the street as the car zoomed past, and between the headlights and the darkness—it was a new moon, and there weren't that many streetlights around here—he couldn't make out anything distinctive about the car, beyond the fact that it was a dark sedan.

"Dammit!" he screamed, not caring who noticed him right now.

Dean went back to the building and climbed back up the fire escape. Going in the front door would risk another confrontation with Omar, and he didn't trust himself not to just shoot the bastard in the mood he was in.

Of course, Artie Mackey was another story.

Climbing back in through the window, Dean said before Sam could ask: "I lost him."

"Blast," Mackey said.

Sam looked at Mackey. "I didn't think anybody said that outside of comic books."

Mackey shrugged. "I have two children, so I endeavor to use proper language. It's a pity you weren't able to apprehend our killer."

"Yeah," Dean said, not putting his pistol away, "well, if you hadn't barreled in like a rank *amateur*, Artie, we might've caught the bastard."

Again, Mackey looked like he'd been slapped, which was the least of what Dean wanted to do to him. "I *beg* your pardon?"

"Beg all you want, you ain't gettin' it. We'd've *had* the mother if we weren't so busy tripping over you—or if we coulda snuck in quiet-like. Now someone's dead." Dean held up his pistol and pointed it at Mackey. "Any reason why I shouldn't make you *just* as dead, Artie?"

A sheen of sweat beaded on Mackey's high forehead. "Look, it's hardly my fault—"

"Dean." That was Sam's insistent voice.

"What?"

"We couldn't have saved anyone."

"The hell's *that* supposed to—"

"These remains—they've been here for *days*."

Mackey looked over at Sam. "What?"

Dean lowered his pistol and put it back in his jeans. The metal of the barrel felt cold on the small of his back.

He peered down under the floorboards that had been ripped up. A rotten meat smell came crashing down on him, and he had to turn away, but not before he saw a lot of individual body parts, all cut to pieces and rotting.

"You're right," Mackey said, "that poor unfortunate was killed several days ago." He shook his head. "But that makes no sense. The wormwood's fresh, and tonight's the new moon."

Sam looked like a lightbulb went off over his head. "It makes perfect sense."

"How?" Dean asked. "The guy in the brick wall was killed on the full moon, and the kids got beat up by the monkey on the last quarter, right?"

Sam shook his head and started gesturing emphatically. "Yeah, but the critical moments in those two stories were the deaths. In 'Rue Morgue,' the climax is revealing that the orangutan did it. In 'Amontillado,' it's bricking Fortunato up. But in 'Tell-Tale Heart'—"

"Of course!" Mackey exclaimed. "It isn't the old

man's murder that provides the story's climax, but rather when the murderer rips up the floorboards to reveal the sliced-up corpse!"

Nodding at Mackey, Sam then looked at Dean. "That's what he was re-creating."

"Whoever *he* is." Dean glared at Mackey. "Thanks to you, we'll never—"

Holding up both gloved hands, Mackey said, "All right, that's quite enough. I don't even know who you two *are,* and—"

"I'm Sam Winchester, this is my brother, Dean."

Dean shot his brother an annoyed glance. He wasn't anywhere near ready to start sharing anything with this nimrod.

But then Mackey's jaw fell open. "Oh, good heavens—you two are the Winchester brothers? I must say, it's an honor to meet you! I've heard so much about the pair of you—and, of course, I've met your father. Strange man, he is."

The brothers exchanged another glance. Somehow, this latest revelation wasn't much of a surprise.

"I must say, everything I've heard about you two is good—and tonight would seem to bear that out, especially given how easily you got the drop on me." Mackey clapped his hands, which made a slapping sound as latex hit latex. "Well, I wish you'd said something sooner. I'd have gladly de-

faulted to a pair of veteran hunters such as yourselves. I'm afraid I'm more of a researcher than a
field man, but when I saw these Poe-related murders happening, I had to act. It's rather my spe-
cialty, after all. Besides, it's not as if the police
believed me."

Dean pointedly ignored the I-told-you-so look
Sam was giving him.

"And you say that this spell is a fake, eh?"

"Yeah," Dean said, "Samuels was running a
scam. Only really stupid and gullible people believed it," he added pointedly.

Sam took out his Treo.

"Who you calling?" Dean asked.

"McBain. No sense in her sitting around anymore."

"You know Detective McBain?" Mackey asked.

"Yeah," Sam said, "she's checking at Fordham
Road and—"

"What, at St. Nicholas of Tolentine?" Mackey
laughed, which sounded to Dean like a squirrel
dying. Or maybe Manfred Afiri's singing voice.
"Don't be ridiculous. The sigil at that intersection
is the last one. If the sigil isn't traced in the proper
order, the resurrection won't work."

"It won't work no matter what," Dean said
through clenched teeth.

"None of our documentation said that," Sam said,

then talked into the phone. "Detective McBain? Sam Winchester. I've got good news and bad news."

While Sam filled McBain in, Dean looked again at the ripped-up floorboards. Then he went over to the window, pulling a handkerchief out of his pocket. "Gimme a hand here, Artie."

"What is it you're—oh, I see, you're eliminating fingerprint traces. You know, for someone who called *me* an amateur, I'm rather surprised you don't take so simple a precaution as gloves."

Dean focused on wiping the entire windowsill and ignoring Mackey's barb. The fact was, he *hated* rubber gloves, and they seriously messed with his ability to use the gun. Wiping the sill probably got rid of the bad guy's prints, too, but he would have to live with that. As he wiped, he asked, "Hey, Artie, you said you have kids?"

"Yes. It's one of the reasons why I don't do much in the field. Can't leave the kids fatherless, now, can I?"

Somehow, Dean forced himself not to react. When Mackey had mentioned Dad, it was in the present tense, so he didn't know about Dad's death. Not that he was about to go all chick-flick sharing with Mackey now. In fact, he still considered shooting the twerp in the head to be a viable option.

Sam put away his Treo. "McBain said to meet her where she is."

"To do what?" Dean asked.

"Work out our next move."

Dean snarled. "Oh, come on, Sammy, it's bad enough we got *Masterpiece Theatre* here, but now we gotta have the Cop Who Came to Dinner?"

All that got him was the patented Sam Winchester Glare of Outraged Confusion, and Dean just waved him off and said, "Fine, what-the-hell-ever." But he didn't like how crowded this was getting. Every time they added someone to the mix, it went badly: Jo in Philadelphia; Gordon the Vampire Slayer in Montana; hell, even when they hooked up with Dad it went south.

But Sammy had to be Mr. Share and Care Alike, so he just let it go.

They went downstairs, Mackey closing the door to 2B behind him, since he had the stupid gloves, and then they drove—Sam and Dean in the Impala, Mackey in a beat-up old Civic—to Fordham Road and MLK Boulevard. Sam found a spot to park on Fordham, and McBain was waiting for them at the gate to the park, which was closed and locked at this late hour. Unlike the nice suit she wore the other night, this time she was dressed in a snug-fitting John Jay College of Criminal Justice sweatshirt and blue jeans, a wool topcoat over it covering her shoulder holster.

Fordham was a major thoroughfare, and the intersection was a wide one, with plenty of cars about even this late at night. One corner was dominated by a huge gray, two-towered church prominently proclaiming that it was celebrating its hundredth birthday this year.

Without preamble McBain said, "*Please* tell me you guys wiped the place down."

"We didn't touch or bleed on anything," Sam said, holding up his hands defensively.

"Except the windowsill," Dean said, "and I wiped that down."

"Er," Mackey said, "I wore gloves."

McBain noticed Mackey for the first time. "Arthur, what the *hell*'re you doin' here?"

"You know this guy?" Dean asked.

"He's the one who tipped me off to this nonsense in the first place." She glared down at him. "He *also* said he wasn't gonna get involved."

Mackey scuffed a toe on the sidewalk. "Yes, well, I could hardly just sit around, could I?"

"Yeah, actually, you coulda."

Dean couldn't help but smile at the way Mackey tried to make himself smaller. But the smile fell in short order, since they were basically screwed. "Look, we got nothin' now. It's another eight freakin' days until the first quarter, and we don't have jack."

"Well, since you guys didn't contaminate the

crime scene *too* much, I'll call it in. Maybe the lab'll get somethin'." McBain sighed. "Wouldn't count on it, though. Lab's backed up to next year. Only crime scene that's got any kinda priority is the two kids, 'cause the university's leanin' on us, but there ain't nothin' more useless than an outdoor scene on a windy night. But Reyes and whoever you two just found, that'll take weeks to process."

Smirking, Dean said, "So what it boils down to is—we don't have jack."

"Yeah, brushy-top, we got jack, happy?"

"Not really. Only thing we know for sure is that the last part's happenin' next Tuesday somewhere at this intersection," he pointed to the road behind him, "and no idea who. Hell, until tonight, this guy," now he pointed at Mackey, "was who I had my money on."

"Thanks *so* much," Mackey muttered.

McBain shook her head. "Nah, I coulda told you he was a bum lead. I've known this guy for years."

"Yeah, well, I've known you for two and a half seconds," Dean said, "and I'm still not convinced that he wasn't working with our guy."

"I tried to *aid* you!" Mackey's voice went all squeaky.

Sam, finally, spoke up. "And mostly you got in our way. I'm sorry, Mr. Mackey, but you fit the profile. You're obsessed with Poe, you—"

"I am not *obsessed*. Yes, I've studied Poe quite a bit, that doesn't make me homicidal. Or will you go after every academic who's studied Poe's life in far greater depth than I can in a simple website?" He shook his head. "In fact, one of them has been sending me e-mails, telling me that it's all a coincidence."

That got Dean's attention. "Who has?"

"Someone at Fordham, actually—a nineteenth-century literature scholar over there. Ironic, since it was in one of his papers that I first found out about Percival Samuels, though that only discussed him as one of many spiritualists."

Dean looked at Sam. "Sounds like someone we should talk to."

McBain looked at them. "What, you're just gonna waltz onto the campus and talk to this guy?"

Mackey said quietly, "Er, his name is Dr. Ross Vincent."

"Fine." Dean shrugged. "We'll go in, say we're with the 'Journal of Poe Studies' or something."

Rolling her eyes, McBain said, "You guys really suck at this, don't you?"

"What's the problem?" Sam asked.

"He's an academic, dumbass, he's gonna know everyone from the journals."

Dean said, "Then we'll go as cops."

At that, McBain burst out laughing. "You two.

As *cops*. Right. Tell me, brushy-top—how have you two managed not to be dead, exactly?"

Bristling, Dean said, "We've been doing just *fine*, thanks. And I wish—"

Sam cut him off, which was probably a good idea, since McBain was also armed, and her gun was in a nice easy-to-access shoulder holster instead of tucked in his pants, so she could probably draw faster than he could. "We usually don't stick around long enough for people to check our credentials." Sam smiled. "Or, by the time they do, things have gotten bad enough that they're more concerned with getting our help than who we are."

"Yeah, well," McBain said, shaking her head, "you been lucky. And luck always runs out eventually. That's the first thing you learn in this job."

Frowning, Sam asked, "You mean the job of hunter or being a cop?"

McBain stared right at Sam with her large brown eyes. "Both."

Everyone was quiet for a moment before Mackey said, "Well, it's late, and the wife will be getting worried. If there's nothing else?"

"Just stay out of our way, okay, Artie?" Dean said.

Mackey twisted his thin lips. "Yes, well, I'd say

I've had more than enough excitement for one night. I'll happily leave it to the pair of you. Unlike your father, I'm sure that you two will handle things well."

That got Dean's back up. "The hell's *that* supposed to mean?"

As Mackey walked over to his Civic, he said, "I mean that the two of you are a good deal better at this than your father is. Which, I suppose, is encouraging—better to see that the next generation is improving." With that, he got into his car and drove down the steep hill that Fordham Road became, heading toward the Major Deegan Expressway.

Dean found he had no idea how to feel about that. This wasn't the first time he'd discovered that he and Sam had any kind of reputation. Gordon had mentioned it back in Montana as well, and it still threw him for a loop. Hell, he was still having trouble wrapping his brain around the notion that there was this whole community of other hunters they didn't know about. He and Sam had always assumed that the few people Dad had introduced them to—Pastor Jim, Caleb, Bobby—were the only ones out there fighting demons.

And now finding out that their rep was *better* than Dad's? That made no sense to him. Dad, whatever his flaws, was a master.

Wasn't he?

Sam said something to McBain that shook him out of his thoughts—he was asking about Roxy.

Squinting, McBain said, "Nah, that doesn't ring a bell offhand—but I'll check the computer when I'm in the office Wednesday."

"Wednesday?" Dean said. "What, you don't work a full week?"

"Yeah, brushy-top, I do—it's just from Wednesday to Sunday. This is my weekend. And believe me, there are people I'd much rather be spendin' my off-duty time with than your sorry asses. Now if you'll excuse me, I'm goin' home."

It took several minutes for him to get his breathing back under control. He had debated whether it was such a hot idea to put up the trip wire, but the last thing he needed was someone barging in on him unannounced. It wasn't likely late at night, but the neighborhood was sufficiently troubling that he couldn't be sure that an empty apartment wouldn't be used for a drug buy or something.

But no, he'd been lucky enough not to have *that* happen.

Instead, it was something far worse.

He didn't recognize the people who came in, but obviously they weren't from the housing authority or angry neighbors or drug dealers. Leaving aside any other consideration, they were a little too white for the neighborhood.

Of course, that didn't automatically disqualify them, but if they were just angry because he was horning in on their "crib" or what have you, he doubted they would have chased him down the fire escape.

Then again, perhaps they were just high on something.

It didn't matter. They didn't catch him. If nothing else, they helped him out by contaminating the crime scene with irrelevant evidence. Not that he left anything behind—he'd been very careful to eliminate as much as possible. He watched *CSI*, he knew how much they could potentially find with the right technology.

They just couldn't bring back the dead with technology.

For that, he had to go to something older. It had taken so long to find the right ritual—so many of them depended on the death being recent. Poe had been dead for 157 years. The only resurrections he could find that would bring back someone dead that long required means he simply did not possess.

Except for Percival Samuels, that underappreciated genius, foolishly imprisoned by an ignorant constabulary.

He just hoped that those three people were merely drug dealers. He had only seen the one who chased him—he never got a good look at the other two.

Three down, one to go. Then, at last, the answer will be mine!

FIFTEEN

As soon as he set foot on the campus of Fordham University, Sam felt his heart pound into his rib cage. He felt like he had come home again, and wanted to run away screaming.

In general, Fordham and Stanford didn't look much alike. Both campuses were built in the nineteenth century, and both had a mix of architectural styles, though Stanford had much more elaborate architecture on the more modern buildings. Being in California, Stanford had plenty of palm trees—most notably on the aptly named Palm Drive, the mile-long entrance to the campus—and a great deal of open space.

Fordham had smaller patches of greenery, more trees (none of them palms), and a tendency toward more old-fashioned architecture, with the buildings much closer together. The campus's centerpiece was Keating Hall, built in 1936. A giant stone edifice that rose above the other buildings on campus, it was topped off by a large antenna from which the campus radio station WFUV broadcast. Laid out in front of Keating was Edward's Parade, a huge green field bordered by a paved pathway and a short iron fence. Had he gone into a coma somewhere else and awakened on the Fordham campus, he would never have guessed he was in New York City. It didn't even *smell* the same— green grass and cold stone and battered wood all teased the nose, where just out the gate onto either Fordham Road or Southern Boulevard you got car exhaust and garbage.

On this cold November day there weren't very many students on the parade, though Sam imagined that in warmer weather the place was packed with scantily clad students sunbathing and throwing Frisbees around.

Looking over at his brother, he decided not to share that image with Dean. It would just distract him.

Their destination was on the other side of the parade from Keating Hall: Dealy Hall, one of two more stone buildings that faced Keating with the parade between them, the other being Hughes Hall, a dormitory. Dealy was the home of the English Department, and they had made an appointment to see Dr. Ross Vincent during his office hours today. They'd tried for yesterday, but he was booked.

Dealy Hall's stately exterior was a contrast to its very traditional interior, as the inside looked just like every school hallway in existence: linoleum floor, brightly painted walls, and old wooden doors with small square windows leading to large rooms filled with small desks.

"You okay, Sam?" Dean asked.

"Uh, yeah," Sam said. "Why?"

"You're twitching."

"I am not," Sam said defensively, even though he knew he was. "I just—this is weird, y'know?"

Grinning, Dean said, "Thought you liked all this academic stuff. Ivy-covered halls, higher learning, all that crap."

"Yeah, and the dead girlfriend," he said bluntly.

Dean opened his mouth and closed it. "Sorry, dude," he said quietly.

Sam found himself unable to respond to that. Dean rarely apologized for anything, and Sam didn't want to cheapen so rare an occurrence with a snarky comment.

They walked to the back of the building where the elevators were, and Dean pushed the up button.

And then they waited.

Several ice ages later the elevator finally arrived, the metal doors sliding open at a glacial pace. Dean looked at Sam. "Shoulda walked."

The elevator then moved up to the fifth floor at a speed that was so slow that if they were going only a hair slower they'd have been going down instead of up.

Eventually they arrived at the top floor of the building and stepped off to see a small wooden desk at which nobody was sitting, and behind it a hallway with several mailboxes hanging on the wall, leading back to a series of cubicles and offices. Sam assumed this was the English Department office, though there was also a hallway behind them that had more offices and cubicles.

A short man with a frizzy red beard and wild brown hair came out wearing the classic professor clothes: corduroy jacket with patches on the elbows, flannel shirt, dark-colored tie, and jeans. Sam couldn't believe it—four years at Stanford, and nobody ever really dressed like that. Yet here this guy was.

"Yolanda? Listen, I—" He saw that the desk was empty, stopped short and looked at Sam and Dean. "Neither one of you is Yolanda."

"No, sir," Sam said quickly before Dean could comment. "We're here to see Dr. Vincent—we have an appointment."

"Well, you're in luck, then. I'm Dr. Vincent. You must be the gentlemen from Lincoln Center." He started walking back the way he came. "Come, come, let us speak."

Sam and Dean followed him back and to the left, past several cubicles on the left and offices on the right, before coming to a particular office, the front door of which was decorated in various bits of Poe memorabilia, much of which Sam recognized from similar items in the Poe Cottage—mostly reproductions of book covers—as well as a few yellowed *Far Side* cartoons.

Vincent sat down on a big leather chair and started fiddling with the gold wedding band on his left ring finger. There was only one other chair in the room, and it was covered in books and papers. "So—which of you is which?"

"Uh, I'm Archie Leach, and this is Marion Morrison."

Dean glared at Sam for a second. Sam managed to keep a straight face. Somehow the fact that his nom de guerre for this particular interview was the real name of John Wayne wasn't enough to mollify Dean's annoyance with being given the name "Marion." Of course, Dean would think that his fake name was from *A Fish Called Wanda*, which it was, but that movie used it for the same reason he did—it was Cary Grant's real name.

In response to Dean's annoyance in the Impala

on the way over, at the names he'd come up with, Sam had just shrugged and said, "This is what happens when I pick the names, man. At least it beats yet another classic-rock pairing."

Dean had pouted most of the rest of the way to Fordham. Not that Dean would admit that he pouted, though Sam didn't know what else to call it when his lips set like that.

"And you gentlemen are taking Dr. Lauer's class, and she recommended you talk to me?" the professor said.

"We're collaborating on a short story for Dr. Lauer's creative writing class," Sam replied. He'd checked Fordham's website and noted that, while this was the main campus, it wasn't Fordham's only location. In addition to the Rose Hill campus in the Bronx, there was the College at Lincoln Center, located on the west side of Manhattan, and another up in Tarrytown. He had pulled Lauer's name as one of the English teachers down there who taught a creative writing class. "It's supposed to be about a historical figure, and we went with Edgar Allan Poe."

Vincent smiled, took a cigarette pack out of his pocket and pulled one out. "Don't worry," he said quickly, "I won't light up. Thanks to the ridiculous new laws, I can't even smoke in the privacy of my own office. Used to be this was a civilized campus. Anyhow, I'm glad you came to me instead of just going to some stupid website."

"Well, we did some research on the web, and we found this one site—"

Grabbing the unlit cigarette out of his mouth, Vincent said, "Please, God, tell me it isn't Wikipedia. I swear, that site should be banned." He leaned back and put his hand to his forehead. "I've had to give out more F's because of numbnut students who think copying an entire Wikipedia page constitutes research. You know what I did one time? I went in and edited one of their idiotic pages and filled it with false information. Sure enough, five students put the wrong information—which was only there for a day, and that day was the one before the paper was due—in their papers. It is to weep." He started fondling the cigarette. "So, what is it you want to know?"

"Actually, the site belonged to someone who calls himself Arthur Gordon—"

"Pym?" Vincent winced, and got up from his chair. Sam, who was standing in the office's doorway next to Dean, stared longingly at it, even as Vincent stood by the window, staring out at several leafless trees and the maroon-brick administration building, which was behind Dealy. "That lunatic gives Poe scholarship a bad name. For one thing, he keeps insisting on definitive scholarship, but there's no such thing when it comes to Poe. Sometimes Poe said he shunned fame and didn't care for it, yet sometimes he claimed he was desperate for it. Sometimes he seemed the prototypical starving artist, other times he seemed to be a money-grubbing hound like most of humanity." Vincent turned around and pointed at Sam with his cigarette. "And then there's his death."

Sam frowned. "He died of alcoholism, I thought."

Vincent threw up his hands. "See? This is *exactly* what I'm talking about! Where'd you get that, eh, Mr. Leach? Probably at www.poeroolz.com, or some other ridiculous website. They should just ban the entire Internet, I swear." He sat back down in his chair. "The fact is, nobody knows precisely what Poe died of, we only know that it happened in Baltimore, and they buried him there."

Dean spoke up. "Professor, there's something I'm wondering. Did Poe ever meet a spritutalist by the name of Percival Samuels? See, what we were thinkin' about our short story being was Poe meeting with Samuels, but we weren't sure if they met. Dr. Lauer said you'd know."

Vincent started tapping the side of his forehead with the cigarette. Sam was starting to wish he'd just light the damn thing up already, city smoking ordinances be damned.

"Interesting that you should ask. We don't have any records of the two meeting, as it happens, although it's certainly possible. Poe, obviously, was interested in the supernatural. You'd think that a proper psychic would have warned him about that awful Vincent Price version of 'Masque of the Red Death,' if nothing else." Vincent chuckled at his own witticism, and Sam gamely smiled back.

"Was Samuels a proper psychic?" Dean asked. "I always thought he was kind of a quack."

Vincent raised an eyebrow. "Well, the man's been dead for some time. I can't imagine we'll ever know for sure. Which is a pity, I can tell you. Drives me mad, really, watching my colleagues bicker about things we can never get solid answers on. It would be nice to know for sure about these things."

Sam and Dean talked for a while longer with Vincent, asking some more questions, many of which had the same answers as the research Sam had dug up over the past few days about Poe, both in the library and on Vincent's hated Internet. After they'd talked for twenty minutes, Vincent suddenly got up and said he had a class and rushed them to the elevator bank. However, the brothers followed him to the staircase, which the professor said was wise. "I didn't have this beard until I had to wait for the thing this morning," he quipped.

As they walked around Edward's Parade on the way back to the parking lot, Sam asked Dean, "Whadja think?"

Dean shrugged. "All college profs like that?"

Chuckling, Sam said, "A lot are, yeah."

"And you liked college, why, exactly?"

Sam shook his head. "I still don't get why anyone would *want* to resurrect Poe."

"What do you mean?" Dean asked.

"Well, it's like Dr. Vincent said, he had a pretty miserable life. His wife died young, his career never really took off while he was alive to the extent that he wanted it to, most of his business ventures failed, and he was depressed most of the time. Hell, if he was born now, he'd probably be on Prozac, Zoloft, and Xanax all at the same time."

They got to the Impala. Dean walked to the passenger side, as he still refused to drive in the Bronx. "Maybe we're goin' about this wrong. Maybe it's somebody who hates Poe—someone who wants him to suffer."

"Who would that be?"

Smirking as he got in the car, Dean said, "Anybody who had to read his work and then write a paper about him."

Sam settled into the driver's side, his left hand on the steering wheel as his right inserted the key. "That doesn't exactly narrow our list of suspects."

Before Dean could reply, "Smoke on the Water" sounded from his jacket pocket. He pulled the phone out, flipped it open and said, "Hey, Manfred."

Sam pulled out of the spot as he heard Manfred's

tinny voice over the turned-up earpiece. "Hey, Dean, I was just chattin' with some of the guys here over lunch, an' I just 'membered somethin' 'bout Roxy."

"What's that, Manfred?"

"Well, see, there was this one time when I slept with her."

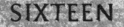

SIXTEEN

The Afiri house
The Bronx, New York
Wednesday 22 November 2006

"Start from the beginning," Dean said angrily.

They were sitting in Manfred's living room. He'd put *Disraeli Gears* by Cream on the turntable, and "Tales of Brave Ulysses" was playing. Manfred was in the easy chair, with Sam and Dean on the couch. Dean was about ready to haul off and belt Manfred, since if Manfred had mentioned this sooner, he might have been spared having to listen to Scottso for a second and third night.

Manfred was holding a beer bottle in his lap and staring down into the bottle's mouth. "Look, it was a while ago, okay? It was way back, when Roxy was still high on everything, y'know? Mary

Jane, coke, speed, booze—you name it, she smoked it, snorted it, drank it, or popped it. She came with some friends to the Park in Rear—this was when we was first startin' out, and we didn't have the weekend gig yet. The friends didn't like us much, an' they left."

Gee, what a shock. Somehow, Dean forced himself not to say that out loud.

After gulping down some beer, Manfred went on. "She stayed behind, though, an' after the show she didn't have nowhere to go. So I offered her a ride back to her place, which was this dump in Morris Park, so I said, 'I got a house,' and we came back here, did a few lines, spun a few disks, then went upstairs."

"And you didn't remember this until now?" Dean asked angrily.

"I forgot it was her! Look, fellas, it was just the one time. Okay, two times—she came back for a couple more gigs—but she was *seriously* messed up by then, an' then she went into rehab. By the time I saw her again, it was a year later, and she was all cleaned up. Hell, I didn't *recognize* her the first time she walked into the Park in Rear after rehab—no makeup, hair cut shorter, and she wore T-shirts insteada tube tops. Totally different lady. An' she went for Aldo, and that was groovy with me, 'cause I got *real* tireda her temperance act."

Dean looked at Sam as Manfred guzzled the rest of his booze and shook his head.

Sam shrugged, and said, "Manfred, did she ever express any interest in getting back together?"

"Hell, no. Like I said, she was a totally different person. Wouldn't go near me."

"I thought she liked the house," Dean said, suddenly remembering a previous conversation at the Park in Rear.

"Sure, she did. Hell, *everyone* likes the damn house. I got Gina beggin' me to move in here half the time."

"You mean Janine?" Dean asked.

"Yeah, right, my cousin's girl." Manfred gave a gap-toothed smile. "Y'know, Dean, she kinda had a thing for you, looked like." The smile fell. "Don't mess with her, okay? I got enough problems with my cousin. 'Sides, she'll flirt with anything that moves."

"No worries," Dean said. Even if he was interested—and he had to admit, Janine *was* kinda hot—he had no interest in getting involved with this man's family in any way once Roxy's spirit was taken care of. *And the next time Ash needs a favor, he can go bite me.*

"I gotta say," Sam said, "this may be why Roxy's haunting you. She keeps saying, 'Love me,' and it might be that it's directed at you."

Shaking his head, Manfred said, "Well that

don't make no kinda sense. I mean, when she got outta rehab, she was all over Aldo, then she just up and disappeared after that weekend I was in Pennsylvania, and then—"

Dean started. "What weekend you were in Pennsylvania?"

Manfred frowned. "Didn't I tell you 'bout that?"

"About what?" Dean was now on the edge of the couch, ready to leap up and beat Manfred about the head and shoulders.

"Damn, fellas, I'm sorry, I thought I told you 'bout the time Aldo house-sat for me. See, that was the last time I saw Roxy. Well, okay, not *then*, exactly, it was a couple days before. I had a family reunion thing happenin' out in Pennsylvania, and back in those days I had a cat. He passed last year, poor little guy, but he was diabetic and someone had to give him shots. I didn't like boarding him at the vet, 'cause he got all skittish, and he really liked Aldo, and since Aldo lives in this dinky apartment in Mamaroneck, he took me right up on the offer." He got up. "This is assumin' I 'member this all right. I'm gonna get me another beer. You want any?"

"Yeah," Dean said emphatically, as the urge for alcohol was suddenly overwhelming. After Manfred left for the kitchen, he looked at Sam. "Can you believe this?"

"After living in the same house with him for the

better part of a week? Yeah, I believe it. Dean, half the time, I'm stunned he remembers his address. He said it himself, he can barely remember last week. For that matter, he didn't even remember that you two already had that conversation about Janine."

Dean nodded, conceding the point. "So are you thinkin' what I'm thinkin', Pinky?"

"Yup." Sam sighed. "We need to start digging."

Manfred came back into the living room with three beer bottles.

After taking the bottle, Dean took a long swig and then said, "Manfred, listen—we need to dig up your backyard."

That caused Manfred to splutter his beer into his beard. Wiping his mouth with his sleeve, he said, "Excuse me?"

Sam's Treo started to ring then. Jumping up from the couch, he put his beer down on a stray empty spot on the coffee table, pulled the phone out of his pocket and walked over to the hallway entrance. "Hello? Oh, hi, Detective."

Manfred gave Dean a look, and Dean said, "We know someone who works for Missing Persons. We asked her to check on Roxy."

"Uh, okay. What's that gotta do with diggin' up my yard?"

Before Dean could answer, Sam said, "Really? Who else did they talk to? Okay. Okay. Okay, thanks, Detective. Talk to you soon." He disconnected and walked back to the couch. "That was McBain—she said that Roxanne Carmichael was reported missing to the Forty-ninth Precinct on September 23, 2004."

Manfred nodded. "Yeah, that sounds about right. Those reunions, they're always right after Labor Day."

Sam sat back down on the couch and grabbed his beer bottle. "It's still an open case. And according to McBain, they talked to Aldo Emmanuelli, Manfred Afiri, and Tom Daley."

Manfred frowned. "I don't 'member that."

"Also," Sam said, "they identified the body that was cut up and put under the floorboards. It was a woman named Sarah Lowrance. She worked in a Blockbuster Video store on Boston Road. And according to the M.E. report, she was killed anywhere from six to twelve days ago."

"Dammit," Dean muttered. He desperately wanted to blame that little pipsqueak Mackey for that, but he knew better. The Lowrance woman had been dead for a while, probably since before he and Sam even came to New York. There wasn't anything they could do for her, except stop the bastard who killed her and that Reyes guy.

Manfred looked a bit pale. "What in the *hell* are you fellas talkin' 'bout?"

Sam waved him off. "Long story."

Shrugging, Manfred said, "Whatever. Look, I'm sorry I didn't tell you fellas 'bout Roxy 'n' me sooner, but I honestly forgot. Now if I can get you two off this whole cuttin'-up-bodies thing, talk to me about diggin' up my yard."

"We think it's possible," Sam said slowly, "that Aldo and Roxy got into some kind of fight here when he was house-sitting for you that weekend, that Roxy died, and Aldo buried her in your backyard. That's why she's haunting the house."

"And also why she only shows up after gigs," Dean added.

"You sure about this?"

Dean and Sam exchanged a guilty glance. "Well—no," Dean finally said. "It's just a guess."

"But it fits the evidence," Sam added as "Mother's Lament" finished. "We've been doin' this awhile, and we're right more than we're wrong."

Manfred smirked as he got up to change the record. "Well, that puts you one up on me. So, okay, say you find Roxy's corpse. Then what?"

"Salt it and burn it."

"Right, right," Manfred said as he slid *Disraeli Gears* into its sleeve and pulled out Traffic's *The Low Spark of High-Heeled Boys*, "you tol' me that. That whole salt thing just freaks me out, y'know?"

And you remembered, miracle of freakin' miracles. Again Dean managed to restrain himself from saying it out loud.

"Speakin'a freakin' me out," Manfred said, "the thing I don't buy in all this is Aldo. He an' I've been buddies for more years than I can count, and he ain't the murderin' type."

"It could've been an accident," Sam said.

Dean rolled his eyes. That was Sam all over, trying to find the silver lining. Recalling how Aldo had been all skittish when he first mentioned Roxy, Dean had no trouble believing that he was hiding something. Besides, they'd been thinking all along that Aldo knew what happened to her and wasn't telling.

"Of course," Sam added, "if it *was* an accident, he should've reported it."

"Nah, he wouldn't've." Manfred swigged his beer. "Look, I don't buy for a second that Aldo did nothin' wrong, and I can't see him killin' nobody, but—well, if it *was* an accident, he wouldn't'a called no fuzz, I'll tell you that for free. Ain't Aldo's style, y'know?"

"Hang on," Sam said, "maybe we shouldn't go digging up the yard."

Dean looked at his brother like he was crazy. "Exsqueeze me?"

"I'm saying, we shouldn't guess. We don't know for sure the body's there, and if it is, we don't know where exactly, and even if we do find it, then what?"

"Then we salt it and burn it and—"

"And whoever killed her goes free, 'cause we'll have burned the evidence."

That brought Dean up short.

Sam went on. "We always talk about how spirits are out for vengeance, and that may be the case here, but what if she's just out for justice, like that spirit down in Baltimore?"

"That was a death omen," Dean said.

But Sam was on a roll. "Yeah, but she was mainly there to mete out justice. I don't think salting and burning will do the trick. I mean, yeah, it'll get rid of the spirit, but it won't bring whoever killed her to light."

"I don't believe it," Dean said, shaking his head.

Sam frowned. "Believe what?"

"That you actually said, 'mete out justice.' Dude, people don't *talk* like that."

Manfred nodded. "He's right, Sam, that was some seriously whacked-out phrase-turning, there."

"Whatever—I'm right, aren't I?"

Dean sighed. Every instinct he had said that they should find the body and salt and burn it, because, dammit, that was what you *did* with spirits who haunted people's houses.

But if they did that, Aldo got away with murder. And that just did not sit right with him.

"All right, so what do we do, genius? Use a rubber hose on Aldo?"

Sam smiled in a manner that made Dean distinctly nervous. "Not quite."

It had been the preparation work that was the most difficult, really.

In order for the sigil to be properly traced, he had to commit each of the moon-based rituals in a particular spot. Luckily, the margin for error on that spot was wide enough that he had options. For example, he just needed one of the apartments in that building on 199th Street to be empty, and one was. He was even more fortunate with the house on Webb Avenue. He would've settled for finding an abandoned apartment in that area as well, but it worked so much better with a basement.

That was how he knew his cause was just. The fates had laid things out for him perfectly, made it easy for him to accomplish his work.

All he had left was the final stage, and still with five days to prepare. This, he felt, would be the easiest of them.

He was standing now at the corner of Fordham Road and University Avenue—or, as it was called now, Martin Luther King Jr. Boulevard—looking up at the two towers of the Church of St. Nicholas of Tolentine. Both towers had bells, which rang out at the appropriate times on Sundays.

It will ring out next Tuesday as well. His heart pounded with anticipation. Finally, that would be it.

He hadn't gone back to the other place. For all he knew, the police had found the remains of poor Sarah Lowrance. She was a perfectly nice woman, and he was sure that she might have lived a long happy life otherwise. But she was serving a greater purpose now, and perhaps in the fullness of time, when people understood what, exactly, he was doing, her name would be immortalized, along with those of Marc Reyes, those two students, and his victim the following Tuesday—and himself, of course, in showing the world the glories of magicks.

When he thought about it, of course, he knew better. After all, the world didn't appreciate Percival Samuels's genius, and he had lived in a time that was far more accepting of the world of the occult than the modern world, with its websites and fax machines and cell phones and iPods and e-mails and all the other scientific nonsense that got in the way of learning.

But it didn't matter. Because he would bring Poe back, back to a world that would appreciate his genius, back to a world where he could tell them the *truth*.

That was all that mattered. What were the lives

of Marc Reyes and Sarah Lowrance and those two students compared to that?

Not to mention whoever he got for the final ritual.

Technically, he didn't need a person for the final portion. There was a bell tower on the site of the fourth and final sigil, and that meant he simply needed to re-create "The Bells."

The question, of course, was how. He thought back over the lyrics, much of which was the repetition of the word "bells." Poe had a gift for rhythm and onomotopoeia that so many of his fellow American poets lacked. Reading "The Bells" felt like you were amidst the "clamor and the clangor," able to feel the bells' tintinnabulation as you read it aloud.

In particular, he thought of the needs of the ritual. He had chosen "The Cask of Amontillado," "The Murders on the Rue Morgue," and "The Tell-Tale Heart" in part because all three involved corpses, and he knew from his studies that the strongest rituals involved the taking of a life, and a human life was stronger than that of an animal. But "The Bells" had no such death.

Then he recalled one stanza:

In a clamorous appealing to the mercy of the fire,
In a mad expostulation with the deaf and frantic fire,

Leaping higher, higher, higher,
With a desperate desire,
And a resolute endeavor,
Now—now to sit or never,
By the side of the pale-faced moon.

And another:

And his merry bosom swells
With the paean of the bells!
And he dances, and he yells;
Keeping time, time, time,
In a sort of Runic rhyme,
To the paean of the bells
Of the bells.

Yes! That was it. He would find a victim and set him alight even as he rang the bells. A burning human would certainly dance and yell, and his or her bosom would swell in an attempt to breathe.

It's perfect.

The church was closed and locked right now, of course, since it was late at night. Tomorrow, after his day's business was done, he'd return and talk to the priest. Explain that he would need to ring the bells himself on Tuesday at midnight. He would, of course, donate generously to the church. That was the easy part. Acquiring what he needed to perform the rituals in such a way that it would leave no trace for the constabulary was an expensive proposition, but ever since his wife passed away, he had plenty of ready money. In the end, dying was the best thing she did for him, as it provided him with both the money to do what needed to be done and the lack of her nagging presence to stop him.

Thus assured that his plan was set and good to go, needing only a victim—and he had the better part of a week to find one—he turned to head toward where he'd parked his car, several blocks down University Avenue.

However, he was intercepted by a short man in an ugly suit, one whose face he had, of course, seen before, on the front page of a rather tiresome website.

The man, who went by the sobriquet of Arthur Gordon Pym in a misguided and rather tired attempt to show his devotion to the author, said, "It's a truism that criminals return to the scene of the crime, but I find it rather entertaining that you choose to come to the scene of the crime before it is one." Pym shook his head. "I should've known it would be you."

"I'm sorry," he said, "but I haven't the faintest notion what you're talking about." He started to walk past Pym, but the little man simply moved so he was still in the way. "I don't know who you are, but—"

"Yes, you do."

He did, of course, but he saw no reason to let Pym know that. "Look, I'm just someone admiring this lovely church—"

"At eleven o'clock at night on a Wednesday? That strikes me as exceedingly unlikely, especially given that this church is the likely site for the ritual you intend to perform on Tuesday next. I barely missed you Monday night, thanks to that damned trip wire, but I can assure you, good sir, I will not let you kill again."

Now, suddenly, he was nervous. At first he figured to bluff his way out of it, but if Pym saw him at the 199th Street apartment, then there was no hope. He was on to him.

And then he realized that there was plenty of hope. He grinned, giddy with the brilliance of it.

"Something amuses you?"

"Yes. You." And then he punched Pym in the face.

Pain slammed into his knuckles and wrist, and he shook it in agony. People did that sort of thing on television all the time, and the victim always fell to the floor, unconscious. Pym, though, clutched the side of his head, and blood spurted out of his mouth.

"You hit me!" Pym cried, spitting more blood.

Of course I hit you, you nincompoop, it's only too bad you didn't fall down. He had no weapons with him—his .44 was back home—so he was defenseless without what he had thought to be the surefire trick of punching Pym in the face.

Left with no other option, he turned and ran, which had always worked in a pinch.

His legs were longer than Pym's, and he had the element of surprise, so he put quite a bit of distance between himself and the diminutive Poe scholar. Even as he pumped his legs to move faster down the University Avenue sidewalk, passing apartment buildings and town houses, he remembered that he had some fishing line in the car, meant to help secure his victims. He'd needed it in particular to hold Sarah Lowrance still, as she'd been particularly ornery before he was able to apply the sedative.

Reaching into his coat pocket with his good hand—the right one was still throbbing like mad—he pulled out his car's key chain and pushed the button that sprung the trunk open.

Sure enough, the fishing line was right where he remembered it to be. He grabbed it, along with a baseball that had been sitting in there since he got it free at a Yankee game his wife had insisted they go to back when she was alive. Grabbing that as well, he turned around to see Pym running down the sidewalk toward him, a cell phone at his ear.

I don't know who you're calling, but it's not going through if I can help it. He threw the baseball right at Pym's head.

It struck him in the stomach instead, but it was enough to get him to stop running and stumble to the pavement.

He ran up to Pym, now wheezing on the sidewalk, grabbed the cell phone out of his hands and threw it against the wall of a nearby apartment building. Then he yanked Pym's arms behind his back and started binding his wrists.

"What're you doing?" Pym asked between heavy breaths. "Ow!" he added as the fishing line cut into the skin of his wrists.

"Choosing my final victim," was all he said in response as he tied the line tighter. He noticed a few people around, but they minded their own business and didn't say anything. Still, one or more of them might have had a mobile phone, so it behooved him to get out of sight sooner rather than later. "Don't worry—your name will go down in history as aiding in one of the greatest endeavors of humankind." He smirked. "Though I doubt you're in much of a position to appreciate that at present. Worry not, I plan to give you due credit for your sacrifice. After all, citing your sources is the heart of scholarship."

He got up, yanking Pym to his feet by his bound wrists. Once again fate had favored him. This was his destiny, he just *knew* it.

Very soon now the answer will be mine!

SEVENTEEN

A staple of old-fashioned detective fiction, Sam knew, was to gather all the suspects in one room. Poe didn't do that in "The Murders on the Rue Morgue," but that story's descendants certainly did. The real world didn't often work like that, of course, so having a chance to actually do so gave him a bit of what he was sure Dean would call a geeky thrill.

He had told Manfred to have a band meeting Thursday night at his place. Manfred pointed out that they hadn't had a "band meeting" in years— "Matter of fact, I don't think we *ever* had a meetin' that wasn't a rehearsal," he'd said—but he nevertheless called it, getting everyone on the phone and saying to come over to his place instead of rehearsing at Tom Daley's.

Tommy, not surprisingly, was the last one to arrive. Sam had noticed that he was the last one to show up at all the gigs, even though as drummer he had the most setup work to do, since he refused to keep his drum kit at the Park in Rear. "Paid too much for this snare," was what he had said when Sam queried him on the subject Sunday night, though it was unclear why he couldn't just take the expensive snare drum with him and leave the rest to save himself setup and tear-down time.

When Tommy finally showed up, Robbie, the keyboard player, and Aldo were bitching and moaning about their respective day jobs on the couch, Dean and Manfred were standing by the record player discussing the relative merits of the remasterings of Robert Johnson's recordings (leading Sam to wonder if Dean intended to mention that he'd recently met the very demon to whom Johnson had sold his soul), and Eddie, the bass player, was standing by the window, staring out it at the backyard.

"Sorry I'm late," Tommy said. He was wearing a bright pink shirt that Sam suspected could be picked up from orbiting satellites. The other band members were in sweatshirts and jeans, except for Eddie, who had the same all-black ensemble he usually wore on stage. "So what's the up, here?"

For his part, Sam had been going over the spell in his head. It was a simple summoning, which Dad had duly recorded in the notebook (confusingly, on the page right after the one on Reapers and before the one on the Calusa Indians), and Sam had the notebook at hand to consult, but there were some tricky Latin words in there, and mispronunciation could be fatal. (He still recalled, with alarming clarity, the time when he was ten and he had done his first tracking spell, only his Latin was sufficiently poor that he instead summoned a sprite, who then proceeded to wreak havoc on the cabin where they'd been staying. Dad had managed to send it back to where it came from, but he never did get the security deposit back on that place . . .)

"Well," Manfred said after fetching Tommy a requested beer, "you're prob'ly wonderin' why I called y'all here. It's simple, but I don't think you're gonna believe it. See—I been havin' some problems lately here in the house. These two fellas—Sam and Dean—they been helpin' me with it." Dean had, at this point, gotten up to stand next to Sam at the living room entryway.

Robbie frowned. "Thought they was friends'a Ash's."

"We are," Dean said. "That's how we found out about Manfred's problem."

"And this problem has to do with Roxy?" Aldo asked.

Dean smirked. "Gee, Aldo, why would you assume that?"

" 'Cause you been askin' about her all week. It's kinda pissin' me off. That ain't a parta my life I'm all that thrilled with."

"And why would that be, exactly?" Dean asked, moving toward the couch.

"Bitch disappeared on me. No phone calls, no apologies, no 'sorry it didn't work out,' no 'can we be friends,' she just up and left. Pissed me off, all right?"

Sam noticed that Aldo didn't have the usual bright expression on his face. Ever since he first saw the guitarist on stage last Friday night, Aldo always seemed pleased with the world. How much of that was his usual demeanor and how much was due to his enrollment in Alcoholics Anonymous, Sam wouldn't have ventured to guess.

Now, though, Aldo was as skittish as a kitten under a rocking chair, which led him to think their theory was right.

"Thing is," Dean said, "the last time anyone saw Roxy before she went missing was right before you house-sat for Manfred here."

Everyone leaned forward at that—except Eddie, who was his usual bass-player-still self. Tommy, who was seated in the easy chair in recline mode, flipped it back forward. "Missing? She's *missing*?"

"Was reported as a missing person right after that weekend, actually," Dean said.

Now Aldo looked confused. "What the hell're you talkin' about, Sam?"

"I'm Dean."

"What-the-hell-ever, I didn't house-sit for no-body."

Manfred put his hands on his hips. "You damn well did, Aldo—that was when I had Lucille, and you gave her insulin each morning while I was off at the family reunion thing."

Aldo put his head in his hands. "Dammit." He looked up. "Man, I'm sorry, but—look, I'm sorry I didn't tell you, but—I really hated that cat. We didn't get along, so when I said I'd house-sit—I lied."

Sam frowned. This wasn't the reaction he was expecting, though Aldo denying he was in the house made sense if he was guilty.

Standing up from the couch, he walked over to Manfred. "I didn't wanna let you down, but I couldn't be around that stupid moggy for more'n five minutes, so I asked the guys to cover for me on the insulin shots."

"Wait," Robbie said, "this was when you had the reunion, you said? What was it, oh-four?"

Nodding, Manfred said, "Yeah. And I trusted you to—"

Aldo held up his hands. "I know, I know, but—" He turned around. "Tell him, guys."

Robbie and Tommy both nodded. "Yeah, we took care of it."

Sam looked over at Eddie, who was also nodding.

Now Manfred was shaking his head in disbelief. "I never even showed you guys how to give 'er the shot—I just showed Aldo."

Tommy laughed. "Dude, we know how to navigate around a hypodermic, I'm telling you *that* right now."

Sam looked at Dean. Dean shrugged and said, "Well, look, it doesn't change one fact: Roxy's dead."

Everyone turned and looked at Sam and Dean, as if surprised that the two of them were still even in the room. "Say *what*?" Aldo said.

"She's dead," Manfred said. "And the reason I know she's dead is 'cause her ghost's been hauntin' me for a couple weeks now, every time I come back from a gig at the Park in Rear."

There was silence for several seconds after that.

Then Aldo, Robbie, and Tommy burst out laughing. Eddie didn't, but Sam assumed that his face would crack open if he even smiled.

Between guffaws, Robbie said, "I coulda sworn April Fool's Day was in, y'know, *April*."

"We're serious," Dean said.

Aldo shook his head, still laughing. "I always thought Ash wasn't wired too good, and this proves it, if you jokers're his friends."

Dean turned to his brother. "Sam?"

Showtime, Sam thought, and hefted Dad's journal, turning it to the page he'd bookmarked with a paper clip.

"*Phasmates mortua hic ligata admovete audieminique!*"

Robbie frowned. "What is that, German?"

Tommy looked at Robbie. "Nah, that's Latin." At Robbie's dubious look, he said, "What? I took it in high school."

Sam repeated, "*Phasmates mortua hic ligata admovete audieminique!*"

"This is *nuts*!" Aldo said. "There ain't no such thing as—"

For the third and final time, Sam said, "*Phasmates mortua hic ligata admovete audieminique!*"

With a clatter, the windows started rattling and the CDs started vibrating in their racks, the collision of plastic on jewel case making a terrible racket.

Leaping to his feet, Tommy said, "What the *hell*?"

The others were all looking around and at each other and at Sam. He recognized the expressions on their faces because he'd seen it more times than he could count: *This can't be happening. This isn't real. This must be fake. This violates my view of the world. Make it stop!*

Then the cackling started.

Aldo went incredibly pale after that. In a small voice, he said, "Roxy?"

The cackling continued, but Roxy's voice cried, "Love me! Love me! Love me!"

And then she appeared.

The blond hair was stragglier than it had been the last time, and it was harder to make out her eyes, but the Queensrÿche shirt was still visible, and her mouth was wide open, screaming the words, "Love me!"

This time, though, she went straight for the window where Eddie was standing.

Eddie's face changed for the first time in Sam's brief acquaintance with him: His eyes widened, his mouth contorted into a scream, he waved his arms back and forth in front of his face, and he yelled, "Get away from me, you bitch! You're dead! Dead and buried!"

Manfred stared at the bass player. "Eddie, what the *hell*?"

"Love me! Love me!" the spirit of Roxy Carmichael kept screaming.

"I told you no, you stupid bimbo!" Eddie screamed. "Get away from me, you're dead!"

"Love me!"

Tommy and Robbie had run over to the living room entryway where Sam and Dean were standing with Manfred and Aldo. "Make it go away, man," Robbie said.

"Why?" Sam asked.

"What the hell kinda question's that?" Tommy asked. "Get ridda that thing, or I swear, I'll go medieval on your ass, I'm tellin' you *that* right now!"

"Love me! Love me!"

Several CDs fell onto the hardwood floor. The windows rattled harder.

"Go away!" Eddie screamed. "I killed you already, go *away*!"

Dean walked over to the hallway, where he'd hidden his shotgun. Cocking it, he walked into the living room and held it up, taking aim at the spirit.

Predictably, one of the band members objected. Robbie stepped forward, but Sam grabbed his shoulder. "Trust us."

"Hell with that—you brought that thing in here."

"It was here before these fellas got here," Manfred said.

Aldo, Sam noticed, wasn't saying a word, but he looked furious.

"Love me!"

"Cover your ears," Sam said, suiting action to words.

With a deafening blast, Dean fired rock-salt rounds at Roxy's spirit, and she dissipated.

"Ow!" Eddie gripped his right arm with his left. Some of the rock salt had pelted him. Sam couldn't bring himself to be sorry about it.

As soon as Roxy disappeared, two things happened: The house stopped rattling, and Aldo ran across the living room and belted Eddie in the jaw.

Even as Eddie collapsed to the hardwood floor, Aldo kicked him, then bent over to punch him again, screaming, "You son of a *bitch*, you *killed* her!"

Dean grabbed Aldo's wrist. "Don't. I'm right there with you, dude, but don't."

Aldo whirled around. "Let go'a me, Sam."

"I'm Dean, and I ain't lettin' go. Let's give him a chance to talk." Dean looked down at Eddie, who was curled up into a fetal position, tears streaking his cheeks. "If you don't like what he says, then I'll *help* you beat the crap out of him. But if nothing else, we need to know what he did to her—and to her body."

Aldo stared at Dean for several seconds, then nodded, lowering his arm, at which point Dean let go of it.

"It was an accident," Eddie muttered.

Grabbing the bass player by the lapels of his black vest, Dean hauled him to his feet. "Get up. Now talk, or I let him go to town on you. What happened?"

"It was—" Eddie sniffled, and wiped the tears from his eyes. "It was when Manfred was at his reunion. Aldo didn't wanna be near Lucille, so Robbie, Tommy, and me each took turns. I had Saturday night and Sunday mornin', so I could stay the night Saturday. I invited Roxy over."

"*What?*" Aldo screamed.

"I was screwin' her, okay?" Eddie said defensively. "It wasn't a big deal. She told me you didn't satisfy her in bed no more, and I figured what the hell, I'd been wantin' a piece'a her since she came on to Manfred back in the day. But it was nothin', it was just sex."

Aldo stepped forward, fists clenched. "Just sex?"

"Easy," Dean said, a hand on Aldo's shoulder.

"So after we screwed, she put on the Queensrÿche T-shirt and starts talkin' about how we should be together permanent. I didn't want that."

"What, she wasn't good enough for you?" Aldo asked. Sam could hear the fury in his voice, and he wasn't entirely sure Dean would be able to hold him back much longer.

"For screwin' around, sure, but I didn't want the stupid bitch as a *girlfriend*. Woulda messed up the band, for one thing, 'cause if she broke up with you and went with me, it'd be *all* messed up, and I didn't even *like* the stupid bitch. Just liked her body's all."

Manfred said, "So, what, you *killed* her?"

Turning to face Manfred, Eddie said, "No! God, we just—it was an accident, she tripped and fell down the damn staircase, right after we had this big-ass fight. I told her I didn't want a relationship, she said fine, whatever, she was getting something to drink in the kitchen, and she tripped and fell."

"You expect me to believe that?" Aldo asked. "Roxy never tripped in her life."

"Maybe she was drunk," Eddie said lamely.

Shaking his head, Manfred said, "She was sober, man, you knew that. C'mon, we ain't stupid. 'Sides, you just said you killed her and that was, whadayacallit—spur of the moment stuff."

Sam said, "I'm willing to bet all these guys will testify to you admitting you killed her." He hoped that *wouldn't* be the case, honestly, as the other members of Scottso would make awful witnesses, plus the circumstances under which Eddie confessed weren't really repeatable in a court of law. Rather than pursue that, Sam asked, "What did you do with the body?"

"Buried her in the backyard." Eddie shook his head. "Took all freakin' night, too."

Sam felt a vibration in his pocket. He'd muted his Treo, but the vibrate function still worked. Taking out the phone, the display indicated that it was Detective McBain. Stepping out into the hallway, he answered. "Detective, this is a coincidence."

"Why's that?"

"We were just about to call you. Riverdale's part of the, uh, the Five-oh, right?"

McBain snorted. "Oh, you're usin' the lingo now? Real cute. Yeah, the Five-oh covers Riverdale, why?"

"You may want to call your friends there, 'cause we think that missing person, Roxy Carmichael, is buried in the backyard of the house we're staying in."

There was a pause. "Seriously?"

"Uh, yeah. That isn't why you called, obviously. What's up?"

"I'll call the Five-oh when I'm done with you, but then you two need to get your white asses outta there."

Sam nodded. "Yeah, of course." They were still

fugitives, and the police were likely to be there for a while, what with digging up Roxy's body and taking statements from all of Scottso.

"Luckily, I got just the thing to keep you busy. That's why I was callin'. Our buddy Arthur Gordon Pym's gone missing."

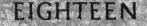

EIGHTEEN

Church of St. Nicholas of Tolentine
The Bronx, New York
Thursday 23 November 2006

Dean had to admit that he had no idea how Sam managed to find his way out of Riverdale. And this was a hard admission, as he had always prided himself on having an excellent sense of direction.

Once they got down the big hill of Riverdale Avenue, one of the neighborhood's major thoroughfares, Dean had no trouble following where they were going. There was an entrance to the Major Deegan Expressway at West 230th Street, and the bottom of that hill put them at the corner of 231st, so Dean knew there were about six ways to get to the expressway from there. And they were going back to the corner of Fordham and MLK, where they'd last parted ways with McBain on Monday night, which was right off the expressway's Fordham Road exit. He could have easily taken over driving from there.

But he had no faith in his ability to drive around Riverdale. And that really pissed him off.

Still, it needed to be done. Frankly, the fact that Mackey was missing just confirmed his suspicion that he was in on it with the sick bastard who was trying to resurrect Poe. But Sam said that McBain thought there was more to it than that. Either way, though, they had to get out of Manfred's house before the cops turned up. Eddie was going to again confess to killing Roxy and burying her in the yard, and Manfred and Aldo both made it crystal clear they would not give Eddie the chance to renege on that statement. Furthermore, they all promised to leave Roxy's spirit out of it—which wasn't a difficult promise to obtain. Tommy's exact words were, "No way I'm tellin' no city cop about no ghost, I'm tellin' you *that* right now."

With luck, this would put Roxy's spirit to rest.

Sam took the Impala up the exit ramp for Fordham Road, made the left turn onto Fordham, then went up the hill to MLK, the entire way spending way too much time at traffic lights. Sam turned right, found McBain's Saturn parked in front of a fire hydrant, and double-parked the Impala in front of it.

"Thanks for comin', guys," McBain said. She was again wearing a sweatshirt and jeans, though this time the jeans were black and the sweatshirt had several Warner Bros. cartoon characters on it, a fashion choice that raised her in Dean's estimation a notch.

"What happened?" Sam asked.

"I was out workin' a case last night. Had my cell off, on account of a sudden ring would've compromised the police work a lot. Unfortunately, my provider sucks ass, so I didn't get my voice mail until this afternoon. There were the usual four hundred phone calls from Aunt Vernetha that I get when I don't call her every hour on the hour, and a message from Arthur."

Sam frowned. "What'd he say?"

"Not a lot." She reached into her coat pocket and took out her cell phone, flipped it open, held down the number one button, then put it on speaker.

A prerecorded voice said: *"You have one saved message."*

Then a familiar whine. Mackey sounded breathless as he said, *"Detective, it's Arthur Gordon Pym. I've made a startling discovery, and you should get do—owlf!"*

Dean then heard some thumping noises, then a few clattering noises, and then: *"Wednesday, 11:39 P.M."*

McBain closed the phone. "That ain't the fun part. I tried calling him back about twelve times and got nothin', not even voice mail, so I traced his cell's transponder." She pointed at the sidewalk where it met the base of an apartment building. "It was lying there." Then she reached back into her coat pocket and took out two broken halves of a single cell phone. "And this is what it looked like."

"That's not good," Sam said.

"Look, I feel sorry for the guy," Dean lied, "but what're we supposed to do?"

McBain stared at him. "*Find* him, brushy-top. He said he made a 'startling discovery,' and that can only mean one thing."

Smirking, Dean said, "He didn't listen to you when you told him to leave this alone?"

To Dean's surprise, McBain actually smirked back. "Okay, two things. The other is that he found our guy, and our guy took him and his phone out with extreme prejudice."

Sam rubbed his pointy little chin. "You think our bad guy kidnapped him and plans to make him victim number five?"

Dean said, "Yeah, but the big day isn't until Tuesday, so—" Then he cut himself off. "The others he planned ahead, though. He had to kidnap the monkey, and he had to have set things up in the empty house and the empty apartment beforehand."

"He killed the Lowrance woman days before the ritual," Sam added.

"Welcome to the conversation," McBain said dryly. "Now I already checked, and there ain't no empty places anywhere in this intersection. The park's too out in the open."

"So were the two kids," Dean pointed out.

"Yeah," McBain said, "but then he had a sedated orangutan. Now he's got an unwilling hostage, and one he wasn't plannin' on. Wherever he's doin' this, it's gotta be outta sight."

Sam was staring down the street toward Fordham Road, his brow furrowed. Dean, knowing that look, said, "What're you thinkin', Sammy?"

"That church at the corner."

"St. Nicholas of Tolentine," McBain said. "What about it?"

"Does it have a bell tower?"

McBain nodded. "Yeah, they ring it out every Saturday night and Sunday when there's mass."

"One of Poe's most famous poems is 'The Bells.' In fact, it was inspired by church bells."

Dean frowned. "Anybody die in that one?"

Sam shook his head. "But that may not stop our guy."

"Especially if he found a short annoying guy in

a polyester suit getting in his business," Dean muttered. "That may also mess up the timetable."

"He's been following the ritual pretty closely," Sam said, "and the phases of the moon are the critical part. However he's re-creating 'The Bells,' he . . ."

After he trailed off, Dean prompted him. "Sam?"

Turning to stare intently at his brother, Sam said, "I just remembered a couple lines of the poem: 'In a' —something something— 'to the mercy of the fire, / In a mad expostulation with the' —something— 'frantic fire, / Leaping higher, higher, higher.'"

Unbidden, images from Dean's nightmare came back to him. The demon who'd killed Mom and Sam's girlfriend Jessica did so by pinning them to the ceiling and consuming them with fire. In his nightmare, Dean saw that happen to several of the women in his and Sam's life that they'd cared about. He would likely never consider Mackey someone he cared about, but he still wouldn't wish immolation on anyone, nor did he have any desire to see it happen again.

McBain started walking toward the corner. "Let's go."

"Oh, this is fine," Dean grumbled to himself. They were the ones who came up with the course of action, and *she* was taking the lead?

He reminded himself that they wouldn't even have been there if not for McBain, and they did need something to do while the cops crawled all over their crash space.

Ultimately, it came down to the fact that he didn't like cops. Never had, mainly because he saw them as ignorant. Of course, so was most of the world, but the law's obliviousness was particularly counterproductive to his and Sam's work. He had long since lost track of the number of times the police had done little but get in their way—since Baltimore, more than ever. True, there were occasional exceptions—there was Ballard, and that deputy in Hibbing. Of course, Hibbing wasn't actually a proper case, as there wasn't anything demonic about the family, so the deputy in question, Kathleen, was still just as ignorant.

McBain, though, appeared to be one of the good guys. And, whether or not he was willing to admit it, she *had* helped out.

But he still didn't like it. He held to his belief that he and Sam worked best alone.

As they walked, McBain said, "Hey, remind me when this is all over—I got somethin' that may interest the two of you."

Dean frowned. "Okay."

That seemed to be all she wanted to say on the subject. When they got to the corner, McBain walked up to the front door—well, one of them.

The church actually had three front doors, and any number of side doors. Wisely, she chose the one in the middle of the front, which was diagonally on the corner of Fordham and MLK, facing the middle of the intersection.

The detective pounded on the ornate wooden door, which was about ten feet high.

"So," Dean said, "the direct approach?"

"I ain't sneakin' into no church, brushy-top. I sinned enough for one life, thanks. Now botha you keep your yaps shut and let me handle this."

Dean looked over at Sam. Sam just shrugged with a "what do you want from me?" look. It wasn't like they hadn't snuck into churches before . . .

After several agonizing seconds, which to Dean felt like several days, the door slid open slowly with a creak. A bleary-eyed man stood on the other side. "Yes?"

McBain held up her badge. "NYPD, Father."

"I'm a deacon, actually," he muttered. "The priests are on retreat for the week."

Lucky bastard, Dean thought. *Gets the place to himself.* He wondered what kind of trouble a deacon could get into while the priests were all away. *Probably not much,* he thought, disappointed.

"I'm sorry, but we have reason to believe that your bell tower has been compromised. May we come in?"

"Compromised?"

"Yes, sir. We need to investigate it."

The deacon seemed to be working the conversation through his brain very slowly. "I don't understand."

Fed up, Dean stepped forward. "Look, Deacon, we think somebody's up there. We need to check it out. Will you let us in?"

"Well . . ." He shook his head. "I suppose. I mean, as long as you're police." He gave a ragged smile. "Besides, all are welcome in the Lord's house."

Dean smiled. "Amen."

As they entered, McBain whispered, "What'd I tell you about lettin' me handle this, brushy-top?"

"I got us in, didn't I?"

McBain just glared at him as they came into the church.

Pointing to a spiral staircase to the left, the deacon said, "The bell towers are that way."

Nodding, McBain said, "Stay down here, please, sir, while we look into it."

"Er, okay." The deacon didn't sound happy, but he didn't argue, either, for which Dean was grateful.

Dean looked around and was surprised to see very little. He could only make out vague shapes inside. He never thought of a church as closing down, but this late at night, with no light coming through the stained glass, and both the electric lights and the candles out, there was nothing to see.

Sam and McBain had already started up the staircase, and Dean followed quickly.

The trio moved up the spiral, McBain in the lead and Sam and Dean close behind. Dean wasn't comfortable with that, but if nothing else, it probably put the deacon at ease, since she was the only one who'd shown a badge.

After climbing up the narrow, winding stairs for about ten days, they finally got past the main part of the church's high ceiling. Dean was never particularly agoraphobic, but being this high up in the open space of the church with only a twisting metal banister between him and plunging to the floor didn't exactly thrill him. He was grateful when the staircase came to an end at a landing. There was a hallway that led down the length of the church, and another staircase that continued upward.

Indicating the staircase with her head, McBain continued up. Dean reached behind his back and took out his pistol, and McBain and Sammy both did likewise at the same time. Again, they didn't want to alarm the deacon, but now that they were out of sight . . .

This was a curvy staircase, but one actually built into the stonework, surrounded by walls on either side with no sheer drops.

Unfortunately, as dark as it was in the church, there had been *some* light, and the hallway at the top of the spiral staircase had some electric lights. This second staircase wasn't illuminated at all.

"Brushy-top," McBain whispered.

I really wish she'd stop calling me that. Dean whispered back, "Yeah?"

"You go first."

Not that he objected, but he had to ask: "Why?"

" 'Cause my night vision sucks ass."

Muttering, "Now she tells us," Dean moved ahead of both Sam and McBain, Sam taking up the rear.

Dean moved slowly, letting his eyes adjust to the growing darkness, weapon at the ready.

As they approached the top, he noticed a trip wire running across the bottom. He might not have seen it in the dim light, but this loser had used that trick once before, so Dean figured he'd go for it again.

"Trip wire," he whispered, pointing at it with his left hand, gun still raised in the right.

Sam and the detective both nodded. Dean stepped over it and moved into a small alcove. There were two more staircases on either side of the alcove, both leading up to the bells themselves, and a small doorway between them. Dean guessed that was where they rang the bells from. Everything was dark stone, giving the place a medieval feel—except for the shiny red fire extinguisher that was on a small shelf next to that small doorway. *Gotta love them fire codes.*

Without even thinking about it, Sam and Dean moved to either side of the door. McBain just stared at them for a second, shook her head, then went straight for the door, yanking it open and jumping back into a kneeling position. At the same time, Dean and Sam leaned in. All three were pointing their weapons.

The room was empty.

Dean shook his head. "The crazy son of a bitch may be up in the bells themselves."

"Or he may not be here at all," Sam said. "This was just a guess."

Suddenly, Dean winced from the echoing report of a pistol being fired, followed by the pinging sound of a bullet ricocheting off stone.

Sam also winced. "Or not."

McBain ran to the bottom of the stairs, but stayed to the side, out of the line of fire—not that there *was* a line of fire with the curved stairs—and said, "NYPD—come down with your hands up."

Dean looked at Sam, and Sam immediately ran to the other staircase.

"No chance of that, I'm afraid. You'll have to come up."

"Don't think I won't," McBain said.

I know that voice, Dean thought. *Where do I know that voice from?* It wasn't Mackey, but it was one he'd heard recently. Not one of Scottso—

they couldn't have gotten here that fast, and this was too well spoken a tone for any of them.

Oh, man. He finally placed it. *Shoulda freakin' known.*

Aloud, he said, "The jig's up, Vincent!"

McBain whirled around and looked up at him, mouthing the words, *Say what?*

After a pause, the voice of Dr. Ross Vincent asked, "Who is that?"

"Doesn't matter, Professor, it's over. I know you kept trying to convince everyone on that message board that there wasn't a connection between the murders. Makes sense for you to do that if you were trying to keep people away from your bogus ritual."

"It isn't 'bogus'!" Vincent screamed, his voice getting closer. "Percival Samuels was a genius, and his methods will provide the answer at last!"

"To what?" Dean asked.

Two figures came into view. One was Vincent—he had looked slightly manic in his office on Fordham's campus, but now he was out-and-out crazed. Dean couldn't see his eyes in the dim light, but his body language was completely messed up.

The other figure was Mackey, at whose head Vincent was pointing the muzzle of a .44 caliber pistol.

I just love Mexican standoffs, Dean thought.

"The *truth!* Don't you see? No one knows *how* Poe died! Now we can learn that, and *so* much more! So much of his life was a mystery, and we scholars waste *so* much limited time and useless effort to solve it, but we *cannot*—not without the original! So I am using Samuels's genius to—"

"It's a fake, you dork!" Dean said. "The ritual's a dud. Samuels was just using it to con the rubes out of their dough."

"You're lying!"

McBain said, "You ain't never findin' out. Drop your weapon."

"No. No, you can't! I'm so close! On Tuesday, everything will come together, you'll see! You'll see! Poe will return and then everyone will know the truth!"

Vincent whirled around and said, "Don't move!" Only then did Dean see Sam approaching from the other side.

"Don't worry about me," Mackey said in a strained voice, "just please shoot this imbecile!"

"Fine by me," Dean muttered.

McBain said, "Don't even *think* it, brushy-top."

Dean wouldn't endanger Mackey's life, of course, but *damn* was it tempting.

Although Sam hadn't moved, Vincent cried, "I said, don't *move*, damn you!" He then shot toward the ground.

Dean could hear the bullet ricochet off the stone,

then hit something metal. *Probably one of the bells,* he thought.

"That was a warning shot. I don't wish to hurt anyone beyond the confines of the ritual, but I *will* kill you before I let you stop me."

"Ain't nowhere you can go, Professor," McBain said. "We can stand here all night, but sooner or later—"

"Scholarship is at stake, madam," Vincent said, his .44 now again pointed at Mackey. "I assure you, I can stand here with my gun at Mr. Pym's throat until Tuesday, if necessary. I've come this far, I will *not* be stopped!"

Dean heard dripping. *What the hell?* Figuring that McBain and Sam both had Vincent covered, he was willing to take his eyes off the bastard long enough to look down at the stairs. Something was running down the staircase in rivulets, each one caused by the three sets of feet on the staircase.

A second later he smelled gas.

Sonofabitch. That wasn't a bell he hit, that was a gas can. Vincent was probably gonna use it for the fire Sammy was talking about.

Holding up his pistol, Dean said, "I'm holstering my weapon, okay, Professor?"

Angrily, McBain said, "Brushy-top, what the *hell* you doin'?"

"Trust me," Dean said as he put the gun in the

back of his waistband. He looked up at Vincent. "Listen to me, Professor, I got something I wanna show you, okay?"

"Do *not* try anything, Mr. Morrison."

McBain gave Dean a quick sidelong glance of confusion, but kept her focus on Vincent.

Dean reached into his jacket pocket slowly, not taking his eye off Vincent, feeling around for the item he needed. He put his thumb in the right position and hoped this would work.

Sam suddenly said, "Professor, look out!"

"What?"

Thank you, Sammy! Vincent turned his head, giving Dean the precious second he needed to pull out his lighter, flick it on, and toss it at the dripping gas.

Within seconds the entire staircase was on fire. Dean felt it at his back as he ran to the fire extinguisher. Turning, he saw that Sam had grabbed Mackey, and that Vincent himself was on fire and screaming.

Dean immediately hit him with the fire extinguisher. White foam sprayed out, smothering the flames. He turned the hose on the stairs, and within seconds everything was fine.

McBain was staring at Dean with an incredulous expression. "What the *hell* was that, brushy-top?"

"Stoppin' the bad guy," Dean said.

"By startin' a fire?"

Dean shrugged. "Hey, he's the one who shot the gas can. It woulda gone off if anyone fired. At least this way we had some control over it."

The detective looked like she wanted to argue, but instead she just shook her head, holstered her pistol, and took out her handcuffs. "What's this asshole's name?" she asked Dean.

"Ross Vincent. He's the Poe expert Mackey sent us to."

McBain put the handcuffs on the burned form of their perp. "Ross Vincent, you are under arrest on suspicion of the murders of Marc Reyes, Sarah Lowrance, John Soeder, and Kevin Bayer, the kidnapping of Arthur Mackey, resisting arrest, and whatever the hell else I feel like charging you with. You have the right to remain silent . . ."

"*Thank* you, gentlemen," Mackey said as Sam led him down the stairs. "That was quite unpleasant."

"Yeah, well, it would've been worse come Tuesday," Sam said.

"Indeed. 'In a mad expostulation with the deaf and frantic fire.' I feared I would never see my wife and children again." Mackey's beady eyes went wide once again. "Oh dear, I must call them. Do either of you have a phone I may borrow?"

Sam handed over his Treo, which proved once

again that he was more generous than Dean, as Dean didn't want this guy touching his stuff. Okay, so Mackey wasn't the bad guy, something he hadn't been a hundred percent sold on until he saw Vincent holding a .44 to his head, but still . . .

McBain had finished reading Vincent his Miranda nights and asked, "You okay, Arthur?"

Into Sam's Treo, he said, "One moment, love." He looked up. "A bit worse for the wear, Detective, but I'll live—probably." Back to the phone: "I must go, my dear, but I promise to be home as soon as I can. I'll probably have to give a statement to the police. Yes, all right. Kiss the kids for me. I love you all. Good night." He handed Sam the phone back and said, "Thank you."

"No problem," Sam said with a friendly smile.

Meanwhile, McBain was on her own cell phone calling for backup and an ambulance for Vincent.

Dean thought back to what Vincent had said in his office about wasting time arguing over things they couldn't know and the importance of truth, and he was kicking himself for not figuring out he was the guy sooner. *Too focused on Mackey, I guess.* Aloud, he said, "I can't believe he did all this just to find out how Poe died."

Mackey laughed. "Really? Obviously, you haven't met very many academics. I can think of several dozen who would think nothing of committing four murders if it meant furthering the cause of scholarship."

Staring at Sam, Dean said, "And you wanted to go to grad school."

"Well," Sam said defensively, "law school."

"Yeah," McBain said, having finished her phone call, " 'cause what we really need is more lawyers. Hell, this guy prob'ly has some suit on retainer that'll get his ass off with insanity." Staring intently at Dean, McBain then said, "Why don't you guys go wait for the backup to show up?"

"Good idea," Dean said emphatically, getting the hint that they should vamoose *before* that backup arrived.

"Definitely," Sam said with a nod.

Dean just hoped the cops were done at Manfred's place.

"Uh, hello?" came a voice from the spiral staircase. It sounded like the deacon.

Sighing, McBain said to Dean and Sam, "Send his holiness up here on your way out. I'll fill him in. Oh, and don't forget, we got that meeting tomorrow morning at six at the parking area just off the 97th Street exit on the West Side Highway."

Confused, Dean asked, "We do?"

"Yeah, brushy-top, we do."

Dean let out a long sigh. He assumed this was

the other thing she had said she wanted to share with them. "Fine. Let's go, Sammy."

Grinning, Sam said, "After you, brushy-top."

Only the fact that he was in a church kept Dean from beating the crap out of his brother.

EPILOGUE

McBain was waiting for them when the Impala veered off the West Side Highway and then veered again when the road split. The left fork continued under the highway to Ninety-seventh Street; the right fork, which the brothers took, went to a small parking lot that overlooked the Hudson River.

Sam took a moment to admire the view. It was a windy morning, and the Hudson was full of small whitecaps. A large boat was sailing up toward them, which soon became visible as the Circle Line, a boat that went around the island of Manhattan. There were only a few people on it, and they were bundled against the frigidity—it had to feel ten degrees colder on the water, Sam thought as he pulled his coat tight to his chest—but they seemed to be enjoying themselves.

On the other side of the river was New Jersey, including the lengthy strip along the river that, according to what he'd read on the web, had been built up over the last ten years or so as a major shopping area.

McBain was leaning against her Saturn and holding a folder, which she handed to Dean.

"What's this?" he asked as he took it.

"I ain't the first NYPD cop to walk the spook beat. Guy before me was a cranky old bastard named Landesberg. He used to keep an eye on the crazy-ass stuff back in the seventies. He left me a box full of folders, and I dig through it every once in a while. Found this, and figured you guys might be able to do something about it."

Dean stared at the contents of the folder, then closed it and handed it to Sam.

Sam saw several yellowing newspaper clippings from a Cedar Wells, Arizona, newspaper in 1966, with notes made in simply awful handwriting, as well as several 8½-by-11-inch sheets of paper.

"It's down near the Grand Canyon," McBain said. "There were a series of unexplained killings in early December 1926 and then again at the same time in 1966."

"Every forty years," Sam said, looking at the

pages, which turned out to be photocopies of clippings from 1926.

"Yeah, and we're comin' up on the anniversary." She indicated the Impala with her head. "I figure that tank oughtta get you cross-country in time."

"Definitely," Dean said with pride. Sam tried not to roll his eyes.

"It's worth checking out, certainly," Sam said. "Can we keep this?"

McBain snorted. "It's way outta my jurisdiction, so sure. Just try to keep people alive, okay?"

"That's what we do," Dean said. "And if we can't, we make sure it doesn't happen again."

"Yeah, I noticed." McBain smiled. Sam noticed it was a warmer smile than the snarky one she usually gave. "Listen, you guys did good work. Closed several homicides, stopped another one, and put a spirit to rest."

"We're not a hundred percent on that last part," Sam admitted reluctantly. "When we got back to Manfred's, he said that Scottso may be broken up. But still, with Eddie under arrest, I'm guessing Roxy's at peace."

"Hope so," McBain said. "So you guys are headed outta town?"

Holding up the folder, Sam said, "Apparently we have a job."

"Besides, I think Manfred could use some alone time," Dean said with a smirk.

"Well, good luck," McBain said. "It was a pleasure to finally meet you guys. And next time you're in town—"

"We'll call," Sam said quickly.

Dean said, "Probably."

"Very funny, brushy-top," McBain said. "Seeya."

She got into her Saturn and drove off.

Moving toward the Impala, Sam said, "She's not that bad."

Dean just looked at him. "She calls me 'brushy-top.'"

"Like I said, she's not that bad."

"Hardy-har-freakin'-har." Dean headed for the driver's side.

Sam blinked. "You're driving?"

"We're gettin' outta this crazy burg, so yeah, *now* I'm drivin'."

Holding up his hands in surrender, Sam said, "Fine, whatever."

They got into the Impala. Sam kept the folder in his lap so he could consult it while they headed across the bridge. Their best bet was to make most of their way across country on I-80 to Salt Lake City, then down I-15 to Las Vegas, then work their way on the local routes to Cedar Wells from there. That'd take a few days, though, even with Dean's lead-footed driving style, so Sam focused on the folder for now while he waited for Dean to ask the inevitable question, which he fi-

nally asked as he went under the West Side Highway and found himself at the corner of Riverside
Drive and 97th Street, with no real idea how he
got there.

"Dude, how do we get outta here?"

Sam grinned.

Just as she was putting the finishing touches on the
paperwork that would close the Roxy Carmichael
case—at least, as a missing persons case, it was
now a homicide—a voice came from the entryway
to her tiny cubicle:

"Detective Marina McBain?"

Turning around, McBain found herself doing
the same thing Sergeant O'Shaughnessy had done
a week ago. Her first impression was black male
with close-cut hair and a goatee. Then she saw the
impeccably tailored suit that meant he was either
a fed or a lawyer.

"Yeah, I'm McBain."

"Special Agent Victor Hendrickson. I need to
talk to you about two men named Sam and Dean
Winchester."

Great, this must be the fed after Dean. "Names
don't ring a bell, why?"

"Really?" Hendrickson folded his arms. "Now
why don't I believe you?"

"I really don't know, Agent Hendrickson, and I
really don't care. I've got a metric ton of paperwork

to deal with right now. I can go see if these Winchester guys are in the files, but—"

"They're not missing persons, they're fugitives, and I think you've seen 'em."

McBain rolled her eyes. "It's nice that you think that, but I never even heard of 'em."

"Yeah? What were you doing last night?"

"Rescuing one of my CIs," she said, grateful that she'd made Arthur one of her official confidential informants, so her searching for him last night could be justified. "He disappeared in mid-phone call, and I tracked him down. Some nut job had him tied to a bell. Turned out to be a serial killer." She grinned. "Surprised you guys didn't waltz in to step all over it, the way you usually do for serials."

"You notice I ain't laughin'."

McBain's grin widened. "You notice I don't give a damn."

Unfolding his arms, Hendrickson said, "I can make your life a living hell, Detective. Where were you last Saturday night?"

"Home, watching television. My landlord can confirm that." McBain rented the top floor of a two-family house in Queens. She helped get rid of a poltergeist in the house, and since then the landlord was her best friend. Lying to a fed about whether she was home was the least of the favors she'd do.

And O'Shaughnessy wouldn't rat her out to the feds, either, and he was the only one who knew she was on the grid Saturday night. "And if you wanna make my life a living hell, Agent Hendrickson, get in line behind my sergeant, my captain, my inspector, Commissioner Kelly, and Mayor Bloomberg, okay?"

Hendrickson leaned against the side of her cubicle and refolded his arms. His facial expression had yet to change since he arrived. The slightly pissed-off look seemed to be his default. "If you think I won't step on *all* those people to get what I need, Detective, you are *sorely* mistaken."

"I don't *know* what you need, Hendrickson! You been standin' here threatening me, talkin' some nonsense about two people I never even *heard* of—"

"You expect me to believe that, Detective?"

"Agent Hendrickson, on the list of things I give a rat's ass about, what you believe is at the bottom, you feel me? Now unless you have actual police business to discuss with me—"

"Hey!"

McBain turned to see the wiry form of Sergeant Glover, her immediate supervisor, stomping toward her cubicle.

"Who the hell're you?" Hendrickson asked.

"I'm Sergeant Glover, and I'm in charge of this shift. Who the hell're *you*?"

Hendrickson identified himself, even going so far as to show ID, which was more consideration than he'd shown McBain.

"That's nice. Get your fibbie ass out of my house."

Now Hendrickson's facial expression changed—from slightly pissed off to completely pissed off. "Excuse me?"

"You heard me. You got no business harassing my people."

"I have questions for Detective McBain."

"No," Glover said, "you don't, 'cause if you did, you'da done it through proper channels instead of barging through here intimidating people. Now you can leave on your own, or I can call up a couple of uniforms to haul your ass downstairs for trespassing."

Hendrickson stared at Glover, then stared at McBain. He pointed an accusatory finger at her. "I'll be back, Detective."

Giving him a sweet smile, McBain said, "My door's always open, Agent Hendrickson."

With another nasty look at Glover, Hendrickson turned on his polished heel and left.

Glover looked at McBain. "What the hell was that?"

"Sergeant, I talked to him for five minutes, and I still can't tell you."

Shaking his head, Glover said, "Damn fibbies."

As her shift commander wandered off, McBain turned around and let out a long breath, never more grateful for the rivalry bordering on hatred between federal and local law enforcement.

Watch your asses, guys, she thought in the general direction of Sam and Dean Winchester as they worked their way to the thing in Arizona.

Roxy was satisfied.

She loved watching the cops come and take that bastard Eddie away. She wished she had it on camera so she could watch it over and over and over and over.

It was over. He didn't love her, but at least he was paying for not loving her, the creep.

She hated him. She hated everything about him. She loved seeing him suffer, and watching him break down and confess like that in front of the whole band.

It was *great.*

But now she didn't know what to do.

Uncle Cal didn't come back, so she didn't know what was next. Would she just stay here? Would she fade away? Would she go to the right afterlife?

Maybe she could just hang out here. Manfred probably wouldn't mind. She always kinda liked Manfred. Maybe she should've been with him all along. He wasn't that bad. She had thought after rehab that someone like Aldo would be better, but that turned out to be *so* not the case. And she had always really really liked this house.

Still, she figured, even if she was sticking around, she wouldn't make so much noise. Manfred might call those two creeps back, and she didn't want that. She still hated the way those shots felt, and she wasn't eager to repeat it.

So she stayed quiet, and would just live here in peace. Or die here in peace.

Or something.

Author's Note

While composing *Nevermore*, I had a special *Supernatural* iTunes playlist going in my headphones. It included the following songs, which I recommend as a listening soundtrack while reading the book:

AC/DC: "Back in Black." (Living Colour's version works nicely, too)
The Allman Brothers: "Ramblin' Man"
George Baker: "Little Green Bag"
The Band: "Chest Fever," "The Shape I'm In," "The W.S. Wolcott Medicine Show"
Black Sabbath: "Paranoid"
Blind Faith: "Can't Find My Way Home"
Blue Öyster Cult: "(Don't Fear) The Reaper"
Blue Swede: "Hooked on a Feeling"
Nick Cave & the Bad Seeds: "Up Jumped the Devil"

The Chambers Brothers: "Time has Come Today"

Eric Clapton: "Cocaine," "Further on up the Road"

Cream: "Badge," "Sunshine of Your Love," "Tales of Brave Ulysses"

Creedence Clearwater Revival: "Bad Moon Rising"

Deep Purple: "Smoke on the Water"

Def Leppard: "Rock of Ages"

Derek & the Dominoes: "Layla"

Bob Dylan: "Knockin' on Heaven's Door," "Like a Rolling Stone" (the original's okay, but I loudly recommend the live version on *Before the Flood*, which is transcendent; all respect to Al Kooper, but Garth Hudson leaves him in the dust)

Electric Light Orchestra: "Turn to Stone"

David Essex: "Rock On"

Iron Butterfly: "In-A-Gada-Da-Vida"

Jefferson Airplane: "White Rabbit"

Jethro Tull: "A New Day Yesterday," "Aqualung," "For a Thousand Mothers," "We Used to Know"

Robert Johnson: "Cross Road Blues" (Eric Clapton's version of this works, too), "Hellhound on My Trail," "Walkin' Blues" (versions of "Walkin' Blues" by Hindu Love Gods, Eric Clapton, and the Jump Kings are also excellent and recommended)

Journey: "Wheel in the Sky"

Kansas: "Carry on, Wayward Son"

Lynyrd Skynyrd: "Down South Jukin'"

Metallica: "Enter Sandman," "Some Kind of Monster"

Ted Nugent: "Stranglehold"

Queen & David Bowie: "Under Pressure"

The Rolling Stones: "Gimme Shelter," "Have You Seen Your Mother, Baby," "Sympathy for the Devil"

Rush: "Working Man"

Bob Seger & the Silver Bullet Band: "Katmandu," "Lookin' Back," "Turn the Page"

Spinal Tap: "Stonehenge"

Stealers Wheel: "Stuck in the Middle with You"

Steppenwolf: "Born to be Wild," "Magic Carpet Ride"

Styx: "Renegade"

Tito & Tarantula: "Angry Cockroaches," "Strange Face of Love"

Traffic: "The Low Spark of High-Heeled Boys"

Joe Walsh: "Turn to Stone"

The Who: "5:15," "Goin' Mobile," "In a Hand or a Face," "Love Reign O'er Me"

Warren Zevon: "Werewolves of London"

About the Author

Keith R.A. DeCandido wrote the first *Farscape* novel (*House of Cards*), the first *Gene Roddenberry's Andromeda* novel (*Destruction of Illusions*), the first *Command and Conquer* novel (*Tiberium Wars*), and now the first *Supernatural* novel. This means absolutely nothing, but he likes mentioning it anyhow, 'cause it almost sounds cool.

In total, Keith has written more than thirty novels, as well as a mess of short stories, a smattering of novellas, a dollop of essays, and a gaggle of eBooks. Most are in various media universes—besides the ones mentioned: *Star Trek* (most recently the *Next Generation* novel *Q&A*), *Buffy the Vampire Slayer* (most recently *The Deathless*), *World of Warcraft* (*Cycle of Hatred*), *Doctor Who* (a story in the *Short Trips: Destination Prague* anthology), *StarCraft* (*Nova*), *Resident Evil* (the novelizations of all three films), *Spider-Man* (*Down These Mean Streets*), *CSI:NY* (the upcoming *Four Walls*), and whole bunches more. The majority of his original work is in the world of his 2004 novel *Dragon Precinct*.

Keith is also an editor—he's responsible for the monthly *Star Trek* eBook line and has edited dozens of anthologies, including the upcoming *Doctor Who: Short Trips: The Quality of Leadership*—and a musician—currently the percussionist for the parody band the Boogie Knights. A fan of classic rock (Dean Winchester would approve of much of his iTunes "favorites" playlist), Keith is also a practitioner of *Kenshikai* karate and a devoted fan of the New York Yankees. As should be blindingly obvious from the book you've just read, Keith was born, raised, and educated in the Bronx, and still lives there with his fiancée and two insane cats. Learn less about Keith at his official website at DeCandido.net, read his tiresome ramblings at kradical.livejournal.com, or send him your Bronx cheers directly to keith@decandido.net.